THE SHELTERING STONES SERIES

3

# THE MAKING OF A TOWN

A NOVEL OF HISTORICAL FICTION

## JOANN KLUSMEYER

Published by Innovo Publishing, LLC
www.innovopublishing.com
1-888-546-2111

Providing Full-Service Publishing Services for Christian Authors, Artists &
Ministries: Books, eBooks, Audiobooks, Music, Screenplays, Film & Curricula

**THE SHELTERING STONES HISTORICAL FICTION SERIES**

Book 3

**THE MAKING OF A TOWN:**
*A Novel of Historical Fiction*

ISBN: 978-1-61314-733-7

Cover Design & Interior Layout: Innovo Publishing, LLC

Printed in the United States of America
U.S. Printing History
First Edition: 2021

Has God called you to create a Christian book, ebook, audiobook, music album,
screenplay, film, or curricula? If so, visit the ChristianPublishingPortal.com to
learn how to accomplish your calling with excellence. Learn to do everything
yourself, or hire trusted Christian Experts from our Marketplace to help.

# CONTENTS

*Chapter 1* ........................................................... *7*

*Chapter 2* ........................................................... *27*

*Chapter 3* ........................................................... *47*

*Chapter 4* ........................................................... *67*

*Chapter 5* ........................................................... *87*

*Chapter 6* ........................................................... *107*

*Chapter 7* ........................................................... *127*

*Chapter 8* ........................................................... *147*

*Chapter 9* ........................................................... *167*

Epilogue ........................................................... 179

Excerpt from The Enchanted Fortress ................................... 217

Additional Book Series by Joann Klusmeyer ........................... 230

# CHAPTER 1

In was in the year of 1898 that Francine Canfield's life began to fall into place. Francine had always known this would happen, she just didn't know when... or exactly how. The thing she had known, however, from the age of four was that at some moment she would know, without a doubt, what she wanted for the rest of her life.

At age four, she had sat with her older sister and three-year-old brother in a moving covered wagon headed to where she did not know... nor care. She was busily admiring the many doll dresses received as a gift from the same grandmother who provided her future inheritance and chatting with the brother who was busily admiring the set of animals and farm equipment from the same grandmother.

Young Francine knew, at that moment, that she would someday have many beautiful dresses, and they would be for something special that she would later learn about.

It was during two years at the PRAIRIE ACADEMY that Francine had learned in detail what she would do with her life. She would teach school in the Territory to children who had no other school. She didn't know where, but that was not a problem. She would be ready when the place became available, and that was why she was making the ten outfits of clothing. These beautiful new dresses would give her the dignity and confidence she thought she needed to impress small boys into obedience and be a role model to inspire small girls... the way that Miss Josie had inspired her. Her career would begin in the neighboring town of Shady Ridge.

If a teacher for Shady Ridge had been available from the fledgling Board of Education, the salary would have been $376.00 a year for one who was Certification Qualified.

A Shady Ridge parent wondered, "What kind of a teacher would we git for that kinda money?"

Answer, "Whoever was willin'. It'd be someone that was likely turned down by the school board of any big community, if they was to be able to get someone better. She, or he, could be anywhere from 14 years old to still breathin'. They's places that are letting a 11-year-old girl teach' cause they can't do no better. They call 'em 'teachers in training'. Sometimes they call 'em 'parlor schools'."

"But there's them New York trained girls Gray Eagle told us about.... What about them?"

"Well, the question now is, can we get one of them girls. It'd cost money for one thing. I can say $1.50 a month'd strain me a bit, but I'd manage. Some way. You speck we could figger a way to get one of 'em girls?"

"Wouldn't know till we tried. We could count noses'a them that's interested, and have ourselves another meetin' in a week or two."

"How long you thinkin' it'd take to get the buildin' up, John?"

As it happened, the folks at Shady Ridge had a mind to work. By the last of March, the building material was on site and shaped into a large cabin that literally grew up out of the prairie soil, liberally fertilized by the sweat of concerned fathers. It turned out to be 40 feet long and 20 feet wide... totally adequate, everyone agreed. There would be a classroom of 20 by 30 and a private room for the teacher measuring 20 by 10.

In due time the offer was made to Miss Francine Canfield to be the teacher of the Shady Ridge children.

It was later that day that Sam Canfield watched his life's partner as she struggled with her thoughts. Maybe he could help her... at least he should try.

"Julie? Let's talk on this. I don't like it tearin' you to pieces this a'way."

The girl's mother was having a pang at losing her younger daughter, not yet 14 years old, but her father put it another way, and pointed out, "I know. But think on it. Shady Ridge, that's a heap sight closer'n Oklahoma City… or even Argyle, for that matter. And here's the thing that'll comfort us… those ladies from Shady Ridge said the community'd be happy if she was to marry someone close and maybe stay on. That'd never happen if she was to take a job with the Board of Learnin' in the city. If she went to Shady Ridge, she'd pretty nearly be the boss'a herself, and you know how our Francine is. She knows how she wants things to be, and she's mostly right in her ideas. Seems like them folks want her so bad they'd do 'most anything to get her, and they come here a'beggin', almost. Think on it… beggin' for our little girl to come and do what she wants to do already."

And that is the way it happened to cause Francine to shine up her worn shoes and put on new dress number three. She had just completed dress number seven and was looking forward to the next three, which would be skirt and blouse combinations. Mrs. O'Grady had encouraged her in that direction, explaining that skirts grew with young girls as they became taller, and that shirtwaists could be made to expand in selected areas. When that could not be done, they could be replaced much more easily than an entire dress. Francine had listened carefully, and within her own mind could see that styles for shirtwaists changed more often, as well.

So it was that she and her parents traveled the three miles to the west for a visit. They were treated to coffee and cake and given a tour of the new schoolhouse in Shady Ridge. It was a cheerful thing to see the freshly painted sign bravely stating: SHADY RIDGE ACADEMY.

The almost 14-year-old girl glanced about the classroom still smelling of new lumber, checked out the size of the closet, and examined the small stove.

Annabelle Martin offered, "Now, Miss Francine, we can put in a bed…'

Whereupon Francine reassured them, "No, thank you. I'll bring the one from my room. What about school books?"

On learning none had yet been purchased, Francine nodded agreeably. "That's all right. Don't bother about books, I'll bring them when I move in. Next August." Which was what she wanted to do, anyway.

The Canfields left two happy ladies with wide grins of satisfaction. Success! Wasn't it wonderful, after all their work and talking and planning? They had a teacher! A real New York trained teacher!

On the journey home, Francine's mother hesitantly asked her, "Honey, how're you feelin' now?"

After her usual hesitation, the girl calmly answered, "Pretty much how I expected to feel. I know I'm ready."

Such confidence was scary to her mother. The girl sounded so much like her father had sounded when he had announced that he planned to make a run for property in the Territory. She had asked him, "Do you think you can?"

The answer had been, "I feel very confident. I know I'm ready." And he had been.

It would be necessary for Francine to have transportation home for weekends, so her father purchased for her a lady's buggy, a small one made for a couple of friends to shop with or take an outing. The abbreviated cab was so narrow that two large persons would not have fitted well, and even two smaller persons would need to be good friends. It was perfect for Francine.

The horse was also perfect. He was a Connemara from the breeding stock of Jefferson Wilson, Miss Josie's cousin. The horse's only problem had been that he was not born with a coat of dark gray displaying the signature charcoal face and feet. The fact was, the animal did not match any pattern that Jeff was working for. He aimed for the matched carriage horses that would bring a high price. Francine bought the animal at the first sight of him.

Francine's choice of a horse had been born an offshoot of the northern animals introduced into the Irish stock by the Vikings, and his color was a medium chocolate. Also instead of smooth coat, his was somewhat shaggy in a texture which, along with the color, was deemed by the northern newcomers to Ireland to be more adaptable to the cold dampness of the climate. It showed his true Viking heritage.

In the case of Francine's horse, the animal was the winner. The girl took one look at the dark animal and knew he was the one she wanted. The buggy was duly found by her father and painted the same shade of chocolate as the horse's slightly shaggy coat. The horse and buggy pair cut into Francine's inheritance money a bit, but there were still funds to buy the necessary books for the library and enough slates for every student to have at least two for their assignments. With some left over.

The animal, whose name was reduced from "Chocolate" to "Chock," amiably trotted between the double trees of the buggy, answering her commands with no objection.

Into the small buggy seat, on the floorboard and into the small boot at the back were the books, chalk boxes, slates, and more. Later on, the students would be required to furnish their own… and a few rulers. There were a number of other things for her own desk. Also, there were her clothes, extra bedding, and kitchen items that would come later.

She had hardly pulled into the yard before a girl of about eleven and a half came running to meet her. She recognized the girl as Isabel Brown, oldest daughter of her host family.

"Oh, Miss Francine! My ma said I could help you carry things in if I wouldn't get in the way! I got to come over yesterday and put the coverlet on the bed. I smoothed the mattress and felt how soft and fluffy the feathers were, and I plumped up the pillows. I brought the three boxes to slide under the bed for other things like ma said you'd need. Can I help?"

With a smile of greeting, Francine called her to the buggy. "See all these books? I suspect you can guess where they go?"

"I can! I can! Let me carry them all!" insisted the excited child. Well, that was Francine's best offer of help for the day until a boy came racing across the road. "I'm Troy Cameron from over there." An elbow pointed to the house across the street. "My ma said I could be the one to take care'a your pony if it was all right with you. I can do as well as anybody else, and I know how to brush their coats to dry 'em out when they get sweaty. Do you want me to take him now?"

"Not today, Troy, and I would be very glad to have you take care of Chock. Later, I'll tell you about special things I want done for him and for the buggy. I just came to deliver things today."

"Then can I help you carry something?"

"I believe you'd have to ask Isabel. She thinks it's her job."

The two children worked together on the loads of books, Troy carrying and Isabel arranging them on the bookshelves that had been constructed all the way along the side of the classroom. In due time, Troy was called home, and Isabel looked for things to do to get to stay. On impulse, Francine asked the girl, "How are you at reading?"

A hesitation. "I can read. Some."

Selecting a book of about second level, she opened to a page and handed it to her. "Let's see how you do."

The girl took the book and began with a bit of hesitation. Most of the words she knew, but she had no confidence and read in a monotone. When she came to the word 'cabin,' she substituted the word 'house'. Francine nodded to herself. The girl was looking at the illustration of a house, and the word 'cabin' was the one used in the text.

If Isabel, being one of the oldest, stumbled on that word, it indicated a strong need for phonics… the sounding of each of the letters. She had imagined, actually, that the whole group could be introduced to sounds at one time, and the younger ones would learn as well by listening.

In time, Isabel was called home, leaving Francine alone. The long, long bookcase was over half filled leaving space for the future. The tables and benches were arranged. Her desk was stocked, and she stood, looking around in all directions. Alone.

Her chest became heavy, and her breath labored. Her eyes filled, and she could not stop the sobs. Sitting at her desk, she buried her face in her arms and the tears flowed. A depression settled upon her like a sudden spring shower, weighing her down. Soggy and dripping. There was no way she could conduct a classroom like Miss Josie did. Why did she come here? She didn't have to do this!

Her shoulders heaved, and her stomach tightened. She had to get out of here somehow. She was only fourteen years old! What had given her the idea she could teach this class?

A deep breath. "FRANCINE," she shouted at herself. "STOP IT, THIS INSTANT! WHAT DO YOU THINK YOU'RE DOING? YOU'RE SCARING YOURSELF!"

Squaring her shoulders, she reached in into her carpet bag and brought out a large, efficient handkerchief. This was no job for a tiny lace hanky! She had more to say to herself, now that she had her own attention.

"Francine, you big baby, don't you ever do this to me again! You can do what you learned how to do. You taught lessons when Miss Josie was not in the room. You were so busy you didn't notice when she went in and out.

"Why do you think I worked so hard these past three years, studying, teaching, and sewing for you? Do you remember when I sat at the table with Rosie and Raymond, and we studied for two hours after supper. Sometimes three hours, and there was more the next morning while we ate breakfast. Why do you think I did that? Maybe you thought it was so you could bawl like a baby. If you thought that was it, you were WRONG! WRONG! WRONG! Don't you ever let another tear fall about teaching. You can cry about other things, maybe, if we got the time, but not about teaching."

At this point she stood, lifted her head, and sniffed loudly. She crammed the cloth of the handkerchief into her eyes, blotting them dry. Her tight stomach began to relax and produce a couple of final hiccoughs.

Stepping back into her tiny living quarters, a room ten feet by twenty feet, she surveyed it critically. The narrow bed fit perfectly against the left wall. The closet was at the foot of the bed, and there was just enough room to open the doors without bumping the bed. Near the foot of the bed was the slipper stool.

She sat down on the stool and pulled out one of the boxes from under the bed. Roomy and sanded smooth, they were, and about a foot deep and two feet square. Perfect. Handy for so many things. Near her pillow was the tiny stand with a place for shoes below, and it had a small drawer above. Hardly more than a foot square. A kerosene lamp she had brought was placed there. Cut glass and as sparkly as pond ice. It was one she had ordered from Aunt Sharon in New York because she liked Miss Josie's lamps.

The table was a hinged shelf that let down when not in use. Saved space. Francine had planned to have her meals at her desk in the classroom when she didn't want to eat with the family so she might not need the shelf.

On the right-hand side of the room was the kitchen. Tiny cabinet with a few dishes. Two small kettles hanging on the wall. A washstand with a water pitcher and wash bowl and under the stand was soap and a space for other things. Next to the cabinet was another small stand holding the miniature kerosene stove, with extra heating oil on a shelf under it. A match container hung on the wall. A small chest of drawers would serve well as a dressing table. She only needed a mirror.

The far wall contained a door and a small porch with a roof over it. Everything looked good. Perfect for her. She was not particularly interested in engaging in food preparation. There was a small tea pot, and she'd likely get herself a coffee pot. Maybe in a week or two. She had taken a liking to that expensive brew while she was at the Academy. Miss Josie really liked it. Smiling at the thought, she told herself perhaps she'd teach like Miss Josie if she drank enough coffee.

Whatever she had forgotten to bring, she would be home every weekend, at least until bad weather. If she needed something bought quickly, her pa would see to it.

Next trip, she would bring her clothing, quilts, and slippers. Certainly a mirror, comb, and brush. A fluffy rug for when the floor was cold. Maybe she could buy a wolf skin rug from Mrs. Gray Owl. The ones the old woman brought to the Academy were handy and cozy, and shook clean so easily.

A shelf high on the wall held a candle in a tin pan holder. Safety factor. If she should go to sleep with the candle lit, it would eventually put itself out. She would use her lamp to read by, and she must bring the huge poem book Miss Josie gave her. No one else ever checked it out, and Miss Josie said it had been ordered especially for her, anyway.

And she'd need composition books to put in the tiny drawer of the nightstand. She never really knew when a poem would happen, but when it did, she had to write it down or it would keep bothering her until she did.

At first she was a bit embarrassed that she liked writing about common things like snow, turtles, cats, or whatever. Miss Josie showed her in the poem book that a poet in England even wrote about a field mouse he'd turned over with the plow. Also, about a louse that crawled on a woman's bonnet in church.

Her teacher had insisted that she MUST write down every poem that came to her, and that she, Miss Josie, wanted a copy of every one. Strange! Very flattering, though! It seemed to Francine that it was normal to think in poetry... she used to think to that everyone did, but it didn't seem to be that way.

With a sigh, she took a last look at the tiny living quarters, turned back to the classroom, and saw the tear-soggy cloth on her desk. She snatched it up with disgust and crammed it into her carpet bag. Whatever had gotten into her? Anyway, she had gotten it over with, and she didn't expect to have time to go through that again.

She heard a jingle of harness as Chock fidgeted and tossed impatiently at the stinging flies. Time to go. She locked the schoolroom door with the key they had given her and stepped aboard the buggy. She just loved the buggy her pa had picked out. It fit her just right, and she dearly loved things to be just right. Pa was a good shopper.

A click of the tongue turned the animal toward home, and he trotted along with no further direction. He knew where he was headed. She set herself to thinking about Troy and what she would have him do. Curry Chock several times a week. Keep straw for him to sleep on. She wanted to get linseed oil and have Troy oil the leather of the small bench in the buggy and the leather harness lines. She wanted the buggy to last for a long time. Maybe she'd have him oil the wheel axels occasionally.

The Cameron's had suggested they keep the buggy in their barn. It was so small, it would take up very little room they'd said. That should be worth a dime every week for the ten year old. Maybe a bit extra when she wanted something special done.

With a sharp turn and a quick stop, the small horse had brought her home. Twenty minutes later, she had him out of his harness and turned into the pasture. A sigh of accomplishment. One more trip to take the last things, and another for the welcoming party the Shady

Ridge parents wanted to give her… the one where she could make a speech if she wanted to. Should she make notes on what she should say? Or maybe just see what she felt like saying? Well, that was next week, and she had plenty of time.

But the time passed quickly. Hot! It was hot! Just as it usually was at the end of August. The classroom would be crowded with the eight or nine families of the new students. Then there was her own family, along with classmate, Carmelita, who said there was no way she would not be there. And Miss Josie and her husband, of course.

What would she wear…? well… The royal blue broadcloth skirt with the "prairie point" trim on the hem and waistband. It flashed through her mind that she had made the extra solid seam in the waistband. It wouldn't do to have a fabric separation because a child had perhaps tugged at her skirt for attention.

Then the white shirtwaist that had been treated to lye soap bubbles until it glistened… as did all her white shirtwaists. Crocheted collar and sleeve trim. Short sleeved, reaching barely to her elbows. That would be about as cool as anything she had.

Not… a hat…? Hmmm… no, she was not going to town. But this WAS a party! And it was being held where she would teach these parents' children. A bow. That would be best. There was the white velvet bow with the very secure clasp… simple and attractive. If she twisted her long, heavy mane of dark hair up from the neckline to the crown, and pin it securely, then the bow would fit well and the clasp would hold solidly for the evening. Yes. And her white, pearl button shoes, as there would not be many times to wear them after she went to work. Black would be best in the classroom.

That taken care of, she thought of her… speech…? She would for certain be asked to say something. She could make notes, or she could wait and see what seemed right. Which…? This being her first experience at this, she had no idea which way was right, but her knowledge of herself said for her to wait. So often, the exact right thing came to her at the moment she needed it, and then she would know what should come next. Yes. She would wait.

The Shady Ridge schoolyard was a seethe of activity. The half-grown pig had been butchered yesterday. It was much too hot in August to butcher any animal that could not be immediately consumed, but that would not be a concern at this time. The rise of community excitement promised the ladies of town that every crumb of every food product was sure to be gobbled up.

Egg salad, potato salad, pickles (cucumber and beet), heaps of sliced onions. Biscuits and cornbread. Angel food cake and fruit cookies sweetened by persimmon sugar and crammed full of toasted pecan and hazelnut kernels. There were even sacks of store-bought marshmallows for the children to toast on sticks over the coals.

The pig on the spit turned slowly, juices and fat oozing as it turned… dripping onto the coals. A tormentingly fragrant smoke floated into the surrounding trees. Older boys were drafted to turn the spit handle slowly and evenly, creating a flavorful crust on all portions.

Tables were created on the sawhorses used in the building of the classroom. White sheets covered the boards giving them a festive look. Older girls were drafted to keep flies from the table as it was being loaded with food.

Francine smiled to herself as she remembered her decision on words to say. NO ONE would want to hear very many words with the aroma of this treat waiting just outside the building! They would be thinking of what would be waiting under the covering bed sheets, placed there to protect the food from insects while words were being said.

Francine sat with her family and watched as they approached the schoolhouse. A numbness settled over her, as though she was having a dream and she knew the events would happen totally without her. It seemed amazing, though, that her inner self realized that she, Francine, had made this possible.

Not that she was surprised, but more a sense of satisfaction that she saw events happening as she had expected they would. Like climbing a ladder, one step followed the last one, and nearer the top, there might be apprehensions, but her apprehensions were not so strong as the knowledge that she WOULD reach the top and that there was a solid place for her feet when she got there.

Folding chairs and benches filled the classroom, and she was directed to her reserved place by John William Brown. Her own family and Miss Josie were settled around her.

Stretched across the end of the room on the wall above her desk, a sign proclaimed, "Welcome to Miss Francine." Words were said, and an applause spread through the group, but the words were lost on the fourteen-year-old girl who was the center of the celebration.

Then she was standing before them. Smiles! Nods of heads! These people wanted her to be here, and they were proud of themselves because they had secured her. She was acutely aware of that. A small shiver of thankfulness flowed from the nape of her neck down her arms. Hers! These were her people, and she would make them proud!

"Thank you so much, everyone. You will never know how excited and pleased I am to be here, and so thankful to you for asking me. I promise that I will try to be all you are expecting.

"I do have a few small things to say, and I'll speak fast because of the aroma coming in through the windows." A chuckle sprinkled through the grownups, and a few giggles and restless movements passed through the younger children.

She continued, "The discussion of the tuition was made and set without consulting me, and I feel I must make a change." Profound silence met these words. "The amount of $2.00 per child per month is very flattering to me, and I appreciate it, but this is what it will actually be. The amount of $2.00 will be for the first child of any family, and the rest of the children will attend free, except for the bushel of cow pats which will certainly be needed." A relieved twitter of surprise was the only sound.

"On to other things. Discipline. With a class of 20 children, there can be no willful disturbances by any child. The first instance of misbehavior will be discussed with the child. The second will be discussed with the parents. The third will be that the child no longer attends the school. No exceptions. It is clearly not fair to allow one child to take up the time of the children who want to learn and whose parents are paying for their education.

"Next thing. The lessons taught here will NOT be easy. Miss Josie, whom you see here, will agree with me on this. My brother and sister and I used a great quantity of kerosene every night at the kitchen table. We were expected to have our assigned lessons prepared, no matter how long it took. There were times that my sister and I took our outside reading to our beds and read by candle light. You see on your left the long bookcase someone so kindly built us, and it is stocked with books arranged by Miss Isabel Brown. These books are not here just because they look nice. Your children will read them. They will read so many that there will be times they will hate me, and you parents may not be really happy, either, but that is my requirement. I refuse to waste my time. I expect to be successful with every child. I just need for every parent to understand that at the beginning.

"Now, just one more thing. I see the nice shed that contains the bin for the cow pats, also the bench for the privy. It is very nice, but I have one concern. All children will have recess at the same time, and I expect their needs to be taken care of then, and the children will want a few minutes to play. For that reason, I ask that as soon as possible, another privy be constructed. That would be one for the girls, and the current one reserved for the boys, as they will also be responsible for storing the cow pats.

"I am so pleased that Miss Josie could be here. She is very important to me, and if she had not been forced by her family misfortune to be here in the Territory, then I would not be standing here tonight. It is because of her that my sister and I could make up four years of lost education in only one year. It is because of her that I had an additional year and a year of practice to be sure I could do this job. It is because of Miss Josie that I lost a lot of sleep, and that my parents bought a lot of kerosene. I might possibly have been mad at her, sometimes, if I had had time, but I was too busy working to even think of it."

Miss Josie seemed to be having trouble with her eyes. Smoke from the roasting spit…? One hand plunged into her bag to search for protection, but Mr. Brad was quicker. He thrust into her hand a more adequate item than she would have found in her bag. She dabbed against her eyes and sniffled a bit.

"Miss Josie, would you please stand for just a minute? I want everyone to see the person who made it possible for me to be here."

Josie Wheeler Cullen stood and looked around. Applause rippled and then thundered. She nodded her thanks and seated herself again.

"Thank you, Miss Josie. One more thing. My parents, Samuel and Julia Canfield did not expect any chores or other duties from myself or my brother and sister during the time we went to school. It was truly a sacrifice on their part. They made it their sacrifice for their children, and they never, even once, mentioned it to us. Please stand, pa and ma."

Sam Canfield turned beet red, and Julia hid her face in confusion, but they stood for a few seconds. More applause. Francine studied the faces of the adults. Did they really understand what would be required of them? Likely not.

"Last, just for the fun of it, I want my sister and my very good friend to stand. This is Carmelita Wilson, cousin of Miss Josie, and Rosalie Canfield, my sister. I'll leave you to decide which is which." A twitter that grew into a guffaw passed through the parents. A giggle from the two girls, their appearances so different. One of them leaned toward a mirror image of Francine, herself, and the other was a girl with tight, red-gold curls and a delicate pink tint highlighting the pale skin and dimpled features. The girls seated themselves giggling noisily and hiding their faces in their hands.

"Now, if there is anything else I need to say, I'll send a note home with your child." Guarded chuckles. Very likely this teacher meant it, and they might just as well be prepared. How did this 'child' speak with such authority… like she was at least fifty years old?

Francine again. "That's all. Let's go eat that wonderful food on the outside tables." Now a thunder of applause. Children raced through the door, and parents gathered around Francine. Smiles. Pats. Encouraging nods. And then it was over.

By the time she and her family had reached the laden tables, the trees had been festooned with lighted lanterns and two of the men were wielding sharp knives, stacking thick slices of meat onto platters to be set along the tables. The fourteen-year-old guest of honor didn't remember much after that. She had said what she wanted to say… intended to say… and now it was time to do what she intended to do.

In time they were headed home. In the rumble and jiggle of the wagon on the rutted roads as the family headed back east, Francine had the thrill and chill of emotion that so often happened after a recitation of poetry in Miss Josie's class… one that she had worked hard on. It was as though something flowed through her arms and body like…? What? Energy…? Excitement…? No, not really. But she remembered one special time that this feeling had happened.

There was the poem that someone had written about the voyage of Columbus, the time when his crew was begging him to go back because they had seen no land for many days. Surely, they would fall off the edge of the earth at any moment.

The second man in charge, called the mate, had pled with Columbus. The poem went, "The Good Mate said, 'Now we must pray, for Lo! The very stars are gone! Brave Admiral, speak! What shall I say?' But Columbus said, 'Why say, Sail on! Sail on! Sail on!'"

Days later the Good Mate again pled, "My men grow mutinous day by day. My men grow ghastly, wan and weak." A salty spray blew over the deck, and he continued, "If we sight naught but seas at dawn?" Columbus answered, "Why, you shall say, at break of day, 'Sail on! Sail on! Sail on and on!'" Reciting the words in her mind, she again felt the thrill bumps of excitement raise on her arms.

And aboard Columbus' ship things had gotten worse. The mate argued. "Why now, not even God would know… Should I and all my men fall dead. These very winds forget their way, for God, from these dread seas, is gone. Now speak, Brave Admiral, speak and say!" But he had said, "Sail on, sail on!"

*They sailed. They sailed. Then spake the mate,*
*"This mad sea shows his teeth tonight.*
*He curls his lip, he lies in wait,*
*He lifts his teeth as if to bite!*
*Brave Admiral! Say but one good word*
*What shall we do when hope is gone?"*
*The words leaped like a leaping sword:*

'Sail on! Sail on! Sail on and on!"

Then even Columbus himself was seemingly discouraged. He walked the deck and looked in every direction.

*Then pale and worn, he paced his deck,*
*And peered through darkness. Ah, that night*
*Of all dark nights! And then a speck—*
*A light! A light! At last a Light!*
*It grew, a starlit flag unfurled!*
*It grew to be times' burst of dawn!*
*He gained a world! He GAVE that world*
*Its grandest lesson! "On! Sail on!"*

One hand held to the jiggling seat of the wagon, and the other reached to her eyes. Of course, she could never expect do anything like Columbus did. His voyage to America made it possible for the parents and grandparents of the people of Shady Ridge to be here. That was his part. And now it was up to her to play her part. The excited chill again raised goose flesh on her arms.

Columbus only did what was already inside himself to do. That's all anyone can do. Tonight, she felt a kinship with Columbus… now that it was her turn. She would be the best teacher that Shady Ridge would ever have because Miss Josie had brought her a dream. She swallowed hard against the lump in her throat.

The horses stopped at the barn, and the family walked through the familiar yard in darkness. Weariness. Tomorrow was another day. A day that work had to be done.

It was much later when they were finally in their bed, that Sam Canfield commented to his life's mate, "Julie, did you take note'a our girl bein' so quiet on the way home… after a party that was just for her?"

A hesitation. "I took note'a Francine bein' Francine. She was busy feelin' things, like when she practiced them poems Miss Josie assigned. She was livin' inside'a some other place and wasn't even in the wagon with us. She was bein' part'a the words and part'a her own thoughts, and that's what happened on the way home. I was lookin' at 'er on purpose."

Sam hesitated. "So you're thinkin' we did right by them youngens'a ours? Who'd'a thought she'd say what she did about us?"

Julia Canfield grinned to herself in the darkness. Such a clever daughter they had! "Yeah, well it weren't all for us. She was a'warnin' all them parents what she expected them to do for their youngens. We was just bein' part'a the lesson."

Sam Canfield reached across in the darkness and patted his wife's shoulder. Then he turned over to a cooler place on his pillow. Sleep. Get some rest. Tomorrow was another day.

Julia Canfield stared at the dark ceiling. Thoughts rolled about in her head. If the evening had been for Rosalie, it would have gone so much differently. She and her friend, Carmelita, would have chatted and giggled the whole way home. They would still have been wrapped up in the festivities of the evening, discussing what was served and what was said, and how people looked. So different her girls were for all the fact that they would almost pass for twins if Francine had not been a bit taller. So very different, but inside each of them was the same determination. Rock hard and permanent.

The girls could both be hard as nails when they made up their minds, but the paths they took were so different. If Francine had taken the job at the rock ledge school, she would have been hard to work with because she KNEW what she wanted and she would get it done. By herself. If Rosalie had taken the Shady Ridge job, she would have been uneasy and apprehensive at first, and lonely for a coworker later on… someone to share decisions and successes.

Life was interesting. Their son, Raymond was next, and he would likely go in yet another direction. She turned her face to a cooler place on the pillow and shut her eyes. Sleep. Tomorrow was another day.

Francine opened the window higher to capture every breeze possible. The night was as dark as the ink in the bottle in her desk drawer. She, too, was full of thoughts and possibilities. She stared into the darkness. She felt she was standing on a bridge. Tonight and tomorrow night would be her last times to sleep in this bed before she moved.

Sunday afternoon she would take Chock and her darling chocolate colored buggy to Shady Ridge, and she would spend the night on the narrow bed in the schoolroom. A new life. She smiled with satisfaction, turned her face to a cooler spot on her pillow. Sleep. There were things to do before she left, and tomorrow was another day.

Miss Josie Wheeler Cullen was silent as she prepared for bed. Brad was understanding and also kept silent. The night breeze moved over the bed as she stretched out. Thoughts crowded together.

Francine had spoken very much as Josie had expected. Friendly, businesslike and to the point. She left no wiggle room for slackers or discipline problems. The first few months might be a bit scary for the students and their parents, but Josie would bet the farm and her Cinderella carriage, that before Christmas the parents would be singing her praises. Cutting back on the tuition was a thoughtful move. They would not forget that.

She nodded to the darkness. Francine was a teacher. Teachers were not made, they were born. Training made a teacher a better teacher, but it could not make a teacher from one who was not a teacher. Josie was comfortable in her assignment, because she, herself, was not a teacher and she knew it. She had never thought for a moment that she was.

She stretched back against the cool sheets with a bit of selfish satisfaction. She was not a teacher, but her gift to the Territory was the creation of teachers. So far, there had been four. Her cousin Carmelita, Rosalie and Francine Canfield, and Eve Adams who now taught in a classroom three miles south. If she did nothing more, she would feel satisfied that she had done what was handed her to do.

Francine's praise of her had been unexpected. Not that she did not know Francine was thankful, but that she expressed it so well, also using the praise as a warning to the parents of what they could expect. Very clever. And being only fourteen, Francine would only get better in the next few years.

Another nod of satisfaction. Francine may marry and have a family, but it will not keep her from her dream. If she had taken a public-school job, that would not be possible. Just another tiny little thing that she, Josie, could pass on. She had been so favored in having a private tutor, she knew that the gifts of ability that she could give were very important. There was a lot more to think about over the next months and years.

She sighed a relaxed sigh and turned her face on her pillow. Tomorrow was another day.

Mr. John William Brown was silent as he prepared for sleep. The lanterns had been taken from the trees and the scraps of leftover food retrieved by the preparers. Tomorrow, he would again store the saw horse tables. Now that the school was started, there would be other times for the saw horses to be used.

Elsie was also silent, but not for long. "John William, you comprehend the words comin' outta the mouth'a that child? You'd'a thought she was fifty years old! She spoke like no fourteen-year-old girl I ever saw." John William was silent, knowing there were more words to come.

"Can you even think on all the words that'll be tossed around Shady Ridge for the next weeks? I'm figgerin' the youngens are going to get a word'a warnin' about puttin' their heads down to learn. I don't think our Isabel took her eyes off that teacher to even blink. I can see her thinkin' on copyin' her in talkin' and walkin' and maybe even dressin'." A hesitation as John William raised the window a bit higher and sat on the bed. Elsie stretched out on the cool sheets, and he laid down beside her.

"What'd'ya think, Elsie, that we may'a prayed for a shower and got us a toad strangler flood?"

A sigh "No. More like we set a trap for a wren and caught ourselves a bird'a'paradise. You reckon Shady Ridge is ready for a bird'a'paradise?"

John William thought for the best answer. He knew Elsie was looking for comfort. "Elsie, honey, if we ain't quite ready for a bird'a'paradise, give that girl a year or two, and she'll get us ready. Top'a that, we'll be glad she did. That's what I'm thinkin'."

"Then I'll think that, too. We been worried, some of us women, that she'd not be up to the discipline, but I changed my mind on that. Still yet, it'll be good to have another grownup there for accidents or such." Then she added, "'Course, I'll be here just a yell away."

John William knew there would be a lot more words said, but they would come in the next few days. Just now he was plum wore out, so he turned his face toward the open window. Sleep. Tomorrow was another day.

Someone else was awake after the party. Margie Van Pelt, fifteen, tall and slim, sunshiny yellow hair braided into a thick crown around her head (hair a gift from her Dutch mother). Pale, pale complexion that required constant protection from the prairie sun and a smile that set off her chin dimple and her pronounced cheek bones. She had gone to the party with her brother's family because his two little girls, five and six, would be going to the school.

Margie slipped into her nightdress and blew out her lamp. There was nothing she needed light for, so she looked out the window at the stars. Thoughts raced themselves around in her head, and ideas tried to form and themselves together, whirling around like clouds in the wind, just out of reach. She had the feeling that she was nearing something, but it needed more thought. Seating herself on the floor below the window, she prepared to spend another sleepless night.

Margie had a problem. One of her feet was perfectly normal. The other was not. Her left foot required trimmed and reshaped shoes to accommodate an ankle that was totally turned in. This caused Margie to walk with only a slight limp, but caused a weakness that kept her from so many of the duties that the territory required. Heavy lifting, extensive walking as well as extreme sun-sensivity created a multiple problem.

Family disasters had decreed that she migrate west when her brother won land in the run. Somewhere in the circle of family problems, health problems, and scarcity of schools, it had left Margie with no education. She felt the lack severely. Not that her brother had much schooling, but his was more than hers, and it was different for healthy men... they could DO things. Her sister-in-law could read... almost. She could not help Margie with more than a few words. But she had a husband to make up the lack. Margie had only herself.

Now, Margie knew about the new teacher who was coming. She also knew that the teacher would need help in the form of another person, just in case of accident or something unforeseen. She listened to the teacher speak, and excitement played up and down the nerves in her arms. Somehow...? She just must try...!

# CHAPTER 2

She'd talk with her sister-in-law and brother. If someone had to be at the school, how could the busy women of the town manage it? There was so much for them to do, especially in the mornings. Margie, herself, had very little to do in the mornings. The girls dressed themselves, the new baby was at least six months away, and the breakfast dishes could be done when she came home.

Now, if she could just sit at school until noon, there would be a lot of words said, and she would learn a lot just by listening to the lessons. She was actually very quick to learn. She was certain of that. If she needed to be home by noon, then one of the other ladies could take the afternoons, and that would give them mornings to do the things all farm women had to do… cooking, taking care of the milk, putting on the beans, picking and canning garden produce. In short, here was the question. Would there be a way to put it to her brother and others that would make it seem to be a help to them if she got to be in the classroom where reading was taught?

When would be the best time to suggest it, and would maybe one or the other of them need to go with her? Who would make the decision as to whether she was capable enough? Would the beautiful girl who was to be the teacher… care… if she just sat and listened in?

Where she had sat in the classroom at the party, she had been so close to the bookcase that she could have reached out and touched the books. She didn't, though. Instead, she had stared at them, feeling a grain of an idea forming in her head. The idea was still growing, and it was certainly past midnight.

Stretching out on her bed, the thoughts continued. Around and around they raced, looking for a place to break out. Ideas! She was still chasing the BIG IDEA when the first rooster sounded off in the barnyard.

During the morning meal and on into the Saturday, her thoughts continued to chase themselves. Here she was, fifteen years

THE MAKING OF A TOWN

old, and nothing had happened. Her memory was dim when she thought of the place called New York City. Smells and smoke, of course, but they were normal. She had stayed in the house with the neighbors. Their big girl, Annetje was fun to play with, and Margie's other brother Hendrick carried something called "new papers." Then he got sick with something, and he was gone. Her other brother worked until dark, then he came for her and took her home to Ma and Pa. Nobody played. Too tired. Pa leaned into his plate to eat... too tired to sit up straight, she guessed. Ma spread oil on her red, raw hands. Hands rubbed raw by the cloth she sewed. Her eyes were red and weepy. Every day. Nothing different.

They talked the other language they didn't want her to hear. Sometimes Ma cried, and Pa hugged her, shaking his head. Every day.

Clearer was the memory of leaving town. Her biggest brother, Jakob, and Annetje moved her into a wagon with a roof and they took a long trip. She missed Pa and Ma but so much happened. Food cooked beside the road. Being wrapped in a blanket and put to sleep under the wagon seat. And she would drift off to sleep with the breathing sounds of her brother and Annetje (who she was now supposed to call 'Anita'.)

New things to see along the way. Anita had held the straps that guided the pair of horses, and Jakob (Jacob) rode the really big horse alongside.

Sometimes she was allowed on the ground to walk alongside the wagon, and she could run... but not very fast. She didn't know why she had a different kind of foot, but she didn't think of it very long. When she got tired, she climbed into the wagon... or sometimes were special, and she got to ride on the big horse with Jacob.

She knew they were supposed to speak with the new words that were hard to say. She didn't know why, but she DID know that it was important. Her brother and sister-in-law had a lot to say to each other in the evenings while she played about. After supper, they mostly sat close together talking low, struggling with the new words while they held cups of hot tea. Sitting close to the fire with their cups held like they wanted to warm their hands... even though it wasn't cold. That was years ago.

On her fifteenth birthday, a few months ago, Margie realized she was the exact age of her sister-in-law when Anita had decided to leave her family and go with seventeen-year-old Jacob to the Big River. Such a terribly brave thing for her to do! And here she, Margie, was. And she had never done anything brave in her life. She helped with the housework and spent a lot of time with Edith and Susan, born in the same year. Diapers to change and wash. Food to cook while Anita was working with Jacob. Teaching the girls to walk. Singing them to sleep, always with the new words.

But now? Her lungs seemed to swell out at the thought, and excitement popped out in thrill bumps along her arms. She would… somehow… figure on how to spend some time at the schoolhouse. These thoughts occupied her through the whole day.

Jacob and Anita Van Pelt also spent a sleepless night and a thoughtful day.

Anita first. In the darkness of the bedroom, she touched his arm. "Jacob, that girl at the school… she wasn't even as old as Margie, but did you notice her words? We're even luckier than we thought that the girls get to go listen to her."

Jacob had not been asleep, either. "Yeah, it'll take a chunk'a time to get 'em over there and back. Mile and half, that'd be too far for 'em at barely six. I was thinkin'a ridin' 'em double on the horse, but that'll make a slow start in the work here. No way to help it, though, and like you said, we're really lucky. It'll be easier for them to say their words in American if they get to listen to that girl. Miss Francine, did they say?"

"I can take the girls," Anita insisted, bravely.

"No." Jacob's voice was firm. "You're sick in the mornin's, and we ain't takin' no chances after losin' the other one. I'll figure a way. Maybe Margie? Could hitch up the cart. 'Course that'd take her away for over an hour… two times a day."

Anita then. "We'd manage. I wish it'd be so she could stay there. She'd likely be a help, and we already thought she'd have to go in my place when it came my turn go. That girl don't hardly get anything fun, and the way she is…"

Yes, the way she was. That doubled over foot had gotten no better, as they had hoped would happen as she got older. She just learned how to manage it. She was slower, but she got a lot done. Ironing. Darning socks and sewing up rips. Cleaning the floor. Never complained, but Jacob had noticed her silence and her yearning look during the party. Reminded him of someone looking through the window of a candy store, knowing they could never go in.

"Days she stays, she'll have to leave the horse hooked onto the cart. Not good for an animal, but I don't see no other way. Don't reckon she could ride on a saddle…?"

"I don't think so. She's a girl, remember. Almost a lady and it wouldn't be proper ridin' straddle in a skirt." Anita sighed, wearily. "Gotta keep thinkin'."

"Well, listen here. There's a way for women to ride. It's called a side saddle but I don't know what that is. I'm wonderin', no farther than it is, could she sit with one leg around the saddle horn to be steady? Old Plodder, he's so slow…" He paused for Anita's response. It was slow in coming.

"That'd be for her to decide. It'd take a burden off both of us if she could. And here's this, if she could go one day when it was my turn, why couldn't she go more days if she liked it. It'd do her good to hear the American words, and if she's ever to have a husband, he'd surely be American. And you remember that she missed school entirely, and she might pick up readin'… or somethin'…?"

Jacob wisely remembered that another day would be coming. "Let's go to sleep and talk tomorrow. Could be we'd get a good idea… or something'."

It was after the evening meal that Margie pulled together enough courage to put forth her idea. "Anita, you and Jacob got time to listen for a minute? I keep thinkin' on that party last night. That teacher, Miss Francine, she had words like I never heard anyone say. I could'a listened all night. I remembered how they said someone would need to be at the schoolhouse in case of an accident… or somethin'?

"I'm thinkin' I could walk that far of a morning, takin' my time, and you'd not have to bother with it. At least, till the weather gets bad. If I could do that every day, and stay till they had lunch, the other ladies could have their mornings at home. Everyone's got so much to do in the mornin'." She hesitated, watching their faces to see the reaction. All she saw was interest, so she proceeded. They could always tell her if she was on the wrong kind of thinking.

"I was thinkin' the girls was big enough to walk that far. The way they skip and run, that'd be no trick for them." She saw her brother look toward her sister-in-law, with a meaningful expression, so she waited.

"Margie, sis, we been thinkin', too. If you'd be brave, could be I got an idea. We think we got somethin' that'd work."

Margie sucked in a sudden breath of surprise and pleasure. "Oh, do you think so! And I'd make up the time I was gone. The ironin' I can do in the afternoon, and the cleanin'. And I'd take darnin' along with me, or whatever needed doin'. That'd be such a pleasure to listen to Miss Francine talk to the classes! I thought I'd look for a stick to carry, maybe helpin' me walk faster. I can be really brave but it's not even two miles to the school, and I'd take care'a the girls, like always! It didn't seem from the talks that whoever stayed had to know somethin' special. They just had to be there." She caught her breath and suddenly ran out of words.

Then Jacob. "Margie, sis, that wasn't the brave I meant. I'll go take care of somethin', and then I'll call you outside." With that, he was gone.

Margie looked at Anita to supply an answer, but she just smiled and shook her head. "This here's your brother's idea."

Later, as she stood in the yard and looked up at the saddled horse, Margie began to think it might, indeed, take some bravery. There the massive animal stood beside a sturdy box.

"Can you step up on the box and turn your back to the horse?" She did and watched her brother's face, wondering.

"Now, reach back and see if you can pull yourself up into the saddle. Don't be concerned as how you're sitting. Reach back and hold to the saddle horn. If this works, I'll make you something better."

She was not particularly athletic, her foot being what it was, but she managed to pull herself up into the saddle, her skirt bundling about her legs. The old horse bent his head around and looked her with a puzzled expression, but he stood patiently.

"Now, sis, I know it's shakey up there, but here's what I want you to do. Your right leg, there, bend at the knee and hook your leg over the saddle horn. Easy now, Old Plodder'll get used to it."

Careful to hold to her dress and protect her modesty, she did as she was instructed. She saw the look of concern in Anita's eyes.

"But, Jacob, that'll make her foot go to sleep, won't it?"

"Not on a two mile trip, I don't think. It won't take more'n fifteen or twenty minutes to get there. And see here, there's room for the girls on behind. I'll lift 'em up today, but I can make it so they can climb up by themselves."

First one giggling girl, then the other, snugging up against Margie's back. "Now, Edith, you hold tight to Margie, and Susan, you hold to Edith. I'm going to walk around the yard and see how it works." The old horse responded to the lead line and ploded calmly behind his master, seeming to disregard the strange load on his back and the squealing and giggling of the small humans.

Following a wide circle and returning, he asked, "How did it go, sis?" A smile and an energetic series of nods was his answer. "And you, Anita?" He knew without looking at her that he had her answer. He lifted his daughters to the ground and turned his attention to his sister.

"Now we get down to work. Margie, you are going to have to learn to guide this fellow, at least for the first week or so. Then he'll know what he's supposed to do. Say 'Come on' and try to sound like me. At the same time, kick your heel against his ribs and jiggle the reins."

The old horse took another look behind him, then a glance at his master, finally lifting his feet into a solid plod. Around the circle of the yard, he went.

"All right, Margie, I want you to ride him around until it begins to bother your leg. I'll step into the barn and do a few things, but you just yell if you need me." With a reassuring smile, he left her. He heard her encouraging voice, "Come on, Plodder."

When she called, almost an hour later, he helped her down and reassured her, "For the first day or two, I'll ride along, to see if everything works out all right. You know, Sis, if you can go alone with the girls like this, it'll really take a burden off Anita and me. It's so important that the little girls go where they talk American words and not the way we say them. They're going to live here, just like you are, and they need to know, just as you do. Thanks for being brave."

As she returned to the house, Margie told herself, "HE was thanking ME? He's sounding like I can do this every day! Not just on Anita's day." She felt so energetic, she thought she could burst from the excitement of it. Books! Children! American words from the teacher! Words she so sorely needed. Pronounced so beautifully and musically!

As Jacob Van Pelt went about his work, his thoughts traveled over the last twelve years.

Back to the ship. He was not yet clear in his mind why they must leave Holland. It seemed his mother was the driving force and that there were good and important reasons for the voyage, most of them centering around himself and his brother, Henrick.

Crowded ship! Hardly room to sneeze with families jammed up together just looking for a dry place to sleep. It was summer, but for some reason the ship was always cold. Waves blew salt spray over the rails and into the hold where the passengers huddled.

Anita's family was pushed up against his family, and the children of all families became very well acquainted. They had to. The proximity forced them into each other's private conversations as though they were in the same room.

Riddles, string games, puzzles. That was all the children had to amuse themselves during the weeks on the ship. Grownups had their fears to occupy their thoughts, and the faint hope of a better life. Food was scanty and poor, and better food was available for those with gold coins, but most of the travelers, if they had coins, were certainly not going to spend them here. They would just suffer, and if hunger made them a bit more miserable, so be it.

Jacob's family was no different, and he remembered cold, hungry, and worried faces of his parents. He was almost ten, and his brother was three years younger. Anita (then Annetje Buijs) was eight. When cholera hit, Anita's two younger brothers were victims and were buried at sea, along with many other children and a few grownups.

They came ashore, the two families, easily carrying all their possessions. Their first home was one room in a huge house. Anita's family had an adjoining room. The privy was three floors down and in the alley. Water came from a faucet protruding from the ground in the front yard and must be carried up. They knew they were lucky to get the room after spending only one night on the street.

Mrs. Buijs was again expecting. Very bad timing. But what could one do? Children came when they came. The men were put to work immediately digging at the excavation to widen the channel of the river. More water was needed in the city. It was dangerous, but it paid coins.

Jacob's mother went to work in a factory, leaving Henrick with the Buijs' between his paper routes. As soon as Henrick could read American numbers, he had been set to work, and he was lucky to get the job. Older boys would have liked the job. Jacob, himself, was even more fortunate. He went to work in a stable where dozens of horses were kept for city work. He carried feed and water and mucked out the wastes. He hated it because of the smell that arose from the hot buildings, but he was glad to have the job. It paid coins and many others, including men with families, would love to have had the chance to smell the wastes.

The smell stuck to his clothes, and the waste gummed up his only shoes. Later he was able to buy rubber boots. Then the two families were able to get an apartment with water in the room. They shared the kitchen but had three rooms to each family. So much better. Unbelievably wonderful, actually.

They stayed there for years. He remembered the times his mother hopefully asked, could they, somehow, finally go west to the big river? Things would be better there. Pa agreed, but insisted the time was not right. He and Mr. Buijs would know when, and then they would go. It would need to be early spring, but not THIS spring.

The factory where his mother worked sewed heavy fabric into work pants, jackets and sometimes bags. There was no way to wear gloves, and the rough fabric fairly took the skin from her fingers. Blood! But she couldn't even be permitted to bleed, as it would ruin the item she was sewing. Deep creases of resignation settled into her face, and her coughs grew worse. Lint from the fabric, she insisted. Just one of the many things to be endured.

Jacob learned everything there was to know about horses. At times, after he was thirteen and fourteen, he was permitted to drive someone somewhere, and sometimes he even got a few extra coins for doing it.

He often wondered what jobs there would be at the Big River to the west. He thought there would come a time to go, but Pa could never agree that it was right. Pa was becoming stooped and haggard. He was not cut out for heavy digging. In the old country he was a carpenter, doing finish work inside houses, and building sturdy, classic furniture in a shop, but there did not seem to be that kind of work for him here. Perhaps it would be better at the Big River, but if Ma couldn't talk him into making the move, certainly his son couldn't.

Little brother Henrick got older, but he was of a small, slender build. The weight of the papers and the hurrying it took to deliver on time were about more than he could do. He seemed too tired to talk when he got home, and only wanted to curl up by the fire and doze.

Thinking back later, Jacob wondered if his brother had not already given up and was too tired to go on. His parents seemed not have noticed, but their son's problems may have gotten drowned within the problems of food, clothing and coal for the stove. Then a man appeared at the door carrying Henrick in his arms. He seemed to have no trouble carrying the frail body that still held breath, but the blood that soaked his clothing told the future. No one could lose that much blood and live… and he hadn't.

The driver of the carriage wept when he told of there being no way he could avoid the 'child who walked calmly into the path of his four-in-hand teams.' Sixteen horse hoofs had done the damage, and it was a miracle that the boy was recognizable. He blessedly never regained consciousness.

Then his mother was pregnant with Margie. Very poor timing, but what could one do? Children came when they came. The cough became worse, and she wanted to go west to the Big River, but Pa seemed unable to tear himself away from the grave of his son, though he had no time or strength to visit it. One more year, he promised, and there would be enough money, and the baby would be born.

The baby was born, and Ma went back to the sewing factory, leaving Margie with Anita's family. Silent and haggard, she dragged herself to work, coughing. Coughing. Gagging and coughing. It was more than the lint from the fabric. In was the dull and dingy rooms, filthy streets, noise and germs, and no sunshine.

Margie was four when the end came. Ma had called him to her bed, privately. "Son… you're my last hope." Her voice was now a whisper, and her coughs brought up flecks of blood. "You will promise me one thing. I will be gone, but…" and Jacob had stopped her words. "No, Ma, you'll get well!"

"Don't stop me. I may not have much time. Under the mattress I have stored the winter coats and my heavy blue cape. Today, I want you to lift up the mattress and take out the cape. Sewn in the cape is a number of gold coins and a few pieces of jewelry. You till keep it a secret even from Pa, but you will persuade your Pa to take you and your sister to the Big River. When you get there, you'll know what to do."

"But, Ma… I can't keep a secret from Pa… can I?"

"You must. You must finish my dream for you. I KNOW we should go to the Big River, but your Pa is stubborn and afraid. If he knew about the coins, he would spend them to make life better for us here, and it will never be better until we leave. Don't open the seams of the cape until you have made plans to go. I haven't kept it all the way from the old country to lose it now before my dream comes true."

"But, Ma, I'm only sixteen. What can I do to make Pa hear me?"

"Jacob, my son, you are only sixteen on the outside. Inside you are older than your Pa. There is money in the jar at the bottom of the flour barrel. You know that. There is enough money to take you to the Big River, and you keep the blue cape with you all the time. It is warm and heavy and will wrap around your sister in the winter. Don't let it get away. Don't wait till spring. Make your plans now…" Her words were cut away by the coughing that shook her shoulders and produced blood on the cloth.

Now, in the hot September Saturday on his own place in the Oklahoma Territory, the strong, young Hollander shook as with a chill. His height clearing six foot four, broad shouldered and filled out, a head full of yellow hair and a curly beard of reddish gold, he seemed not one to cry, but his memories didn't know that. Laying down his pitchfork, he hid his face in his shirt sleeve and wept.

That had been the last day of seeing his mother alive. It was in the night that Pa woke him up and wept on his shoulder. It was also then that Jacob sincerely hoped that he was older than sixteen on the inside, because his father's strength seemed to have turned to water.

His mother was put into the New York soil near her son, and Pa silently picked up his shovel and headed for the excavation. Jacob lifted the mattress and took out the blue cape. It was heavy, made of wool fabric and lined with fur. So many times he had seen it on his mother, and even now it carried the smell of her. He would like to have cried, but he hadn't the time.

Reaching to the bottom of the flour barrel he took out the family's banking jar. Heavy. A lot of coins, though he did not know how many it would take to get to the Big River, it was time to make plans. His mother had given him instructions, and he had always obeyed.

Wagon and a team. A solid wagon with a canvas cover to protect the people and possessions from the weather and furnish a bit of privacy. He paid for them and left them in storage where he worked.

His greatest pain was leaving Anita as they had become fast friends. They had talked of marriage… sometime. Jacob nodded in agreement with himself, as he knew the 'sometime' had come and he must, somehow, persuade her to come with him. She was only fifteen, but like his mother had said of him, she, also, was older than fifteen on the inside.

His worst problem would be Pa. He would find it terribly hard to leave the graves, but Jacob would persuade him. He would finally threaten to take little Margie and go without him. He was considerably bigger than Pa, and a lot stronger. But when Pa dragged himself home each night, Jacob found he hardly had the heart. How could he badger the old and weak person that was his Pa? And each day followed its yesterday.

His mother had been in the ground for six weeks when the rain came in a downpour that seemed determined to wash away the entire city. The muddy streets were practically impassable, and trash and filth floated down toward the river.

Still Pa went to work. Dangerous. The river raged and the metal equipment was water logged and sunken into the soft river banks. Finally the soaked ground could hold no more water and turned into a moving morass of soggy dirt. Water slamming against the machine that operated the drag-line... it lifted the wheels, turning the whole piece of equipment over. Two men were under it, and the first one was not breathing when he was dug out. The other one had a leg crushed, and he had passed out from pain, though he was still breathing.

Jacob was rushed to the hospital just as the surgeons were about to amputate. He leaned down to his father's ears. "Pa! You'll be fine. The doctors are here...."

The surprising response. "Son, go to the Big River. I should'a listened to your Ma. She always did know...."

"What, Pa? Say more!"

"Go. Take your..." The breath left the tired, discouraged old body before the surgeons had been required to cause even more damage to the leg.

Go. Take your... it would surely have been 'sister' if Pa had had another breath. Jacob stood looking down at his father as the doctors were silent in the presence of his grief. He could not cry. That would be later. Now he must do what he must do.

The mud was dipped aside for the pine box that was placed beside the raw hole dug a month and a half ago.

The Buijs family enclosed him with all they had of sympathy, but it did not... could not... help. That's when he told them. He'd had enough of pain and loss, and he had been instructed by both parents to go west to the Big River. The one with the snakie letters in its name. The big one that split the whole of America in half.

They could not add any advice. Jacob must do what he must do. He wisely waited two days before he told them he wished to take Anita with him. He had the covered wagon and three healthy animals. He needed Anita to help him decide what else to take. They had always planned to be together, and now was time. Everyone knew there were good jobs at the Big River.

Girls grew up fast in those times. Fifteen did not seem so young as it did when he now looked at his sister. He bravely brought his two girls, one almost five and one fifteen, to the Big River, and there were indeed jobs of every description. They found a room, and he went to work on the river. Steveadore. Lifting and loading. Boarding and unloading. Working off some of the depression of the last year. The air was musty and damp from the river, but was not heavy, smoky and putrid as was the place he had left.

There was talk of the land run in the territory of Oklahoma where, if he was lucky and fast, he could earn a quarter section of land all his own. A lot of the young men talked of going. Some actually made plans. Jacob, though, knew for a total and true fact that he was going, and his brave and wonderful wife would be by his side.

She spent money from the jar taken from the flour bin. Clothes. Food that would travel. So clever was his Anita. He had not told her of the value of the blue cape, but had cautioned his Anita that his mother had wanted him to keep the cape because it was so warm and would wrap completely around little Margie. It made sense to Anita. Warmth was something they'd need to think on.

Then it became time to leave. He crossed the Big River in mid-February during a spell of blowing, freezing rain. The three horses and the wagon pulled onto the ferry, and the paddle wheels churned through the brown water. The weather obscured the last sight of the Big River as Jacob leaned over the ferry railing and stared at the rolling, twisting flow.

You were right, Ma. When I got here, I got a job, and I knew what I should do next. Sorry about Pa, but I guess you know that now. I got Anita here with me, and Margie is wrapped up in your blue cape... covers over every other bit of clothing she has. She and Anita are huddled under a blanket, giggling at nothing... you know the way they always did? Don't you worry none, Ma, I'll make your dream come true. Me and my two girls, we'll do it." He forcibly attempted to swallow the lump in his throat. It could have been so different, but maybe this was the way it was supposed to be. If they had come when Ma first wanted to, Anita would have been twelve and been left behind. It was better this way. At least for him.

A jolt told him the ferry had reached the other side of the Mississippi River, and he must be ready to drive off. He'd need to find a place for the horses until the storm blew over, and there must be somewhere that he could take the girls, but in spite of the ice slivers stabbing against his cheeks, he was happy and light hearted and even warm inside his heavy sheep-skin lined coat.

They spent a day and another night in the lobby of a hotel, along with other families caught in the same blizzard. At least, food could be bought.

The trip across Arkansas was accomplished with no major mishaps. Another ferry crossing happened over one of the tributaries to the Arkansas River, and another one would come when they again met the twisting Arkansas River at the border town of Fort Smith.

The wagon was re-provisioned at Fort Smith, and they moved into Oklahoma. Leaving the hills behind, they traveled the flat lands toward the center of the territory to where the land race was to be held.

Jacob left his 'girls' at the border of the unassigned land because the wagon could not keep up the pace required to win a parcel of land. He had left word with her and attempted to extract a promise that, if he did not return in two weeks' time, she would go back to Fort Smith and safety. Anita could not agree though she led him to believe she would. She knew she would live in Oklahoma. She would find a way.

Jacob also had firm plans to stay. If he should be so unfortunate as to miss out in the race, he planned to find employment with someone who had won. He would do that before he went back to collect his wagon.

He was dismayed that he was forced to travel so far, and take the time to register his land, and then to get back to the border. He was in fear that the two weeks would have passed, and Anita would have headed back, but he found them laughing and happy with the others at the border, being fully assured that he would be successful. As he was.

The land he acquired was flat and without any improvements. A small creek ran through it and that was its biggest plus. All the way back to his girls, he ran through his mind how he would quickly manage protection for the family, acquire a cow or goat and plant a garden that would see them through all of the months before winter set in. And he didn't even know how fierce the winters were in Oklahoma, but he knew he would make it.

With a sharp ax, he made a shed from cottonwood poles and the brushy limbs he removed from them. People needed shade. The Oklahoma Territorial sun was already hot and it was only May.

Next he spaded the garden, with Anita busy on the rake and hoe breaking clods of earth. It was clear that the sod had not been broken since it had been created by the Good Lord and was impossible to plow with the horses. Precious seed finally in the ground, he turned again to the shelter. He closed in two sides of the shed with more cottonwood logs, chinking the cracks with clay from the creek. A cow was not available for any price, without making a two- or three-day trip, so he settled for a goat. It was a good choice. They took up less room.

Next came the larger garden. Potatoes and turnips, winter squash and tomatoes. The land nearer the creek was not so tightly sodded, and the work went faster. A neighbor wished to borrow the horses for a day, and he agreed to lend a horse if he could borrow their wagon for another day. On that day, he made two trips to the sawmill five miles away to bring dimension lumber for the house.

A storm blew in, and the house lumber was quickly used to board up the shed to keep possessions from blowing away. The shed was divided using one half to cover his wagon in which they were still living, and the other half for the animals. Then he used two precious days cutting swaths of prairie hay for the animals. Swinging the heavy scythe was efficient but exhausting. As the hay fell to the ground, Anita wielded the rake to pull it into windrows to dry. They had yet to roll it together and haul it to the shed. When that was done, it had to be stored in the part where they lived to keep the animals from starting to eat it immediately.

41

Back to the house. By now it was October, and the nights were often cold. The protection of the shed created a warmth that was livable, but would not stand the brunt of the winter. Anita was patient and toiled as hard as he, and her only complaint was that she could not carry water and heat it on their small camp stove fast enough to keep themselves and their clothing clean. Not surprising.

He had to have more boards, and that meant taking the cover from the wagon and using it to haul the lumber, though it was too small to be efficient. Also, the shed was very cold without the wagon to crawl into and to sleep in.

Bedding on the hay was warmer, but the gnawing of the field mice working on the hayseeds kept them awake. Providence, however, sent a stray cat into their midst, and in addition to eliminating the mice, it made a plaything for Margie, now going on seven.

It took two weeks of hauling to bring in the amount of lumber needed. On one of the trips, he stopped in the settlement of Argyle and placed an order from the catalog of Montgomery Ward. A cooking stove, a potbelly for the parlor, large washtubs and a pair of bedsteads. He'd get those home, and Anita would have to decide on what else was absolutely necessary.

Now that he had lumber, he created a table and benches from rocks and boards. The boards would later be part of the new house. Anita was joyous. She had enough backache from work without cooking while bending over to the ground. Also, a bench and a table seemed like a luxury.

By Christmas, he had three rooms boarded and rafters up. He had never made his own shingles and thought this might not be the time to learn. Using more of the lumber, he boarded the rafters solid and covered them over with tar paper tacked firmly and oiled thoroughly. Roofing would have been nice, but it was in non-existent supply.

The day they moved into the house was a day of laughing and playing. Jacob had gone to Argyle for the catalog order, and Anita and Margie carried… dragged… and rolled their possessions onto the floor made of actual boards and not hay-covered dirt. They stacked their two mattresses in what would be a bedroom and snuggled together, hugging each other joyfully. It did not matter to them that there were no doors yet, and that the windows were square holes in the wall.

It was the middle of the night that the weary horses plodded into the yard and to the small warmth of the shed. The exhausted man removed the harnesses from the animals and stumbled into the house, aided by the light of the wagon lantern. Locating his 'girls' he lifted the edge of the top mattress and slipped under it, clothes and all, grateful for the warmth of the two feather-stuffed mattress ticks.

The next day he put in windows… store bought with glass panes. The doors had yet to be made but he now had the hinges.

Daylight had brought happy examination of the purchases. Among them was a cheeping box of fluffy two-legged fuzz balls. Also a roll of something called chicken wire. Anita and Margie constructed a shelter to contain the tiny fowls before the efficient cat considered them to be dessert. Margie squealed with pleasure as she pounded left-over biscuits small enough for their tiny beaks.

Soap, he also brought, and it created tears of joy in Anita's eyes. Better than gold and diamonds, and now she might be able to clean the clothes in half the time.

Margie was outgrowing her shoes and dresses, but the blue cape was still a 'perfect fit.' Jacob had been obliged to tell Anita of the hidden coins before she decided on another use for the fabric. There were more coins than expected, as well as a gold chain necklace with a red pendant, a string of pearls, a ring with a red set, and a number of broaches. The jewelry Jacob's ma had said might be valuable, but to save it if they could for Margie.

The plunder money was put in jars and buried by a massive cottonwood tree. They didn't need it yet, but certainly would before income came in.

Anita had not a moment that was not filled with exhausting work, but Jacob did not know how they would have made it with her strength and ability. He was sure, now, that her exhaustion was the cause of his son entering the world three months too early. Well, he'd not let that happen again.

He made the trip back to Argyle with the girls, and Anita was able to pick out what she needed, and place another order. Margie's new coat was extra big, and her shoes were heavy and serviceable.

Such a shame that the left one had to be cut, shaped and sewed with leather strips to fit her foot.

Before Margie was ten, Anita was again pregnant. Jacob insisted that she must do less strenuous work, and she obeyed him… when she took the notion. Things had to be done, and she did them. Margie was able to help a lot, now. Time consuming tasks such as rubbing clothes on the rub board, hanging clothes on the line, and pressing out the wrinkles with the heavy metal 'sad iron' became Margie's jobs. Picking vegetables and drying them was everyone's job as it must be done when the vegetable was ripe. Nature didn't wait.

Jacob found time to construct a log smokehouse by the time the pig was ready to butcher. He'd need a bigger one later, but it took precious time to fell the cottonwood trees.

The chickens were now laying their eggs and even hatching some. The babies had to be pinned up and fed at first, but soon they learned to take wing and fly into the trees to roost. The cat didn't bother them… there were too many other goodies there on the ground.

Baby Edith was born, pink and round, and that gave Margie another duty. It became her favorite. A little 'sister' to play with. Eleven months later, Susan was added to the family. Sky blue eyes and golden hair like her sister… and her aunt and parents. Holland could produce such lovely blond hair!

Six months later small Edith uttered her first word… her face dimpling with pleasure over her success. It was difficult to actually discern what the word was, but for a positive fact, it was not part of the Dutch language, or even tinged with German. Also very clear was the knowledge that the word was not English.

Wide eyes and raised eyebrows met between the parents. Of course the time would come, but it surprised them anyway. Jacob looked at his wife and cleared his throat with dignity. "From here on we will speak nothing but English. Even though it is hard and we know our English is not the same as our neighbors, we must try. We must listen carefully and try to copy what we hear. These little girls must know English first, and if ours is the best we can teach them now, they will learn better, later. That goes for you, too, Margie. You can be a help because they MUST not learn any Dutch words."

He looked full face on to each of his girls and was answered with a rapid nod. English it would be, no matter how difficult it was. Jacob had something else to add. "Not even to ourselves, or each other when no one else is listening. Not even in the darkness of our bedrooms. We must make it easier for them than it is for us."

Each year Jacob had managed to add another room to the house. A growing family required a growing house, but other problems arose with the growth. Food being taken care of, duties with the garden and the animals, his attention turned to the fact that Anita still stacked clothing and other things on shelves constructed of rough boards. She had no wardrobe closets or bureau of drawers. There had been no complaints on this score, but he should have noticed.

He lay in the dark, thinking. His thoughts drifted to the old country and his father's shop. Solid and stunning furniture built to last for centuries. Smooth grained wood. Planned to the silkiness of a baby's skin with the sharp blade of the hand planner in his shop. Rubbed with fine sand to bring up the straight, smooth grain of the white oaks. Lumber was not produced in Holland, but shipped from England or from the coast of Labrador.

Hadn't he spent a lifetime in the shop? Didn't he know exactly how the pieces should fit together? Pa's special, well-worn and used tools had been sold. Impossible to bring on the ship. Too bad, because if they had brought the tools, his father would not have used up his life at the end of a shovel.

The sawmill had lumber, but it was rough pine or blackjack oak, native to the soil of the Territory. If he just had the right wood, he could make a bureau of drawers for Anita... better than could be bought. Certainly she should have closets to keep the dust from their better clothing. By now they should be attending community gatherings, and better clothing was hoped for.

He ached to build. It had been the pounding together on the step platform to assist his sister into the horse's saddle that brought on the feeling. Actually, he had made two of the platforms. One would stay in the yard, and the other would be taken to the school. Tomorrow they would talk with the teacher when they picked up the children after the first school day.

45

A comforting peace settled over him as he made his plans… and as he had assured himself that a place had been found for Margie. She certainly deserved it. Like Anita, she never complained about what she had to do, but she must make some changes. Meet people. Have friends. Surely, this was the first step toward accomplishing this.

Miss Francine Canfield, teacher, prepared to return to her classroom in Shady Ridge. Freshly ironed dresses, hair brushes, and other items of personal use were packed.

Chock tossed his shaggy, chocolate head, seeming eager to be harnessed and on the road. Three miles. He willingly backed his shaggy rump between the doubletree poles and waited for the straps. Jeff Wilson had been a good trainer.

Key in hand, Francine opened the door and entered the building that would be her second home for the next… years? Hanging her clothes and putting her personal items in the top bureau drawer, she walked out the back door and into the face of Elsie Brown coming toward her.

"Good to see you, honey. I was comin' over to talk about food and…"

Chuckling, Francine answered, "I was coming over for the same thing."

"Then come on over. I took apple cake outta the oven and it's still a'steamin'. Water's hot for tea. We'll talk."

Seated at the huge table with the tea and cake, Francine began. "My ma made me promise to tell you some things… about how picky I am with my eggs. I always boil them myself and peel 'em so hot I burn my fingers. Then I slather on butter. So she told me to say to you that I'd cook my own eggs, and she even sent a week's supply with me."

"Well, that's all right, honey. 'Course, I'd do my best, but you gotta do what your ma says. I was gonna say that I ring the bell for every meal. I never know where everybody is, what with my bunch and the three nephews we got stayin' here.

"Now for breakfast, I make biscuits and gravy, some kind'a meat and a platter'a eggs. Along with oatmeal. I got honey and jelly."

# CHAPTER 3

Francine grinned. "My ma sent jelly and honey, too. But I'd like to come over when I hear the bell and get oatmeal and biscuits and meat to make my lunch. I'll eat with the students. But I'll be really hungry for supper, and I would like to eat with your family unless I've got lessons I'm working on. Then, I'll just make up a plate and bring it home with me. Ma told me to be careful not to make you extra trouble so I'm hoping I don't. It takes quite a lot of time to be ready for three different classes for seven hours every day. It's the same as I did over at Prairie Academy, so I'm use to it."

The older woman nodded. "Well, dear, that certainly won't cause trouble to me. I just want you to feel free in my kitchen, any time you want something, and take any thing you find that you like. Cook something yourself if you want to."

Now Francine chuckled. "No chance of that. I don't cook if there's anything around that doesn't need cooking. I can do lots of things, but I'd rather not eat my own cooking if I don't have to. I've got no problem with boiling water and dropping in the breakfast eggs, but that isn't really cooking."

That settled, Francine returned to her apartment, armed with a generous hunk of the apple cake topped with a puddle of melting butter. She stowed the cake in her tiny pie safe with the tight door against varmints and insects. Stepping through the door to the classroom, she settled into her chair behind her desk and propped her chin on her elbows. It was time to think.

She had not planned her first day, counting, instead, on an inspiration and an instant knowledge of what to do. As always. As dark descended at the end of the long Oklahoma Territory day, Francine made a cup of peppermint tea to eat with her fresh apple cake. Then she lit her bedside lamp and opened her book of poems written by English poets... the one given to her as a gift by Miss Josie. It was her favorite bedtime book.

Morning. The children arrived early, each with a parent in tow to furnish birthdates and directions to their homes. Most of them had a sibling nine or ten years old who was fully capable of finding their way home and leading younger family members. Most of the children were playing noisily in the yard, delighted to see other children to play with in this land of distances and sparse inhabitants.

As she stood on her step at the front door, she saw a sight that opened her eyes with interest. She had come through a period of being interested in her Norsemen ancestors… the Vikings from the northland with their snake ships who came to England to plunder but later to live among their former victims. Pictures in the book showed the snake ships with their highly lifted prows, usually carved with dragons or sometimes with the head of a woman with flowing hair. For a period of time, she had found them interesting, and then she had gone on to the other fascinating things in the books at Miss Josie's Prairie Academy.

What she now saw brought her attention sharply back to the Vikings as she saw the stern face with yellow hair flowing in the wind, chin covered with red-gold curly beard, and astride a horse of rich chestnut color. The horse head was held high as it trotted down the rutted track of State Highway. The long mane of the horse flowed out from the neck of the beast, giving an impression of the dragon head. Behind the saddle of this tall, broad shouldered 'Viking' rode two small girls, confidently holding to the overall straps, their eyes trained on herself and the schoolroom. The long hairs of the horse's tail flowed behind, completing the picture of a snake ship from Norway heading confidently toward the steps where she stood.

Blinking her eyes to refocus them, she saw an ordinary man from the settlement with two small girls riding behind him. Directing the animal into the school yard, the man swung down from the saddle and lifted one, then the other, of the girls down beside him.

He spoke in an accent obviously not English, and some words seemed to require thought. He was Jacob Van Pelt, and he lived a mile down State Highway and left for a half a mile on Sandy Creek Road. His daughters were Edith, a bit over six, and Susan, hardly more than five. His tuition had, of course, been paid to John William Brown, who would be keeping the records.

Jacob was a man of few words. After patting the heads of his daughters, he ducked his own head in what might be a quick bow toward Francine, and turned back to the horse, swung aboard, clicked and jiggled the rein, and he was gone. Francine led the girls into the classroom and rang the bell. The day had started. Almost.

Somewhat breathless, Grandma Catlin bustled in, bonneted and carrying a basket of yarn. "I come to stay the day, Miss Francine. You needin' something, you got only to ask me. I'll be sittin' and knittin' socks till you do."

Hmm. Francine was not exactly confident about the old lady, but from her apartment she brought a comfortable chair, with cushion, to the corner of the room and got the old woman seated.

The eight youngest students were seated at the lower table made especially for them. She carefully placed the Van Pelt sisters on opposite sides and ends of the table. She was acquainted with closely spaced sisters, and she did not want Edith in position of helping Susan, or Susan expecting help as she may have at home. Francine knew she would know quickly enough if Susan, a barely five, could keep up. She clearly remembered Tray Cullen and Lily Gray Owl from Miss Josie's class. They had no trouble. It must have been the way Miss Josie taught.

The second level had six students… four boys and two girls. McGregor twins, Dorcas and Donald. Also, Dorcas' friend, Mary Ellen Tall Tree. She set the two girls together and Troy Cameron, the oldest boy on their side, with the other three boys opposite. She'd see how it went. Could be, she'd have to change the seating every few days.

The third level fascinated her. They were four girls, the same as Miss Josie's first year. Two of them were sisters, as had been herself and Rosalie. There had been no problems or competition between them. Girls were different, and she hoped these girls would work together the way she and her sister had worked with Carmelita and Carlotta.

She knew she could not play favorites, but Isabel Brown had won her heart. Huge brown eyes and fly-away hair, escaping from whatever restraint was chosen for that day. Turned up nose and ears slightly protruding, sharp elbows and a bit of clumsiness. Dress

49

always seeming to be askew, and sash ends hanging loose. It almost seemed that her dress and even her hair and other features had difficulty keeping up with her, but none of that was noticeable when she smiled. Her smiles used up her whole face and maybe even her hair. Bright, open and inquisitive. She would be interesting to watch.

Grandma (call me Katie) Catlin settled into the corner chair and took out her knitting needles. The charcoal and gray yarn made the half-done stocking grow rapidly.

Francine decided the first week or two would be spent on memorizing the alphabet and the beginning of letter sounds. All 20 of her students were silent and attentive, but she knew that would change. Soon.

By noon Miz Catlin was nodding. Her needles drooping into her lap. Francine hoped she would not fall out of the chair.

She passed around Second Grade McGuffey Readers to level three and told them to work on the first story. The others repeated the first seven letters of the alphabet and their sounds.

In the afternoon she put out sheets of paper to level three and told them to divide up the letters in their first motto, and draw them on the paper sheets as big as they could. First motto, A BOOK IS A PACKAGE OF THOUGHT.

This done, she handed the lettered sheets among the students of level one along with color crayons. Color the picture any way you want, they were told. When the younger students had scribbled thoroughly on the letters, the sheets were divided among level two along with several pairs of scissors. "Cut along the line," she told them, "and don't bother where the colors are. Just cut out the letters, and tomorrow we'll do something with them."

By later afternoon, the old woman in the corner had given up and was sleeping soundly, her head leaning back into the corner. As she seemed to be safe from falling, Francine gave the matter no further concern. It was a decision for later.

Then it was bell time again, and the students were told to stand and WALK to the door, being polite to smaller classmates. Most of them walked on home, but the two Van Pelt sisters were strolling around, looking at the wonderful things in the room. Francine, at the door saw the blond Viking again, this time walking beside the small, two-wheeled cart, locally called a 'dog cart.' Riding in the cart were two women, their butter yellow hair fluffing out from their bonnets in the slight breeze. Also in the cart was a strange object looking like a short staircase... maybe.

The man stopped the cart, and a tall, slim lady in a sky-blue dress stepped out and came toward her, the man took the staircase to the back of the school yard. The tall girl in the blue dress proceeded toward her, walking with a slight limp but managing quite well.

Francine waited. "Miss Francine? My name M.. (she almost said Marteja). I'm Margie. I come to ask a.. question.. maybe." The strange lilt to her words were the same as the man's and also the young sisters. She continued. "We come to party, and you talk. We liked the way, and my brother is good.. no, happy little girls can hear you talk. Is hard to learn new talk. Not like the old country and very hard for big...?"

She raised her hand above her head. "No.. tall ones to learn. Little girls have good time... to know how to say... speak." She took a deep breath, frightened, but knowing that she must continue.

"Brother and his... wife, say I come to hear. I do not have any school. Say you might not care I stay. Maybe mornings. I can help if little ones have uh... hurt, like accident?" She tapped her shapely fingers against her cheek. "I need hear good talk. They say I listen with little ones, and it make me... help me learn. Do I say good for you to hear?"

Francine had listened to the agonized attempt at English, wanting to help but knew she shouldn't. Best she smile with encouragement and wait. Margie knew very plainly she was not doing well.

"Come in, will you Margie? I'm so glad you came. Let me see if I know what you'd like. I had old Miz Catlin here today, and she went to sleep. If I needed help, I would have had to wake her." Margie understood the English perfectly and smiled at Francine's words.

"I think you want to come with the little girls and help me if I need it, and maybe English words will be easier. Is that what you'd like?"

Margie impulsively reached for one of Francine's hands with both of hers. "Yah! I mean, yes! If it can be, I can come next day and stay for noon or more. I can sit quiet and not sleep. I want... need for hearing words like you say. English so not like Dutch." She smiled and shook her head with dismay, spreading her hands wide to display the huge difference.

"Margie, I would like very much for you to come. Stay as long as you like, and it would be a very big help to me. I won't let you go to sleep, because there will be things to do. Do you mind that?"

A rapid nod of the head inside the snow-white bonnet. "I do all if you say what. Here come my brother's wife. She is Anita, and she care for me when I was... like little girls? Ten years. Like big sister. Now she work harder so I can come and talk better."

Anita stood at a polite distance and smiled. Jacob came back from the rear of the school with the little sisters in the dogcart. Anita stepped aboard, and the family waited.

"Brother bring step so I can get off horse when I come. He was sure you say yes. So I come next day." With a smile and a wave, she turned and boarded the dogcart.

"Good bye! See you tomorrow!" Well, that took care of Miz Catlin and the dozing off. Whoever came tomorrow would be sure to be very glad to go back home. This could work out very well if Margie could just hold out. Actually, though, she must have had a lot of experience with her nieces, so she might just be ready for it.

Francine was in her bed opening her poetry book when Margie's words ran through her mind... the way she said that her brother wanted her to come, and that the sister-in-law was willing to make up the sacrifice of time. Woman in the Territory never had a totally spare minute, and freeing Margie to come was a gift from her family that no amount of money could buy. Fingering her way through her favorite book, she read for a few minutes, then blew out the light.

End of a full day. Problem solved, maybe. And a delicious supper of chicken dumplings and fresh garden vegetables. Apple cobbler. She had brought hers home with her to eat while she worked, and had just finished it. Full day. She was soon asleep.

Children were gathering in the schoolyard, playing noisily. Francine stood at the front door, watching as the huge chestnut horse trotted toward her. Instead of the yellow flowing hair and red-gold beard, the rider was wearing a dark blue bonnet with white trim. Behind the rider sat the two small yellow haired girls.

The horse came willingly into the schoolyard, made his way through the squealing children directly to the step platform in the edge of the trees. Margie stepped comfortably onto the platform and held each girl's hand as she slid off the horse to stand beside her. Skipping down the platform steps, they left her behind to join the other children.

Margie made her way carefully down the steps and tied the horse to a nearby tree. Then came to the front of the schoolroom, meeting Francine with a happy smile. She settled her bag of socks to be darned beneath the corner chair just as Francine rang the bell.

Level one made their way noisily to their low table and scuttled into the places they were assigned yesterday. The others did the same, after a bit of tusseling among the level two boys.

Looking around the room, their eyes settled on the page-sized cut-outs stuck to the wall with tacks. "A BOOK IS A PACKAGE OF THOUGHT." Ha! That's what those letters were for!

"Students, we will read this together. Then we will talk about the sounds of the letters so we can read any words we ever see." Several students had no trouble with the first attempt.

"Now, this first word has only one letter. When a word has only one letter like "A" or "I" it will say its name, so the first word is "A-ay." Think about the next word while I talk with Miss Margie."

Picking up a handful of nine of the slates and a cup full of chalk pieces, she went to level one table. "Miss Margie, will you bring your chair over here please?" And it was done. "I would really like a little help if you could, and that would be to pass out the slates to each child, and keep one for yourself. Most of them will not have used a slate," and she held up the eight by twelve item made of rough black material, bordered with a binding of wood.

"I would like you to help them get used to using chalk on the slate and erasing it with these cloths. They may draw what they like, or they may start with circles, like this. Then they must erase and draw something else." She demonstrated by drawing a row of small circles and rubbing them away with the cloth.

Of course, Margie, herself, had never heard of something called a slate, but she was game. With a smile and a nod, she took the board from Francine's hand and picked up a chalk stick. "Boys and girls, we get to do something we like. We think a minute what to make, while I make a tree." Holding the slate so the children could see, she made two marks up and down, topping the pillar with a scalloped ball. "See? Is good to make picture. Watch and I make a bird." A small oval appeared over the tree and sprouted a pair of wings. The children giggled, appreciatively.

"Now I give each one a… slate. You take chalk to be ready. Make a horse if you want. Maybe house."

Francine sighed happily. Margie was a natural with children. In a moment eight slates were being slathered with chalk marks. They giggled shyly as they displayed their creations to their seatmates. Totally unnoticed, the teacher walked away.

Back with the wall motto, she began. "We start with a "B," just like what makes honey. Two zeros are an "U-ooh," and a "K" makes a sound like "cake." Put together they make a… what?"

A few students timidly suggested 'book'?

"Exactly. Today, we will take this motto word by word and learn a lot about sounds. We will then copy the motto on our slates." An excited murmur passed through the two tables. "Next week we'll work on the entire alphabet, the whole package of letters. Some of you have not had the chance to learn the alphabet, but it is very important to learn it first."

Letter by letter she went, sounding each letter in the motto until she came to the 'gh' in thought. She pinned a blank scrap of paper over these two letters and continued to sound those remaining. Then, "Now here is the interesting thing about learning words. Some letters are just thrown in, and they have no sound at all. They could be left out, but they aren't, so we learn to put up with them like flies in the daytime and mosquitoes at night." A chuckle from the students.

"Now you will get slates, and I want you to print the motto. If you need more room, you'll see the slate has two sides, and you may use the back. If anyone has a problem, just quietly lift your hand, and I'll help." Ten heads with tousled, play-messed hair bent over their desks, looking up occasionally with frown-furrowed brows to determine the proper shape of the letter.

Miss Francine came back to level one table. "My, my, what a good job. Everyone knows how to use the chalk. Now I want you to erase all your marks, and we do something new. Pick up the chalk with one hand and put the other hand on the slate like this. Very carefully make a mark all the way around your hand. Miss Margie, will you put your hand on the slate while I show them?"

Margie's shapely hand fit properly in the center, with slightly spread fingers. Francine traced her hand with the chalk. "When you have your hand traced, we'll count our fingers." That done, with a bit of help from Margie, Francine held the slate so they all could see. "We're going to name this little finger 'one.'" She drew the number over the pinkie finger. Over the next she drew a two, explaining as she went through all five.

"I know that this will be very hard for your hands because your fingers aren't very big, but Miss Margie will help you when you need it. She'll tell you the names of the numbers if you forget. After everyone has finished, we'll erase everything and do it again. I'm so proud of you! Everyone is working so hard and doing so well. I'll be back after while, and I want to see how well you do." With a reassuring smile she handed Miss Margie's handprint to her and walked away.

She had decided to have the first few math lessons together to see where their skill level stood. She was eager to have them using the study cards she made over the summer, copying the ones made by Miss Josie. The study cards had the wonderful advantage of participation by the students, drawing them into the activity.

On the back of the slate, she told them, "Write 2 and 3. Draw a line under and tell me how many 2 and 3 make. Put that number at the bottom like this. See the 5? Now put 6 under the five and how many do you have?" Some were stumped. They weren't sure how to make a 6 or how many that was. Ha. Now we know, she told herself, sadly.

"Students, erase everything, and we'll go about this another way. Write these numbers across the top, 1 to 5. Midway down write 6, 7, 8, 9, 10. Now, beneath the 1, put one dot. Beneath 2 put two dots. If you have trouble, lift your hand, and I'll help."

Level three had no trouble. Part of level two were stumped on the larger numbers. So… that told her a lot. Classes separated, and the four older girls could move on. At least in numbers.

When she came back to the youngest, she had a bowl of small stones. "I need to hear everyone count. Miss Margie will count with you to help. Let's go… One, Two, Three, Four, Five. Very good. Again." They did. After four repetitions, she said, "It's time for you to say the numbers without Miss Margie." She especially watched small Susan Van Pelt. The pink mouth clearly repeated the numbers. Good! Fantastic! She was going to do fine!

"Class, I want each of you to reach quietly into the bowl and take out exactly five stones. Before you start, we'll count one more time. One, Two, Three, Four, Five. Very good. Take turns and do not throw or drop your stones. If you have trouble, lift your hand, and Miss Margie will help." With that, she walked away.

Back to the older girls. "I want someone to go to the motto and point to each letter telling me what sound it says. Who will start?"

Isabel's hand shot up from her lap like a bird off a nest when a cat leaps up the tree. "Isabel, come and point to each letter with this stick as you say the sounds." After Isabel, the others took a turn with varying success. "Very good. Now I am going to write another motto and see how many of the sounds you can pick out."

"A PACKAGE OF SOUNDS MAKES A WORD." The word "sounds" created a studious pause and some help with the diphthong, but they managed. Not bad. She told them to open the second grade McGuffy reader. Each girl read the one-page story, with Isabel going first. Some required a lot of help.

Lunch bell sounded. The children stood and walked to the door as instructed. Francine wondered how long that would last till she had to remind them again that the littler ones could not always get out of the way, and besides, running made a lot of noise.

She came to the low table and sat on it. "I think we did a good job. How did it go with you? You didn't get to work with your sewing? Did I take up too much time?"

"Oh, no! No! No! I had good time. Learned a lot. I want... always... to help. I thought... listen but help is better. Do the little ones read... words in a book? I want so much to... know words."

Francine held up three fingers. "Wait three weeks, and you will read words. Wait four weeks, and you will read more than one hundred words. That is a promise. All you have to do is come every day and stay all day." She reached in the bookcase and took out a fourth-grade reader. Opening it, she pointed to the first story. Before the year is over, you will read this page. Maybe before Christmas you will read the page."

Margie stared expressionless at Francine. "Can it be?" was all she could force her throat to utter. She stared at Francine and her nodding head, then lowered her face into her hands. It was just too much to comprehend.

"Lunch time. We have work to do this afternoon." She decided the knowledge was about too much for Margie, so she went into her apartment and heated a cup of tea while she ate her biscuit and sausage sandwiches and munched on the late radishes, fiery hot as all fall radishes turn. Her comfortable bedroom chair still drawing duty in the classroom, she sat on her slipper stool and leaned back against her soft feather mattress, smiling contentedly.

During the afternoon she moved between the tables, introducing activities that would come in the next days, correcting misshapen letters and numbers, watching her four older girls as they looked at the second story in their McGuffy reader. A lifted hand gave the answer when they stumbled. She would not hold her older class to phonics as she would the others. The girls already knew a lot of words by sight and seemed eager to move ahead. She didn't want to risk slowing them down. It was necessary that they move into the fourth reader with comfort.

It was late in the afternoon, and level two was becoming restless. It was clearly time to move the bowl of stones to their table.

"Each of you must lift out 4 stones. Put them in a pile. Then pick out 2 more and put them in the same pile. Count them. How many?" Hands shot up and Troy Cameron blurted out, "Six!"

"Very good. Write on your slates, 4 with 2 under. Draw a line and put six below. Four plus two equals six. Now put 3 more in the pile. Count them and write down the equation on your slate."

Six pairs of eyes looked at her, questioningly. "I want you to look at the example on your slates and figure out what to do. Think hard." Dorcas reached for her chalk and printed 6 over 3, a line and a 9. Then she covered her work with her hand. "Dorcas, why have you covered your work?"

"I think it might be wrong, and I don't want you to see." Her tablemates jerked their eyes up to the teacher. What would she do if the equation was wrong? "Hold up your slate so the class can see. Dorcas is right. Also, I want to remind you that it is all right to be wrong. If you knew everything, then you wouldn't be coming to school. You would be at home chopping weeds with a hoe. Always do your best. If you happen to be wrong, we'll work it out together."

A sigh of relief. "Put your stones back in the bowl. Now take out 2. Then 5. Then 1. Then 4. Look at your stones and write the equation with the result." A quick scribble, a line and a result, 12. A hand shot up.

"Yes, Donald?"

"We all put down four numbers. Troy has three. But we got the same answer." He pointed to Troy's slate. 5 plus 3 plus 4.

"Troy, why do you have only three numbers?"

Blue eyes stared into her face, lips drawn firm with seriousness. "I looked and my head said 2 and 1 were 3. So I just wrote 3. Is it wrong?"

"No. You took a shortcut. It's like you cut through someone's cow pasture on your way home instead of going around the road. You still get home, if a bull doesn't hook you with his horns." A relieved titter passed through the children. "Mostly, short cuts are good if you get the right answer. In fact, we'll be needing to use them with some of the problems we'll have. Erase your slates and stack them on the table.

"It's almost time to go, but I have something to say first." She picked up a canvas bag about 1 foot square. Each of you will need one of these bags, and we will write your name on it, so you'll know it's yours. Today you will not be taking anything home, but that is unusual. Most often, there will be something to go in the bag for you to do before you come back in the morning. Inside the bag there are two sheets of cardboard. When you need to take home your slate, you will slip it between the cardboards, so the bag will not erase your work.

"You will be taking home your McGuffy readers a lot of the time, and you will practice your assignments until you do them well. We have no time for sloppy preparation. There are books in the library shelves that you will be required to read. They can only be taken home inside the bag and not taken out until you get home. When you are reading a library book, you will not lay it down without putting it back in your bag. Even if you are told to go draw a pail of water for your mother, you will put the book in the bag.

"When you get here early in the morning, you will bring your bag inside and put it on your table. Do not leave it outside while you play. I am very proud of you today, and I intend to be proud of you tomorrow, so goodbye now." And she rang the bell for dismissal.

Margie reached for her un-opened sack of un-darned socks, turned to Francine and tapped both hands on her cheeks. "Feels good to hear new things. Makes thinking!" With that she waved, walked out the door and to the standing horse. Climbing the steps, she positioned herself on the saddle, Susan scrambling up behind her with a gently push on the rear end by her sister. Then Edith lifted her skirt and slipped a leg over the haunches of the chestnut mare.

A click of Margie's tongue and the animal moved out, breaking into a trot at the road. Two little faces turned back to her, and two small hands waved. Francine smiled as she waved back.

Anita was a very good cook. Preparation and blending of the food from the garden seemed to come naturally to her. The squashes, both summer and winter, were a challenge. Holland did not grow gourds like these, and neither had they been available in the heart of the New York immigration district.

Butter was good as a flavoring, but her mind kept saying 'cheese.' A variety of kinds of cheeses were made in the old country, many flavored with herbs, blended and aged. Some pungent as a prairie skunk, others mild as an apple. The milk of the goats made good cheese, but it could be better.

Back in the old country, the cheeses were mostly made from the milk of the black and white cows that did so well on Holland's low and moist soil. If she just had some milk from the Holstein cows of her childhood, she would be happy... The very thought of the round, rich tasting cheese that was used to richen and flavor so many foods... even deserts... made her sigh. It should work well on the American gourds.

She didn't say much, but Jacob knew her so well, it was no secret from him. Of course, she was expecting their third child, and he had heard that pregnant women sometimes had urges for something different. Even so, what Anita thought she wanted was something he would get for her if he could.

Old Mac at Argyle was a fountain of information. "Yes, let me think. It was over to the east there was that fellow that had them kind'a animals. Black and white spotted, they were, and gave a spate'a milk like you wouldn't believe. Folks here wasn't of a notion to like them cows. Didn't have the thick yeller cream for cookin'. Seems I 'member they had some kind'a foreign name like you said. I could make you a map 'cause that feller could be havin' more cows than he wants. Could be, he'd be glad to load some off on you." The shopkeeper picked up a scrap of paper and a pencil, sketching the section line roads to reach the cows.

Jacob had come this far, so he might as well go on. Four miles it turned out to be. He knew he had gotten there when he saw the field containing at least a dozen of the familiar black and white spots grazing on the last of the prairie grass.

A fellow Duchmen. Hans Theunis slapped him on the back in friendship. "Know'd there'd be a 'nuther one'a us show up here sooner or later! You bet I got cows, and there ain't no cheese like that from a grass-fed Holstein. How many was you wantin'?"

"Depends on the price. Had in mind three... could do with two for a while. Noticed you had a good bull."

"Nope, you're wrong. I ain't got no GOOD bull. All three'a the ones I got are meaner'n old Nick, hisself. Fact is, if you want three cows, I'll throw in a bull for nothin'." He named a price that made Jacob wince, but then he thought of the taste of the cheeses and his love for Anita. He had no doubt hers would taste the same as those of his boyhood.

"Could be I could barely manage that, on one condition. Could you get the critters over to Argyle? Comin' all the way out here and then getting' on home, that'd take me all night, and my wife ain't in no condition to be left alone any more'n I have to." He felt he should have been embarrassed over using Anita's condition to ask for a favor… but he wasn't. It was the total truth. Bargaining was bargaining, and it was evident this man wanted to get rid of a few of these hay eaters before winter.

"Well, mister, bein' it's for a fellow countryman, I reckon I could manage it next week… say on Monday. I could be there by mid-mornin', and you bring a wagon. No way to get that bull home if you don't tie his nose to the wagon endgate. You bring the coins, and we'll have coffee at Mac's store."

It was now late afternoon, and Jacob was eager to be off. He pushed the animal to his best speed, planning to allow a rest in Argyle. So, now he'd done it. Four more hay-eaters to prepare for. He forgot to ask if the cows had been bred, or even how old they were. Oh well, he never pretended to be a farmer.

Today was Wednesday. His daughters shouted excitedly for him to come to the table and see what they learned. He watched as they both placed their slates on the table and planted a small hand on the black surface. Carefully around each finger went the chalk and just when their papa was prepared to say how wonderful it was, they squealed at him to wait. With wobbley, untrained muscles, they drew the numbers one to five on the appropriate chalk-drawn fingers. Now they had his attention.

Edith instructed her sister, "Now, together." And the two voices excitedly recited, "One, two, three, four, five!" Squealing and giggling with excitement they stared at their dumbstruck father. Their aunt Margie relieved the situation by clapping applause, joined in by their father.

Edith hugged her father's head, whispering in his ear. He looked toward his sister for an interpretation. There was none, only an outgrowth of excitement. Wrong! More was to come. On Friday of their first week at school, the upper classes had worked on the first half of the alphabet, memorizing it in its order before learning all the sounds. Together they had recited 'a b c d e f g h i j k l M!' together. Strong emphasis on the last letter.

Margie, sitting with the youngest students had been monitoring their one to five numbers, attempting to make them more readable.

In the last minutes, Miss Francine had pronounced, firmly, "On Monday, everyone will repeat these 13 letters without mistake. We will then go on to the other 13. If you think you cannot remember them, put the McGuffy reader in your bag and take it home, remembering the rules of the bag." Then she rang the bell, and the room was cleared except for Margie with a scrap of paper, trying to draw the letters. Francine came to watch, and Margie explained, "I need to know these letters. I want… I get them right."

"Oh, no, don't do that. You must take a McGuffy reader in a bag. You may take any of the books you want to look at. We'll just mark one of the bags for you."

"Oh, please, just let me use one time. I make a bag. I can't use student bag."

"It's all right."

"No! Bags for students. I make a bag, but I use one this time for size. Best I learn letter shapes, so I know when little ones learn." Francine nodded. Somehow it made sense, and it was obvious that Margie had a mind of her own… and that was a very good thing.

McGuffy book in the bag, she smiled, waved and went to the waiting horse. Francine's last sight was the small girls waving and the blue bonnet on Margie's head back on her shoulders where it had fallen when the horse broke into its jogging trot.

At her house, Margie heated the flatiron to press the dresses, and as she smoothed it across the cloth, she recited, 'a b c d e f g h i j k l M!' Big finish on the last letter, just as the upper classes had recited.

Outside the sisters were playing on their swing, hung from the limb of a huge cottonwood tree. Edith sat on the swing board, and Susan gave her a shove each time she came close. Together they chanted, 'a b c d e f g h i j k l M!' the last letter shouted firmly into the clear September day. Susan, then shouting, "My turn! You push! We count letters again!" After the transfer, Susan on the seat, the chant began again, treating the last letter with magnificent emphasis.

But still, to papa's untrained ear, it sounded just like the sound of an angel's song.

On Monday morning, class was assembled. Miss Francine instructed everyone to stand to recite the first half of the alphabet. The two upper classes stood, and Miss Margie stood with them. Edith and Susan tried to stand, but they were so small it was certain Miss Francine would not be able to see them, so they stepped upon their benches. They added their voices with the best volume they could produce and by the time they reached the 'e' all other students had turned to see where the sound was coming from.

The sisters recited without a blink of embarrassment all the way to the final 'M' with its proper emphasis. Silence. Then Miss Francine smiled and clapped, and on the second clap, the two upper classes had joined in. "Class, we have just been treated to a five year old reciting perfectly. This week we will include the younger class in our study. Thank you, Edith and Susan.

"Now, second and third classes, take your slates and chalk for an oral problem." A minor groan came from second class. Oral problems were the worst, but Francine decided to let the complaint go… this time.

Jacob Van Pelt had spent the weekend reinforcing parts of the fence on the back corner of his land. The prairie grass was high and still green, so the animals should have all they wanted to eat. He had a concern over the fierceness of the bull, but the truth was that if he was to produce the black and white cows that Anita liked, he would need the bull. Facts were facts, and Anita, the main source of his strength of purpose, deserved all he could provide her.

He started earlier, as the wagon behind the team was slower than single horseback, and he needed to get to Argyle and back as soon as possible. He was not looking forward to the trip, but one did what one had to do. Also, he could remember the taste of the special cheeses from the old country, and that was enough to pull him onward.

As promised, his countryman was hitched in front of Mac's store. The cows were tethered loosely to one corner of his wagon, and the bull to the other corner. The bull's head was tied by the horns so that he must keep his nose down and match his gait to that of the team pulling the wagon.

"Did ya a favor, friend. Put a ring in this old fellow's nose so's he'd give you no trouble. If he gets stubborn, just tap 'im on the nose where it hurts, and it gets his attention. Dealin' with this fellow, you always need a stick. Now when you untie 'im, take this here other rope and tie it to a fence. Don't think you can hold to the rope, least wise till you get use to 'im. Don't untie the rope to the fence till you get the gate shut back of 'im."

He nodded with assurance. "Just a warnin', bein' I think you might not be used to critters like him."

Jacob felt the fright bumps raising on his arms and on the back of his neck. Whatever had he gotten himself into? Had he lost his mind? But then, he repeated to himself, he would HAVE to have the bull sometime, so he may as well learn now. If he lived through it.

He asked, "Do these animals have names I should learn?"

"Yeah, but they don't come lessen' they want to, so you just call 'em whatever comes in your head. You can tell 'em apart by their spot pattern. That'n there," he indicated a cow with more white than black, "She's due first. The one tied to the back, she's still milkin', and the tuther'n, she'll be in heat next month. Gotta keep records. It's easy. Now let's go have a mug'a coffee."

He thought maybe a mug of coffee would calm his nerves. It didn't. Neither did the second cup. Time he headed west to get home before dark… if he lived.

Securely tied to the back of his wagon, the black bull, his pair of horns each over a foot long, grumbled but followed along without incident. The cow who was still producing had a bit of trouble waddling along with her distended udder, but they still arrived with the sun still in the sky. Barely.

Reaching his own plot of land, he urged the confused horses into the cow pasture and back out again, stopping at the gate blocking the exit. That ought to keep the bull from causing trouble. Loosing the cows and driving them away from the gate, he picked up a stick and untied the bull, bracing against the expected attack. The animal lifted his head, stretched his cramped neck, turned and walked off to a huge oak tree where he laid himself down on the grass. He stayed there and looked around with a disinterested expression. He had walked miles with his head ducked down and was in no mood to cause trouble for anyone.

The cows wandered away, Jacob drove the wagon out of the gateway and closed it securely. Driving the horses back to the barn, he realized he still had a cow to milk, and Anita had the starter for the cheese she seemed to crave. The bull had acted tame as a kitty cat. All in all, it had been a good day. So what if he was tired. That was just an ordinary day, for just as soon as he milked the cow, there would be a delicious meal and a night to sleep.

He came into the yard with the full pail of milk to the sound of his daughters at the swing. Edith was giving the swing a shove each time it came toward her, and chanting, "n o p q r s t u v w x y Z!' Now it's my turn!" He smiled and nodded. All in all, it had been a very good day.

It was after classes on Thursday that Margie approached her. "Is it all right for asking a question? I see in the book what I wonder."

"You certainly can ask a question. What is it?"

Margie opened the McGuffy first year book. "See where it say 'a and t' like 'ay..ta' sound. Is row with other sounds in front. I see 's' snake letter in front. Is word 'sa at' like on a chair?"

Francine looked at the questioning eyes. What courage! Trying to figure out words already. "Yes, that's really good! That word is 'sat' but look at the next one with 'b' in front. 'Bat' and 'cat'. Look at the 'f.' What do you think it sounds like?"

"Fa at… fat?" At Francine's nod, she went farther. "Mat, rat, hat? Is fun!" And she almost giggled with happy pleasure.

Francine encouraged, "Look at the 'an' sound. What do you see?"

Margie drew in a breath. "Can, fan, man, pan, ran… Oh, is so fun! I will go. I keep you from work. I can take book… is all right?"

"Certainly. You take the book, and we can talk again tomorrow, if you want."

Francine watched as Margie walked away, limping a bit and careful to hold her skirt safely aside as she went down the front steps. She waited to catch a glimpse of the three of them on the chestnut horse as he broke into his usual trot upon reaching the road. Also, as usual, the sisters looked back and waved, and Francine answered their goodbye signal.

Turning back into the classroom, a satisfaction swept over her. Options. Like Miss Josie, she was giving options, but different from her former teacher, who insisted she was not a teacher, Francine knew for a positive fact that she WAS a teacher and that teaching was what she was born to do. She was also hungry.

Opening her small pie safe, she found nothing but two small sugar cookies. She was much hungrier than two cookies. She could smell the aroma wafting from the Brown's. Ham, it smelled like. Likely, sweet potatoes would go with it. She'd walk over and mention that she'd like her potato without honey baked in. She really liked lots of butter, and if her potato was just lifted out, she would take care of it herself.

She was really so hungry, she might just stay and eat at the table. Cornbread, probably. Turnip greens stewed, and browned in a skillet with onions and crumbled bacon. Maybe she could help in some way.

Later, she felt like something different. Coffee. Roasted peanuts. With her cut glass lamp lighted in her small apartment, the aroma of coffee and her poetry book, she settled onto her bed and read. And ate peanuts.

She had been teaching for almost a month, and was amazed at how quickly her pupils learned. She saw the downcast faces when she assigned homework, but, so far, it had all come back completed. Those four girls in third level… they continuously intrigued her as she remembered her own class.

Could they work harder and not get discouraged? Maybe, if she went about it like Miss Josie. She remembered how Miss Josie told them that she KNEW she was making them work extra hard, but she KNEW they could do it because they could and would work hard enough to do it.

# CHAPTER 4

So… what if she took them from the second book, which they read fairly well, and put them directly in the fourth book? Should she try? They knew they were reading below level, but the fourth book… that was where they should be, age wise. Pride. It was important to build pride! That was something Miss Josie gave her class. Francine would have to decide on the best way to give it to these girls.

She drained the coffee, brushed her teeth and braided her hair out of the way. It was dark outside and the crickets were screaming in the trees, an owl was calling 'Wooo, wooo,' flapping through the trees like a ghost. The Catlin's cow gave a mournful 'Moo,' and that was the last thing Francine heard, until….

The Brown's alarm clock rooster aimed his decibels in the direction of Francine's apartment. Eyes open. Feet eased over the edge feeling for the fluffy rug. Thoughts engaged. *Those four girls are wading along the edge of their learning, and I should be teaching them to swim, and I will. Girls, get ready!*

About twenty minutes into the morning, Margie was helping 6 year old fingers master better skill with chalk, level two was studying the words in level one McGuffy reader, and Francine pulled her stool up to the end of the table to Level three.

"Girls, take a piece of chalk because you will have to write down some numbers. Problem: Mother wants to make 15 cupcakes. Her pan only holds 12 cupcakes. She measures 5 cups of flour into the bowl. Breaks 4 eggs and stirs in a cup of honey. She wants to know how long it will take to bake her 15 cupcakes? If you want me to repeat the question, I will.

Noting four puzzled nods, she repeated the problem. Chins in free hand, chalk poised to write. Isabel was first to peek through her fingers to see what the others were doing. Nothing! Up went her hand.

"Miss Francine? I didn't hear how long those cupcakes had to bake. Angel food takes longer'n raisin cupcakes."

Francine nodded. "So you think you need to know the baking time. Does anyone else have a problem?"

Althea Martin doubtfully raised her hand. "Miss Francine? I don't know why I wrote down 5 and 4 and one cup? Did we ever have this problem before?"

Francine responded, "You think you have too many numbers. Is that the problem?"

Althea nodded, but Carolina, her sister, was still puzzled. "If they're gonna put down the flour and raisins and honey, it ain't gonna raise till it gets soda. Four eggs ain't gonna raise it much."

Connie Cameron became brave. If the others were going to complain, then she had her own differences with the problem. "First thing I gotta know how long it takes that batter to cook. The recipe oughta tell. And if she cooks one pan with 12, it'll take longer'n it will for the 3 in the next batch. Won't it?"

Isabel again. "Maybe she'll put 8 in one batch and 7 in the other one. That'd be more even, but we still gotta know how long they're 'sposed to bake and then add the times together."

Althea again. "Or else we could multiply by 2. We done learned our multiplying tables up to 5, so we could do it that way."

"Girls, you've done very well. Now tell me three things I could do to find out how long it will be before I get 15 cupcakes."

Connie looked up. "If that mother would come to my house, my ma has a pan that holds 20. She could do it at one time."

Then Althea. "But how long would it take to get to your house? We don't even know where this mother lives."

Connie nodded, agreeably. "You're right. Miss Francine? You know what I think?"

"No, I don't, Connie. What do you think?"

"I think that mother don't know what she's doin'. She needs to get smarter about cookin'."

"All right, girls. We've learned a few things. We have more facts than we need to know of some things and not enough of other things, and if we had more knowledge, there would be more than one answer, depending on which way we went."

All elbows on the table, four chins on fists and four grins. Isabel summed up their frustration. "You was just foolin' us, wasn't you?"

"Yes and no. I was fooling because there is no way to answer that problem, but I want each of you to write 2 problems of that kind. Make it about whatever you want, but be SURE there is an answer, and that you can tell the answer to the rest of the class. We'll see how that goes. Take a slate home with you because you might need to write on both sides, and I want it ready in the morning."

She took four of the fourth level readers from the stack in the bookshelves. "Right now, I want you to turn to page four and read as much as you can. Have your slates ready for any word you might not know."

"Level two, get ready to say our times tables for three. I'll be right back." Walking to the youngest group, she carried two copies of The Little Red Hen. One she handed to Margie, opened at the first page, and pointed to the beginning. From the other book she began to read. "Once upon a time there was a..." and from the corner of her eye she saw Margie following along with her finger as the words were pronounced.

Back to level two, she called them to the recitation bench beside her desk. She liked a recitation bench. It gave restless bodies a change of scene, they disturbed the other classes less, and small boys could not 'accidentally' kick the girls' shins under the table. Math finished, she set them to practicing their penmanship... which was very sloppy. Something had to be done about that.

Picking up the story of Little Red Riding Hood she came back to level three. "Put your books aside, and we'll look at your slates later. You remember when we read this book? You know the story well, of course, so we're going to talk about what makes a story.

"There are a lot of writings that are called 'stories' but are really narratives or sometimes just answers to a question. Occasionally, there are stories hidden within the narratives or answers.

"The best description of a story is a writing that has at least three sentences and contains three kinds of information." Francine glanced around the faces: Isabel, Carolina, Althea and Connie. Chins on fists and elbows on the table. She had their attention.

"The three kinds of information are: Situation, Problem, Solution. Here is an example. 'I'm standing here before you.' That is a situation. 'I have given you a problem that had no answer.' That is the problem. 'I expected you to figure that out, and you did.' That is the solution.

"You see, situation means what has happened at that moment or is still happening. Problem means that something has happened to change what is happening, and it may not be very pleasant. Solution means answer, so a story that had something bad that is happening is not a complete unless it is finished, or it is not actually a story.

"I'm going to give you a three-sentence story. 'Connie lifted the blackberry cobbler from the stove to carry it to the table. The cat ran in front of her, and she stumbled, spilling the hot cobbler on her foot. She screamed and yanked off her shoe and stocking and dipped her foot in cold water." By the time she finished the story, the four girls were laughing almost too hard to listen, and all other children had stopped to enjoy the joke.

Holding her finger to her mouth, she quieted them. "Now, did I tell a complete story?" Nods and smiles around the table. Isabel's hand up. "Miss Francine? Do Connie's feet still hurt?" Whereupon Connie ducked her face into her hands and giggled quietly.

"Now, girls. You will tell me a story. Althea will tell the situation, Connie will tell problem, and Isabel will tell the solution, and Carolina will tell us if we told a complete story. Althea, you may begin. The situation may be anything you think of."

The girl paused a moment in deep thought. "My littlest brother, not Marvin, stepped in a mud puddle in his new shoes."

Connie took a deep breath and plunged in. "I knew he would get a whipping, and I didn't want him to because he gets so many."

Carolina was ready. "I think it will be a complete story, won't it?"

Francine nodded approval. "Very good, but let's think. Isabel, what is the solution?"

Without hesitation, she began. "I lifted him out of the puddle and cleaned his shoes so good no one ever knew they were muddy."

"Girls, you did a very good job with something that was new to you. Now we'll talk about letter sounds."

Carolina's hand went up. She whispered, "That was fun. Can we do it again?"

Francine's answer was a smile, a wink and a nod. Absolutely they would be doing it again! And again! And again!

"Level Three. 'A' is like what?" In unison came a shout, "Apron!" Level two. 'B' is like what?" "A ball and bat!"

She nodded approval. "Now we'll talk about 'C'. That letter is like a clown. It hides and pretends to be some other sound. It likes to be a 'K' like a kite and also an 'S' like a snake. If there is a reason for this, we don't know it, but it's one of those things we just learn. Watch this sentence as I write it," and she took chalk to the blackboard.

"A SILLY CLOWN SITS IN A CHAIR IN THE CLOUDY CITY. Where does a 'C' sound like a 'K'? Isabel, read the sentence and tell me."

Isabel read it to herself in a whisper. "Clown and the word next to the end."

"You're right. How did you know the word 'cloudy' was a 'K' even if you didn't know the word?"

"Cause sloudy is a word that can't be said."

"You're right, this time, but there are some words that are just hard to say. We won't have them today, though. Althea, where are the 'C' words?

"Uh… city?"

A hand shot up. "Yes, Troy?"

"What about silly and sit?"

"Troy, you forgot what I asked. I asked for the 'C' words, not 'S' words. 'S' almost always says its name."

Francine turned to the youngest group. "Level one, what is the 'H' sound?" The answer came shouted back, "Huff!" "And the 'P' sound?" Answer, "Puff!" The huff and puff were their favorite ones from the wolf and the pig story.

Sounds were going well. The little sisters learned the alphabet quickly from hearing their Aunt Margie teaching herself, but the others were not far behind.

It was up in the spring that Donald, age almost nine, took his turn at bringing in the pail of drinking water from the Brown's next door. At Francine's insistence, each child, or at least each family, had brought a drinking cup. There seemed to be talk of something called germs that could be spread from drinking after others, and she hoped to contain any sniffles and coughs within families.

She had chanced to dip a dipper of water into her coffee pot and noticed an unaccustomed activity moving about in the pail. On closer examination, the invader was about the size of a raisin and had a pointed tail that propelled it about in the depth of the water.

Quick to note changes in sound in a room full of healthy children, the teacher sensed a hush settle over table two, which seated mostly boys. Trying to keep a straight face, she turned toward the group and addressed them as a whole.

"Students, I fear someone has lost his way. It's just too bad for the poor little thing, because all he wants to do is to grow up, just like you boys at the second table. The little polliwog that somehow got into the drinking pail must be rescued, and I assign you four boys to the job. The big problem is that the little creature has nothing to eat in the pure well water. He has to get back into creek water that has tiny foods so he can grow up.

"So what I want you to do is take the pail outside and take the dipper, too. Dip out enough water to get the little tadpole into the cup and transfer him to a bowl or can, or something.

"Then, rinse out the pail and bring fresh water into the classroom. I'm sorry the little swimmer will have to go hungry today, because I can't spare a boy to go to the creek for water. Starting tomorrow, you boys take turns among you to bring a quart of water from Sandy Creek and each day we'll dip him out and put him in fresh creek water. However the little creature got into the pail, I'm sure he's regretting it sincerely.

"So now get slates and practice penmanship. I'll put your assignment on the board, and later give you a sheet of paper. Make sure your pencils are sharpened."

She turned her back to the class, now pin-drop silent, and began to write. A small scuffle behind her indicated that the boys were obeying. Otherwise the room was silent, except for the scratch of her chalk and Miss Margie's soft voice reading a story from the primer. The teacher wrote:

## BULLFROG ON THE LOG

*Bullfrog on a mossy log,*
 *His bulging eyeballs, all agog.*
*Throat swelled out to sing his song*
 *That sounds like hammers on a gong.*
*Belly white and bulging wide,*
 *Spiders, bugs and flies inside.*
*Snake comes by with tongue a-flash.*
 *He's in the water with a splash.*
*Bullfrog, just a slimy lump*
 *But bullfrog has the brains to jump!*
*Bullfrog on a mossy log?*
 *He's just a grown-up polliwog!*

Just as she had expected, the minute her chalk was put down, a small, feminine hand shot in the air. It was Dorcas, Donald's twin. Dorcas, the curious question asker. Without responding to the hand, Miss Francine stepped into her tiny kitchen and returned with a tin piepan and a spoon.

"Yes, Dorcas?"

"Miss Francine, what is a gong?"

As an answer, the teacher held the pan by a rim and tapped the center with the spoon. A tinny sound rang out. "Now, Dorcas, imagine if I had a washtub and an egg turner. That would be a gong." With a friendly smile, she concluded, "Now, you've learned a new word, and I want your best cursive writing on the sheet of paper I'm passing out."

The tiny wriggler was watched with fascination each day as he went about picking off the invisible bits of food in the creek water. When she saw the tiny bumps just back of the swimmer's tail, she transferred him to a white bowl with a rock in the center. Changing the water was a bit tricky, but exciting as the bumps formed into kicking legs.

At that point, she stretched a thin cheesecloth over the bowl and fastened it on the edges with clothes pegs. Water was removed and changed out with a large spoon under the cloth.

Then the tiny front legs and the shortening of the tail. The excitement of the week was when the class arrived to see the little fellow sitting on the rock, seeming to look about him, wondering what happened.

The second level boys, as a group, were assigned to see that the frog got back to the creek. Francine chuckled to herself as she thought of these same boys, bearded and gray-haired, repeating the incident to their grandchildren, likely with interesting and partly true embellishments.

Spring came. Gardens were planted. Weeds came up. The children were needed at home, and homework must be worked around. And the warm days made them restless. On a warm evening in the middle of May, the end of the term party was held. Excited children, and perhaps even more excited parents came, bearing sweet edibles and buckets of tea.

Level one presented their part of the program. Beginning with the alphabet, they took turns with the letters, telling a word that began with that letter. Starting with Edith Van Pelt, "A is for apron." And passed on to Darlene Garcia. "B is for ball and bat, and also biscuit." Young Marvin Martin, whose mother, Annabelle, had interviewed the teacher for the job, had wriggled excitedly with anticipation, because he had the favorite letter. In a clarion voice, he announced, "C is a clown. He can sound like 'S' in city, and 'K' like in Kitty." With a proud smile he sat back to wait for his applause that quickly came. Taking turns, they finally came to Eddie Brown. "Z is for zero, and that means a circle of nothing." More applause.

After that, they shouted answers to number problems… in unison from cardboard flash cards. Their challenge was to quickly determine if the card said 'plus' or minus.' Much more applause.

After that, the second level repeated the Bullfrog poem in unison, including a lot of giggling from the two girls. Following that came the flashcards with a top number, a question mark, a line, and an answer. They were to quickly determine, by the answer, if the problem was add or subtract and by how much. Appreciative applause was the reward.

The four girls in level three had to repeat, in unison, many rules of grammar and punctuation which, incidentally, would be on their Certification Test. After that, Francine pulled from a favorite memory. The four girls performed a reading of the poem, "COLUMBUS," written about the discovery of America. One of her all-time favorites.

First would be Isabel Brown. As the four girls stood on the small platform, Isabel stepped forward, with a description of the poem.

"We will jointly recite a poem by Joaquin Miller titled "COLUMBUS" but often called by its most important words, "SAIL ON!"

*CAROLINA: "Behind him lay the gray Azores,*
*Behind the gates of Hercules;*
*Before him not the ghost of shores,*
*Before him only shoreless seas.*
*ALTHEA: The good mate said, "Now we must pray*
*For lo! The very stars are gone;*
*Speak, Admiral, what shall I say?"*
*Then CONSTANCE:*
*"Why say, sail on! And on!"*
*ALTHEA: "The first mate said,*
*My men grow mutinous day by day;*
*My men grow ghastly wan and weak."*
*ISABEL: The stout mate thought of home: a spray,*
*A salt wave wash'd his swarthy cheek.*
*ALTHEA: "What shall I say, brave Admiral,*
*If we sight naught but seas at dawn?*
*CONSTANCE: "Why, you shall say, at break of day,*
*'Sail on! Sail on! And on!'"*
*ISABEL: They sailed and sailed, as winds might blow,*
*Until at last the blanched mate said:*
*ALTHEA: "Why now, not even God would know*
*Should I and all my men fall dead.*
*These very winds forget their way,*
*For God from these dread seas is gone.*
*Now speak, brave Admiral, speak and say—"*
*CONSTANCE: He said, "Sail on! And on!"*

75

*ISABEL: They sailed, they sailed, then spoke his mate:*
*CONSTANCE: "This mad sea shows his teeth to-night,*
*He curls his lip, he lies in wait,*
*With lifted teeth as if to bite!*
*Brave Admiral, say but one word:*
*What shall I say when hope is gone?*
*ISABEL: The words leaped as a leaping sword,*
*CONSTANCE: (Shouting) "Sail on! sail on! and on!"*
*ISABEL: Then, pale and worn, he walked his deck,*
*And through the darkness peered that night*
*Ah, darkest night! And then a speck,*
*A light! A light! A light! A light!*

Then all four girls finished the performance in unison, speaking together as perfectly as with one voice.

*It grew..a star-lit flag unfurled!*
*It grew to be Time's burst of dawn;*
*He gained a world! He gave that world*
*Its watch-word: "ON!...ON AND ON!"*

The last four words were almost shouted, and the packed building went pin-drop silent. Several wiped their eyes with hankies, one or two sniffled, and then the applause began. On and on! Everyone stood and clapped, until the girls, overcome by emotion, ran to their parents.

Francine had looked forward to the summer... warm days, family and a lot of time to think. A shiver of contentment spread over her as she climbed aboard her buggy that followed behind the trotting hooves of the chocolate pony.

A handful of books had been sent home for the summer with Margie... levels two to four for practice. She had joyfully reassured Francine that the books would never be put down, except in the canvas bag. She explained that the book bag had its special hook, high enough that Edith and Susan would not be tempted take them out.

Francine smiled appreciation, but she had no doubt in the world that the two little nieces would not be hanging over her shoulders or sitting at her feet when she read. Bright little girls, they were. It would be fun to see how they had progressed during the summer.

Another thing to look forward to was that her girls in level four were all assured that they could spend another year at the school. Such a gift from their families! Young girls of ten to fifteen had so much to do.

She, herself, would be doing a lot of picking and shelling, peeling and canning. Evenings, however, could be spent with the McLaughlin sisters and with Patricia and Bridget with their hat making. They were doing really well, and Miss Josie's Aunt Sharon in New York was continually sending something she thought might interest them.

Francine had bought a darling felt bonnet from them. It was just the color of Chock, her pony. They were talking of taking some of their hats to Argyle to see if the shop there would offer them.

And there were her sister, Rosie and their friends, Carmelita and Carlotta. The four had so much in common, being Miss Josie's first class and taking their certification test together. Also, Carlotta was married, now and had that darling little boy.

As they clipped along, she and Chock, she smiled with pleasure at Miss Josie's attendance to her 'end of school' party. She was one of the ones who touched a hanky to their eyes as her class of four finished the poem. She was beginning to realize how Miss Josie had felt about her first class when she thought of Isabel, Carolina, Althea, and Connie. Another whole year with them! There would be time to try all sorts of things to broaden their knowledge and give them an interest outside the happenings of Shady Ridge and the Corners.

Josie, herself, had come home from the party realizing that she had witnessed the work of a true 'teacher" Francine had the teacher's heart… that was plain to see.

Miss Josie had watched her cousin, Carmelita, and her friend Rosie with their successes in the Prairie Academy, but perhaps Francine was the 'teacher' and would be happy nowhere else. The skill she showed with her program! Josie would never have thought of it. And the poems Francine wrote… where did they come from? Sometimes they seemed to grow, complete, out of a certain occurrence or sight, but other times they were just there… such as 'Grandpa's Overcoat' that went through so many uses and other family members until it ended up on the rear of the baby as a diaper cover. Francine had never seen that happen, so what made her think of it?

The Shady Ridge teacher was bringing her copy book to her, so Josie could copy down what she wanted. Of course, she would want them all… one day she would send some of them to Aunt Sharon, who loved to get 'work assignments' from the Territory. There was certain to be a publisher just breathless to get enough of Francine's poems for a book, if Francine was of a mind to let them go.

Some of the poems were long and descriptive such as 'Summer Storm' but others were short and pithy, but still full of mental pictures. She even let her mind wander through her favorite short one.

## BLOSSOMS IN THE GRASS

*Look up! A vast expanse of skies,*
*As blue as Scottish lassies' eyes.*
*Around! Windswept trees and grass are seen*
*A necklace strip… in shades of green.*
*Look down! Beside the footpath as you pass*
*Are blossoms growing in the grass,*
*Like tiny chips of painted glass!*

So descriptive of a prairie morning with tiny flowers blooming in the dewy grass. How did she learn to put things together so well and make such use of descriptive words? What would she have done with this talent if Josie had not come and been able to introduce her to whole books of famous poetry? Would this talent have just turned into frustration as she rubbed the dirt from overalls, tilled her garden, and canned the produce, while patching skinned knees?

Now, though she may choose to do those things, her mind has something else it can do, and her fingers can make her special copybook writings so others can share the beauty of her words. Josie had lain awake to think, but now she turned to a cool place on the pillow and shut her eyes. She had, actually, accomplished something after all. Hadn't she? One should try to accomplish something lasting with their life. Would the blooms of her own "Blossoms in the Grass" qualify?

By mid-August, Francine was looking forward to the start of school. She would have seven students in level one, maybe more, and her level two, containing Edie and Sue Van Pelt, would be an interesting challenge. Blank slates they were… ready for her chalk!

Troy would be in the third level… maybe the fourth, along with the girls. She smiled as she remembered the snake episode.

It had happened after the tadpole incident that she had walked through the classroom and noticed the loop of snake showing from under the low bookcases. She could, of course, have called for help from anywhere, but she saw Troy grooming her horse as he often did before coming to school, and called him. He had come running across the road, leaping up the steps and landing at her feet.

"Troy, we seem to have a visitor. I thought you might know the best way to tell him to go home. He's right over here."

The boy followed her to the reptile, still in the same position. He stared down at it with a disgusted look. "It's dead, Miss Francine, and I know who put it there. You want'a know?"

With a smile, Francine admitted she was sure it was dead, but said she didn't want to know who did it. If he could just take it out and dispose of it, it would be their secret.

With a wide grin between his freckled cheeks, he nodded acknowledgment. She wanted to turn the tables on the boys.

When class convened, she watched as the other three boys in the class kept trying to peek toward where the snake should be, concerned that it wasn't there, or possibly disappointed that their teacher had not spotted it during class and screamed in fright. Such a worried concern showed on their faces! Troy, himself, buried his head in his book to keep a straight face. Such fun for him to share a secret with his loved teacher!

Donald McGregor, especially, had an anxious look the whole day. Francine smiled at the memory. Now there was another whole year ahead of them. Also, she would be glad to get the pony back into Troy's care, where it would have much more attention. More care than the animal had had all summer at her own hand, certainly!

The classroom, when she went to check it out, had been swept and apparently scrubbed clean. It had the healthy smell of lye soap mixed with the lingering scent of active children, books and chalk, along with the various items they had brought in their lunch buckets.

She pushed up the windows, propping them at their best height, then removed the protective towels she had used to keep dust from the books in the long bookcase. There was plenty of room for the new ones she had in her buggy.

Her tiny kitchen was spotless… all pans and kettles hanging on their hooks. A bouquet of small cedar branches occupied space in a pint Mason jar. A local favorite for deodorizing a kitchen.

Her bed had been freshly made with the spread and sheets she had left there over the summer. Isabel's work, no doubt, as evidenced by the embroidered pot pouri bag enthroned on her fluffed pillow. A revealing sniff. Flower petals and just a touch of cinnamon, along with selected herbs from her mother's garden.

A light tap on her kitchen door, and it was pushed open. The bright face of Isabel appeared.

"Ma says I can ask do you have something to be carried in? But I'm not to keep bothering you. Do you… have… something…?"

With loving caresses, the girl lifted the new books from their boxes and examined them before sliding them into the place she thought they should go. Francine, watching from the corner of her eye, remembered Miss Janine who had assisted Miss Josie. She had done the same thing, showing what was almost a reverence for the brand-new books that still smelled of printer's ink.

As Miss Janine had done, Isabel was working as slowly as she could, making the job last longer. Francine remembered the concern on her mother's face as she had spent another chunk of the inheritance her grandmother had left to her and her brother and sister.

Her pa had winked at her and reassured her mother. "They're the tools of her trade! Just think of them as hammer, saw and drill for a carpenter." Her ma had nodded. Pa had a way of calming her ma's fears with a few words. And he was right… they were her tools and no one knew that better than going-on-thirteen-year-old Isabel. They were to be treated accordingly.

Margie Van Pelt seemed just as happy as Francine to be back. It seemed the little girls still needed transportation, and it was decided that Margie's services could be spared from the household. Or, it might be as her brother had said... just that Margie had been shorted on education due to the migration to the Territory, and it was through no fault of her own. This was a way for her to catch up. Either way, Francine was glad for her company.

Several times, as a special treat for both of them during the summer, she had come over to Shady Ridge and they had ridden back to the Corners in her buggy for some activity. It gave Margie a chance to get acquainted with others her age.

During the summer the school yard had acquired two seesaws that the children called tetter-totters. Also, a metal bar had been installed between two trees for playing skin-the-cat and for hand-walking. Two of the large blackjack oaks had acquired swings made of steel chain with a solid board seat. Wonderful!

Also, just outside the schoolyard was something called a brush arbor. It consisted of pillars holding cross logs and a roof of piled-high brush. Grass clumps had been cleared and a group of split log benches were put into the shady protection of the leafy roof. Apparently, Shady Ridge had grown to the point that there had been occasion for groups to meet together. Business, music, circuit-rider preacher, family parties and a place for young people to meet each other for picnics and such. Even the children made use of it before and after school as a piece of play equipment... walking the benches or looking for privacy for secrets. What a timely addition to the small community!

It was late in the spring of that year that a young man with broad shoulders and sun-bleached hair spotted the girl in the lace bonnet enthroned on the back of the chestnut horseand flanked by two tiny replicas of herself. Hers? Hmmm, no, because she looked entirely too young for children of that age.

Slowing his black mare as much as he could, he followed behind her to longer enjoy the scenery. Sunny yellow hair was tossed about the bonnet in the Oklahoma spring breeze. He had seen her leave the new school house... was she the teacher? Somehow he didn't think so.

A mile farther on State Road, she turned the chestnut, heading him down Sandy Creek Road. Oh! She must be part of the Dutch family on the far corner down by the creek. Following as quietly as possible, he stopped in a grove of trees and watched.

She directed the horse to the stepstand in the yard, dismounted, and walked to the house. A limp. Stone in the shoe? No… the natives knew to stoop and take out the stone because stones never went away by themselves.

All the way to the door, she limped slightly as though accustomed to it. Birth defect? Maybe… but it didn't seem to slow her down. The two smaller girls ran to their tree swing, singing some number song they must have learned from school.

Hmmm… this took some watching. In the girl-famine of the Territory, a fellow had to do what he could! And he, Robert Farmer, now had a mission. His eyes crinkled as he thought of the way he had acquired that last name. His daddy had been a baby when his father brought him from the old country, and the father had spent time on the ship considering his name.

Dutch names were so full of consonants and double vowels that were strung together haphazardly, that they were extremely hard for an Englishman's tongue to manage, and that was bad when one was going to a country highly populated with English people. He'd tried, but no one seemed to be able to pronounce all of his name's Dutch inflections. At that point, the granddaddy began to say, when asked his name, "I'm a farmer," as that was exactly what he expected to be.

At Ellis Island, he had been listed as Johann Farmer, and that was how it was written. Made life a lot simpler, it did! Of course, Van Pelt was easy to say. Robert began to ask about the neighborhood, did anyone know anything about that family… kept to themselves, it seemed. One friend told him, "You know, that girl, she's got a bad foot that makes her limp."

Bob Farmer had taken only a moment to answer. "Wonderful! So when I take 'er somewhere, she won't be wantin' me to dance with 'er. I got four left feet when I try to dance. I can barely walk without tangling my own toes and stepping on my own heels. Why do you reckon I learned to make that fiddle and squeak out a few tunes?"

He did more than 'squeak' out the tunes. He was now in demand at every gathering, and seemingly could play anything he had ever heard. It had been such a good day when a fiddler had come with the circuit preacher, one time, and Bob had studied it as much as he could during the service. He couldn't tell you what the preacher said, but he had sighted and estimated the dimensions of that instrument. It took three tries before he got one made that actually sounded notes. Strings, he had to order from Wards Catalog over in Argyle.

He just HAD to meet this girl! He couldn't just go up and knock on the door, but he had spied on her every chance he got. He had been going down Sandy Creek Road one of his many times, and the answer to his problem just fell into his lap. He looked up into the Provident Heavens with a 'thank you' sigh. What could be better!

There, standing in a grassy ditch, was the bull... fat, shiny black, and long-horned... Ring in his nose... so he had been trouble to someone, had he? Well, it just took skill.

Behind the animal was a gaping hole in the fence, and it appeared, for all the world, that the beast was trying to get back into the pasture he had just left. Horns got in the way... seemed like. Tying his horse nearby and speaking softly, Bob approached the animal. The bull extended his neck and nose toward the outstretched hand. He actually took a few steps toward him.

Hmmm, tame? It appeared that way. Stroking the course curly hair on the animal's face, he moved his hand to a foot-and-a-half long horn. The bull moved closer.

Tugging softly on the horn, he began to lead the animal toward the front gate of the Van Pelt establishment. Safely at the gate, the bull walking docilely beside him, he entered the yard and paused at the step platform. "Hello, the house!" he called in a friendly voice.

A man appeared, stared, and then came hurrying. Before he could say anything, Bob Farmer explained. "Thinkin' this big baby might be your animal. He either made or found a hole in the fence and walked through. Didn't know how to get back in the pasture, but he was a'tryin'. That ring in his nose fooled me, thinkin' he might be vicious, but I'm figgerin' he was glad to see me."

One word led to another, with Jacob Van Pelt volunteering that he didn't know why the bull had a ring. Previous owner said he was a trouble maker, but that hadn't proved to be a fact.

The younger man nodded, knowingly. "Let me ask something. Did the previous owner have a lot of bulls and you got only this one?"

At Jacob's nod, he continued, "Then I know what happened. It has to do with the ladies, and apparently the other bulls were older or stronger and pushed him away. Noticed you got three good looking ladies down there eatin' the same grass as he was. Him the only fellow, what's he got to be mad about, with a deal like that?"

The conversation had gone on, Bob prolonging it as long as he could, when Margie headed for the clothesline with a basket. Limp, and all. Bob wanted to be safe... and now was not the time for a mistake. "That your wife?"

"Who? Oh, no, that's my little sister. She came out here with us. Name's Margie." Then to his sister, "MARGIE? Come over here a minute and meet a neighbor. He was good enough to bring back our old bull that got out. Maybe we could find some coffee and a cookie or two?" They could, and it was an hour later that Bob had wrangled an invitation to return 'sometime' and what could be better than that? Some days just naturally turned out good!

Margie. Beautiful girl! And that foot didn't seem to bother her or slow her down a bit. It certainly didn't bother him! Wonder if she'd like a fiddle...? He had that new one started, and it appeared to have a very attractive wood grain. If it worked out, it should buy him a lot of evenings teaching her to play it, and her brother was welcome to stick around while he was doing it... at least at first!

The young man rode away whistling. He lifted his face upward once more in thankfulness, and could Someone up there please make the bull get out again? Probably not. He was likely on his own, now, in the romance department.

The half-finished fiddle would be a thing of beauty, without doubt. Made mostly from the fine-grained wood of the white oak, it was trimmed with insets of red cedar, patterned with twisty grain as though the tree had experienced tormenting winds. And likely it had.

He had learned from previous mistakes that fiddle making was tricky. Sometimes the wood cured in a way that twisted the whole instrument out of shape, and he had to start over again. Exasperating! He had such a little bit of patience.

This one, however, seemed to be coming along. Perhaps things were turning his way, but what had given him the idea that the beautiful neighbor actually wanted to play a fiddle? There was something about her that... well... it just seemed the thing to do. Or try to do.

Loosening the glue clamps from the instrument, he held his breath. No warping had seemed to occur. Needed light touches with the sanding. He had glued extra fine sand to a patch of very tough canvas, and he now applied it to the neck of the instrument. So far, so good.

He had things to do, and he couldn't actually spare the time to work on this... he had wasted enough time already on trying to find a way to meet her. His own pa counted on his help in the field, and one day he would share in the increase of livestock when he had a place of his own. It was only right he do his share.

With a sigh, he put the musical instrument aside and changed into his plow shoes. Look out, mules! He needed to make up time so he could quit early.

While following the mules through the cornfield the thought came down upon him. A musical. He'd get a musical together. He could locate a couple of French harp players, a drummer was easy to find, and there was that fellow in the next county that played the concertino, the strange, whining little thing folks called a squeeze box. Hey, wasn't there a fellow who played the jug and actually harmonized notes and helped keep time?

The more rows he plowed, the better it all sounded. After all, where did they think this was... Oklahoma City? Even the old folks would welcome a Saturday night away from their cabins to sing songs they remembered from childhood.

Total darkness caught him winding the ends of the strings onto the keys on the instrument's neck. Touchy job. Strings easy to break. Good thing he ordered extra strings from the catalog. Tomorrow was Sunday, no circuit rider preacher. Too bad. The monthly service was a good time to see more people, so he'd just have to put some miles on his horse if he wanted to spread the information about the musical.

Wonder of wonders, he actually succeeded. Of course, he had resorted to a left-handed way of inviting Margie to the musical. He'd sort of changed the theme into a picnic (folks liked to bring foods and eat together), and he asked Margie's brother instead of her. This way she had the safety of her family at first, and he'd see how it went. Possibly he was the only one who was dreaming of possibilities!

Also, he had actually located another instrument. A strange little thing called a banjo (the player of it said that in Tennessee they called it a 'tater bug'). The fellows managed to get together for a "practice" session that consisted of everyone sort of doing his own thing with a lot of laughter. The jug player might actually be the most valuable in the group... hard to believe!

The log benches were packed and crowded. Fried chicken, potato salad and stuffed eggs were everywhere, enough tea to drown an elephant, about four chocolate cakes and a bucket of cookies. Laughing and games, and the half-remembered stepping game where the fellows lined up facing a line of girls singing something like "Skip to my Loo." (Whatever was a 'loo'?) With the music they wove their way through the group, circling and patting hands at a specified time. Turned out to be very popular.

Young Bob Farmer was flying high on a dream. Sometimes things work out, and their wedding was performed in the late spring, set to coincide with the monthly visit of the preacher.

Jacob Van Pelt, his new brother-in-law, insisted he put up a cabin on his land. As he explained it, his sister was entitled to the property as much as he was, as her help had made a lot of things possible. Good enough explanation for Bob.

The big thing happened, though, when Jacob commented that the fellows should understand each other well as they both liked working in wood. As it had turned out, Margie was excited about learning to play the fiddle and showed a lot of talent. Given time, she might even be better than Bob, himself. The rest of that surprise was when Bob saw the bureau with drawers that Jacob had made.

# CHAPTER 5

Anita had been so pleased with it, she insisted on having another one, and one for Margie. While he was at it, Jacob cut and set aside the boards to build bureaus for his daughters. Big ones, just like their mama's. They were growing so fast. Seven and eight, now.

Bob examined the bureau. "Man, you know what kind'a cash those things could go for? I hope you get time to show me what you do. Folks'd pay actual money for those, and there ain't no good market for fiddles. At least, not yet, and they take forever to make."

"Well, I hadn't actually thought...."

"Forget it! We gotta start right now thinkin' on it. I gotta have an income somewhere. Aimin' to have me a family someday. That'd be somethin' to do on a rainy day, or in winter. Could hook it onto farmin'. What'd'ya think?"

The more Jacob thought of it, the better it sounded. There had been so many things to do that could be quicker done by two, that the newly acquired relative looked better and better!

Margie continued to bring Edith and Susan to school. She was not only excellent help, she became a good friend, and had such pleasure in learning. Her new husband insisted she do what she wanted to do. If she had fun at school, then she must go.

At the end of the third year of her teaching, Francine had taken the four girls of the upper level to Oklahoma City, just as Miss Josie had taken her own class. It happened that her brother, Raymond, had something in the city he wanted to see about, now that he was fifteen and had big ideas. Pa went along, too, and rode his mare beside the double buggy.

Raymond had, by now, raised a half a dozen of the huge Clydesdale horses, and had dreams of going into the dirt moving business. Had his eye of a piece of property that might be for sale. Father and son needed to see what equipment was available, and where would be the best place to invest the rest of his inheritance from his grandmother.

Francine shared the overnight room with her four excited pupils, reliving her own testing day. It had seemed like a party, and these girls certainly thought so. Raymond and his pa had spent most of the night comparing drag lines, scrapers, and pulley-operated loaders, along with trailers equipped with heavy springs meant for that type of work.

Isabel giggled when she said that her folks had promised her pearl button shoes if she passed her test. Was there a question of that not happening? The very idea brought on another fit of giggles.

Over the lunch period, the girls were too excited to eat the lunch Francine had bought for them. "Really, Miss Francine, I'd upchuck for sure," Althea insisted, and the others agreed.

It was during the third year that Francine had spent a weekend droopy and pale, and a mother's eye spotted the trouble. "Francine, let me check your throat. You look like you're tryin' to take the mumps."

"No, ma, I couldn't. Remember when Rosie and Raymond had 'em, and I stayed right here in the house with 'em? Don't you suspect I should'a had 'em then?"

Her mother nodded, "Yes, but that wouldn't have been the only thing you did what I didn't expect. I can spot mumps, and you got 'em, so you'd better be talking to Carlotta about fillin' in for you. She had 'em along with Rosie and Carmelita, and she'd be about the only one able to fill in, less'n you want to turn school out for a couple'a weeks."

"Two whole weeks? That's too long!"

"Could be, but that's what it'll be. You're goin' to bed. I don't think the Shady Ridge mothers'd be wantin' you around their little boys. Girls, either, for that matter. Do what I say, now, or it might be longer'n two weeks. I'll send Rosie to see Carlotta soon as she comes in."

With a weary sigh, the girl went to her room. This was one time she was almost glad to obey. She was getting concerned about it anyway. And her throat HURT!

Carlotta's eyes shone with excitement as she listened to what Francine had planned for her classes and saw the notes she had already made. "You can let Margie take over on the little ones if you want. She's pretty good at filling time profitably. She'll know where the flash cards and dominos are. You'll like my bed. They gave me a new feather mattress this year, and it feels about a foot thick."

Her mom wielded an iron hand and kept Francine down the whole two weeks, with the girl insisting she was well, already! When she could return to school, it was late September, at the end of a dry, dry summer. Powder keg dry, the folks said... something was bound to happen. And it did.

It happened on a morning that Margie did not come. She was needed at home to help bring her second little nephew into the world.

Isabel was too excited for words as she was permitted to help. She was busily attending to the new Level One, settling them down to their first year of school when Francine stepped out the front door and stood on the steps for a breath of air, hot as if it came from the oven.

She frowned and sniffed the breeze! What was...? When she saw the billowing smoke in the northeast, every sense within her being was alerted. What she had expected to be another pleasant year of doing what she was meant to do, was not to be. A change in her life was looming just 'down the road a piece.'

It had begun four years ago and a long way away, but it changed Francine's life in a way she would never have guessed. The incident had been cradled in France and had grown up in Shady Ridge.

Young Richarde LaBarr had finally boarded the French ship, le Voux, fulfilling a dream of a lot of years. It was time to move on. Past time, actually. Something within him had pulled him onward, just as something behind him seemed to push.

Two of his older brothers were left tending their father's grape vineyard, and the whole family knew there was no room for another in the small winery. It wasn't that he was not loved, it was just the way it was. A plot of ground supported only so many families.

The young man, Richarde, had been obliged to pay an extra fare to cover the cost of the 1000 young, rooted grape vines he was taking with him. There would be the problem of keeping them damp for the four or five weeks they would be on the Atlantic. He expected to catch enough rainwater during a storm to take care of this because water from the salty Atlantic Ocean would not do.

Just now the roots were wrapped tightly in oiled canvas, as new rooted cuttings often were for the first winter, and they would need to be in the ground by summer. He knew where he wanted to go, and he would have them in the ground in time. Hidden in the lining of his all-weather coat was his share of their father's estate, and he hoped it would be enough.

There was the other thing. So many of his fellow passengers were from Dutch or French origin, and they were intent on changing their names to "Anglicise" their sound. English voices sometimes had trouble with French words.

He had already decided on his new name. He had boarded the ship as Richarde le Barr, and would step off as Richard (accent on the 'Rich') with last name, Barlow. This way, his sons would have an English name to match the English-speaking nation where they would be born.

He was heading west immediately to a place called Ohio. It had a good sound and was surely a place of the sunny, sandy soil that would grow good grapes. Why wouldn't it be the perfect place in this perfect country, and he already had plans for the wonderful report he would send back home... about how well he was doing.

He had met Viola on the ship, and she seemed to be 'the one,' but they would know more, later. First he had to get the vineyard. Which he did, and he then came back to New York to get his bride. It was not his fault or hers that she was a small, delicate girl and had never even seen a farm. Love and youth does not consider these things as important.

They produced two sons, Richard Junior and Stanley. Both boys grew into good hands at caring for the vineyard, and it was not their fault that the heavier, richer soil and position of the summer sun was not the best for their brand of grapes. The latitude was just not the same as France. The three men worked hard but never did figure out what to do to improve the yield.

The plants lived, but did not produce satisfactorily, and the grapes they made had a different taste. The brothers spent a lot of time talking about the problem, and wondered if a more southern exposure would be better, but their father was stubborn.

The old man worked himself into ill health and seemed not to notice how his Viola was failing until there came the day she could not rise up in the morning. He immediately prepared a wagon to take her back to New York where she might get medical care. With total sadness, he left his sons in charge and, with tear-wet eyes, he also walked away from his dreams.

His lovely Viola weakened by the day, and breathed her last just outside a small New York town. A local minister helped him place her in the ground, then wished him well. After that, there was no reason to go on to the east. He bought writing paper from the waitress in a diner and wrote the letter to Viola's parents, giving the waitress postage money. Then he left the diner as in a dream, which had actually become a nightmare.

He paid out his team from the local livery, climbed aboard his wagon, and turned westward toward the beleaguered vineyard.

While he had been gone, the sons took a bold move. They began to create root cuttings of the grape vines, saying nothing to their distraught father who practically spent day and night in the vines, accomplishing nothing. The old man had no idea that his sons were doing exactly what he had originally intended to do... move on and begin again. There was much activity in the states to the west, and it pulled at the sons just as the colonies had pulled at the older man.

It was less than a month later that the boys found their father prone between the rows, face down and arms extended. He had used all the strength he had and had lost his beloved wife, so why was he still here? With a sigh, he had given up. His sons did for him the last thing they could do and sent him to eternal rest in the fields among the roots of the grape vines.

Left on their own, the sons sped up their root making. Richard Junior found time to court and marry Louise who was just as eager as he to set out for the west. Louise was a healthy, strapping girl whose parents had been born on Ohio farms and she had no illusions as to where she would be going or how hard would be the work. She also knew that the success of such a venture would depend a lot on herself.

Preparation was made, and a date was being selected when it was determined that Louise was pregnant. Oh, well, another year would not matter. They'd be just that much better prepared. Two wagons. That would be enough.

The small girl was born, and her mother insisted she be named Violette, after her French grandmother. The emphasis would be on ready to 'sell up.' They took the Santa Fe to Oklahoma Station and bought two horses.

Looking at the postings at every opportunity, they saw a number of possibilities. One looked very good. Quarter section. Partially fenced. House and two out-buildings. Small creek on the property, and a recently punched water well. It was the well that did it, knowing it would be a big thing to Louise and the little one.

Louise was ready and excited when the men returned. Two wagons, packed and loaded well. Louise was good at things like that. The rooted cuttings were dug and wrapped in oiled canvas.

They sold the vineyard for a good price, which they converted into gold pieces, and they bolted the rooted cuttings firmly to the underside of the wagon load of vines. Two teams of strong horses and a spare saddle horse just as a safety measure. It was early in the spring of 1897 that the caravan started out.

Anticipation made the trip an exciting adventure. A house already there and a punched well of water! What was not to be excited about?

It was in late March that they reached Oklahoma Station, now Oklahoma City, and stayed over for two days to let the animals rest and to re-provision. On the night of the second day of travel, they had made good time and darkness was falling. Time to stop for the night.

Ahead of them they saw another wagon had stopped, and a plume of smoke indicated a supper fire. Safety in numbers and all that.

Richard Junior pulled up just behind that wagon, and Stanley snugged his wagon behind. Leaving the brother and sister-in-law to start the evening chores, he leaped into the saddle of the spare horse and headed toward a small hillock to see if he could look about.

Also, it was so good to get off the buckboard seat of the wagon and into his saddle. The animal bounded off through the scrubby brush as though he, too, was glad to shake out his muscles.

Stanley was amused to note that he still wore his large knife… Also, his small hatchet, gun, and his metal drinking cup still dangled on his belt. Should have left them in the wagon. Oh, well.

From the top of the small rise of land, he looked to the west, the place of his dreams. The sun had just sunk below the low purple shadowed hills and streaks of violet-colored clouds festooning the sky. Violet. Such a beautiful color. He gave an instant of thought to his mother, then he cast the thought aside. He had no time now for sadness, and his mother would surely understand. He would, however, be taking her little namesake, Violette, to the new land.

Turning the horse back, he headed toward the rising smoke. SMOKE? There was far too much smoke to be a cooking fire! Digging his heels into the ribs of the animal, he tore through the low shrubbery, holding his breath against the roughness of the land and the presence of prairie dog towns. Horses' legs could break so quickly from unexpected holes.

He shook his head, trying to clear away what he thought he saw, but the sight would not erase. Three blazes leaped toward the sky, fueled by the oiled canvas covering. Shouts and the report of gunfire. The sunlight was gone, and the dimness of dusk was heightened by the broiling billows of dark smoke.

Leaping from the saddle, he tore toward the blaze of the middle wagon. The horses had been cut loose and driven off, the rear of the canvas wagon covering was a blaze and a roar of flames, but the screams of small Violette rose above them. Throwing himself into the front of the wagon and leaping over the seat, he grabbed up the screaming infant of only six months.

Leaping from the burning wagon just before the blazing canvas collapsed, he held the blanket wrapped baby to his shoulder. Looped over his arm was the carrying circle that Louise used to free her hands while holding the child.

His restless horse was whickering and tossing his head. Where were Richard and Louise? Grab the horse. Can't let it dash away. Night falling. Screaming baby. Pounding heart! What to do!

Too horrible to imagine! There was Richard, face down. Blood! In the dim light, he recognized an exit shotgun wound. Beside him, Louise. Blood on her back! Both dead. Impossible to comprehend. This could not be happening.

Exhausted, the baby quieted to soft snubs and hiccoughs. Then another sound…an animal…? She appeared. Old woman, bent and creeping out of the shrubs. Tiny, shriveled being. Must be from the other wagon!

Investigation revealed three more bodies. All shot. The wagons had become a pile of burning embers, melting down into the prairie soil. The oiled canvas coverings had blazed like a torch.

The old woman whimpered softly. Stanley went to her, and she clung to his arm. Name? She wasn't sure. What she finally decided on sounded like Lizzie McMurty. Stanley convinced her to sit on the ground on the baby's blanket, and he tucked the baby into the carrier circle and put her in the old woman's lap.

Hurriedly he felt around for something of value that had escaped the fire. Anything! There was the oil lantern, handle bent, but still containing oil. Matches he had in his pocket.

A bit of weak light from the lantern gave him a better view. Grape vines all gone. Provisions gone. Money all… wait, it was in the metal box attached under the wagon, and the thieves had not had time to find it… had they? Poking into the hot ashes, he located it. Hot but not melted. Gold pieces still inside. With a stick, he shoved it aside and kept looking.

Wagon axels lay in the embers. Cooking pots twisted from the fire. It was really too dark to see anything else, and the strange smells were bound to attract animals. No shovel to make graves, and the hard earth would not permit necessary depth. Also, he didn't know how many persons should be in the other wagon. Only one thing to do.

Hardening his mind against the bodies he left behind on the prairie, the young man turned his attention to the living. Little Lettie was becoming restless. Likely hungry. There was no mother to feed her, though.

Loosing the horse from the shrub where it was tied, he forced the old woman into the saddle, practically lifting her against her protests, and settling her on the animal. Struggling, he managed to get the carrier loop over her neck, and the baby settled into her lap, held within the loop.

Not trusting his sense of direction, he took the compass from his pocket and held it in the light of the lantern. Facing west, he headed toward the little settlement of Argyle that he had seen with his brother. Don't think of what is left behind, he chided himself. Push on ahead.

By now the baby was really setting up a howl. Stanley didn't blame her. He'd squall, too, if he could. So far the old woman, Lizzie?... jogged along and held to the saddle. He was not sure she was aware of what was going on, and that was, for certain, a blessing. There would be help in Argyle, if he just held out to get there.

Stanley held to the rein to lead the horse through the scrubby growth... heading on west toward help. Surely it was not more than five miles away. If he was going straight. If the little town was directly to the west, and not southwest. He'd hate terribly to walk on past it. The going was very slow, and the trail was overgrown.

He forced himself to look at the old woman, fearing she had fallen asleep or dropped the baby, but she appeared to be a tough lady. Hanging on, she seemed to ignore the fidgeting baby. Maybe she had experience with restless, whimpering babies, but Violette had no experience with being hungry. How long could babies go without eating? Would Argyle have something to feed her with? Bottles, maybe? What do they do for babies with no mother?

He plunged through the bushes holding the lantern high on his aching arm to avoid the worse part of the rough land. Sticker bushes. Dried sticks that rolled, or broke noisily underfoot. Tired, smoke damaged eyes searching the horizon for a pattern that was not tree tops. Would it be too much to ask to see a smoking chimney?

It was in the first of the pale morning light that he saw the regular shape of rooftops. The horse plodded tiredly behind the exhausted young man. The baby was howling, but he could see that the old woman had pulled the carrier loop toward her and was holding to the baby. She had seemed to learn to roll with the gait of the horse.

He tried to imagine the picture the four of them (including the confused horse) would make as they walked into the presence of those who had not experienced his night. The old woman, sitting astride the horse, had her dress pushed up revealing her skinny calves, knobby knees and high topped, well-worn shoes. Facial expression firmly set and staring ahead with determination, one arm hugging the baby to her chest.

Something had to be done. He'd have to get her down and let her walk with some dignity into Argyle. Seeing him reach for the baby, she stared a moment, then reluctantly lowered the infant into his arms. The child promptly woke up and began to yell. It was a sloppy yell as both small fists were crammed into her open mouth.

Laying the baby on the ground, he had the sudden knowledge of a lot of moisture on her, and on him. Oh! Babies required diapers! Old Miss Lizzie allowed herself to be lowered to the ground and steadied until she found her balance.

Lifting small Lettie into his arms, Stanley felt his shirt sleeve become instantly soaked from contact with the soggy diaper. So be it! He lifted the rein and spoke to the horse, then he spoke to the woman.

"Miss Lizzie, we're going to walk over to this store and get some help. Can you walk that far?"

By way of response, she adjusted her bonnet over her straggling hair, and shifting her wrinkled skirt into a semblance of straightness, and nodded. Planting her feet firmly one after the other, she followed.

Never was he more relieved than when he saw the scene before him consisting of a large, square building with light coming from the windows. Wrapping the horse's lead lines onto the hitching post, he patted the animal in reassurance and opened the door. Miz Lizzie stepped through, and he followed. A man looked up.

"Sir, we've got a peck'a trouble, and we need help." Nothing like stating his business in one breath.

"Come on in here. I got coffee perkin', water for tea, and the oatmeal porridge is bubbling. What do you need first?"

"Everything. I have a soaked baby who lost her mother yesterday, and she's really hungry. I need clothes, horses, wagon, and rest. Miz Lizzie, here is about done in, and the baby soaked her pretty well, too."

"I got ya'. Miz Lizzie, you just step right over here and sit down. First thing to do is have food." With that he dipped up a generous portion from the bubbling kettle and set it in front of her. "I'll bring tea," he decided for her.

"And you? Right over here. I got diapers by the dozen. You can change her, and I'll have a cook in here in a few minutes to make more than oatmeal." He handed over the package of white diapers.

Stanley took the package and stared at the shopkeeper. He'd never diapered a baby in his life and didn't remember an occasion of observing it done. Old Mac, the owner, was no dummy. "Don't know how to do it, huh? Your wife never let ya. I'll bet."

"Sir, this baby is my niece, and both parents were killed yesterday by robbers. You're right, I don't really know what to do." By now the red-faced baby was screaming hysterically.

Old Mac nodded. "Take advice from an old man. I can help you learn, but you'd best feed her first. How old is she?"

"'Bout six months."

"She's old enough. You just sit here. Oatmeal is the perfect food. I'll fix it. Let's get her quiet, and it looks like you can't get any wetter." The man strained out the smoother part of the porridge and stirred it in the bowl, blowing away the steam. "Now we test the temperature. Double your little finger and dip the knuckle in this stuff. If it doesn't feel hot, it's all right. Here's this spoon and just dip a bit on the tip and blow it." He demonstrated. "Now, put the spoon against her lower lip. I'll hold back her hands back till you get started."

Gratefully, Stanley obeyed. When the spoon touched her lip, the tiny girl began to suck. Down went the oatmeal, and she opened her mouth for more. Mac observed, "Looks like she might'a had a spoon before. Now we can't let her have very much at first, hungry as she is. Or it'll come up faster'n it went down."

After that, he demonstrated the way to affix a diaper to the small bottom. Next came a new flannel gown from the box of

97

baby clothes. Her vocalizing had simmered down to a few snubs and hiccoughs. Eyes drooped from exhaustion. "Look at that," Mac commented. "With luck, she'll take a nap while you take care of yourself."

He brought food, and noticed the woman sitting silently before her empty bowl. "Can I bring you more, ma'am?" Lizzie nodded and eventually consumed three bowls of the hot cereal. As she finished her tea, she sighed in contentment. "Ma'am, come with me and I'll find you a bed."

She shook her head. "Necessary room."

"The what...?"

"Necessary room. Out back."

"Oh, you want the privy. I'll show you where."

That taken care of, she settled onto the canvas soldier-bed and allowed him to cover her. Sighing again, she closed her eyes.

Back to Stanley. "Well, we got your niece and your grandma settled, what can I do for you?"

"Is there someone I can leave the baby with for a few hours? I have to make a trip back to where we were ambushed. I didn't see much in the dark, and I speck they got all six horses. I have to look around, though, because everything I had was there... but the baby. Miz Lizzie was with the other wagon that got burned. I don't know her at all, but she seems to have developed an idea of who I am. She's calling me James, and acts like she may have cared for a baby."

"Couldn't say who her folks were?"

"No. She seems of a mind that I'm part of the family. She was wandering in the brush when I came back to camp, and she said something about looking for supper. I figured she was lookin' for greens, maybe. But the fact is, I'm gonna take her with me. I'm thinkin' the law won't say it's kidnappin'. It may turn out we need each other. Anyway, the first I need is clean clothes and a wagon and team, to either rent or buy. I have need of a safe box if you have one."

Mac digested his situation. "Nothin' I can't handle. I got my own team, and you're welcome. I'll check around for one to buy. Could be, I can help. You go do what you have to do and settle your mind. How far was you headed, anyway?"

"About five or six miles on out west. Bought a place where they proved up and now they're goin' back east."

"Must be the Holtz place. Well, I'll get the wagon, and you pick out what you need from the store. We'll settle up later."

It was a slow journey, and the young man was torn between wishing to get this mission completed and dread for what he may see. The lone horse trotting between the double-tree poles of the small wagon seemed to be enjoying the day.

Compass in hand, Stanley guided himself directly to the scene of the disaster. Three piles of ashes and chunks of debris. At least five lives ended, and who would ever know how many more? He pulled the wagon alongside and stepped out. A quick glance revealed no slain bodies. A guilty sigh of relief. A more through search revealed the truth of it. Nature's clean-up committees at work.

Another guilty sigh. No bodies meant no graves he must preside over. With the shovel he had brought, just in case, he approached the rear pile of ash. To the wagon he had steered into place a hundred years ago yesterday. Seemed like. The oiled canvas coverings must have gone up quickly. There was, however a number of metal tools without handles. Hammer, ax, hatchet. Rake, spade, shovel and two grubbing picks. Good. He knew about handles.

A swipe with the handle-less rake turned over bolts and screws. Parts of leather harness that were too far from the blaze to catch. The lines had been severed with a sharp knife. The thieving, murdering demons had stolen a half a dozen good animals. Maybe that was worth leaving the box of gold coins and not being caught.

He moved on to the next pile of ash. Spoons, forks, knives, kettles, bent but usable. Two chains that had bound a trunk of Louise's valuables that she couldn't live without. Well, she wouldn't have to, now. Louise was an extraordinary girl. Maybe someday he could find one as good.

A few glass dishes. Smoked but not broken. More harness rigging. Put everything in the wagon that had a possible use. Small metal box with a fancy catch. Maybe silver, but in bad shape. With his knife blade he forced open the catch. Necklace. Two rings with colored stone sets. Chain (gold) with heart shaped locket. Inscribed, "To Louise with love. Richard." He remembered that. His brother had given it to her to seal her promise to marry him. Several trinkets with catches on the back to be pinned to garments. Nothing else.

Deep sigh of gratefulness. Something to save. A gift for small Lettie. All he could give her of her parents. He swallowed hard to remove the lump in his throat, but was not successful. Dragged his sleeve roughly across his blurry eyes. Time later for tears.

On to the other pile of ash. Did not belong to him. Yes, it did. He had Miz Lizzie so he should try to find something of hers. Twisted metal box (could be straightened) contained charred… biscuits? More cutlery. More tools without handles. Small pile of charred nails, a very valuable find. Silver spice cans, tarnished but undamaged. Silver must be a very strong metal. More leather tack from the severed harnesses. A box of her clothing would be helpful but was not there.

He walked away and stood in the bushes to look up. What was he meant to do, now? His foot moved aside a rock…? No, it was a shiny object? Colt, 45. Not two feet away was the other one. The shiny new guns he and his brother had bought just before leaving Ohio. It was obvious his brother had pitched them into the brush hoping to keep them away from the robbers. Well, Richard, you were successful. Thanks. I wish you were here, but I'm glad you and Louise are together. I know you're in a better place because there was never a pair of people better than you two. Goodbye now.

He forced his feet to turn back to the horse and small cart containing a surprising number of items. Money…! The other people must have had some money. No one would come out here without something to keep them till the crops came in.

Scrambling around his plunder, he pulled up the handle-less rake and went to the third ash pile. Carefully, from one side, he began to rake away the debris. Grizzly. Pieces of unidentifiable origin. Scorched metal can. Coffee? Lid was stuck. Take the whole can maybe the coffee was still good. Keep raking. Shiny objects. Yes, coins of various denomination. A handful of pennies. Not much for a trip like this, but he found nothing more except a number of colorful buttons.

A thread of memory flashed through his head. Louise… stringing colorful buttons and a few thread spools on a shoestring. "For Lettie," she'd explained with a pleased smile.

Yes, for Lettie. He gathered all the buttons he could find over the next half hour. Surely he could find a shoestring somewhere, or buy one from Mac. Then Lettie would have a toy suitable to her age.

Back to the wagon and the horse was headed west. Patient and plodding, now, and the young man did not care. This was clearly the time and place for the tears. For the groans of agony. Relief that he could turn away from the scene of the disaster, but anger that he could not turn back the time. Sniffles and throat lumps. More tears until his shirt sleeve was almost as wet as it had been when he carried the baby.

Argyle was just ahead. Straighten up the face. He still had a duty.

"Mac, I'm gonna take my saddle horse and run out to the Holtz place. Way my luck's goin', my house may be a hole in the ground. Anyway, I need to check it out before I take my girls out there. I'll be back, maybe after dark. If I don't, you have my safety box, and I'll trust you to do what you have to do." Sometimes one had to depend on kind strangers.

Old Buster was glad to get his four hoofs on the ground, and Stanley was beginning to get a grip on his emotions. Instead of just helping his brother, he now had two individuals who could not do for themselves. He could handle this problem and he would. The Powers Above would not give him too much to bear… that had been a promise made by his Maker. Just move on ahead. Is this what faith was about?

The spring sunshine was warm, and the time was about two o'clock. He'd need to hurry.

There it was. The house, the two outbuildings, and the smokehouse. Fences intact. House had only one broken window. Storm? Animal? Didn't matter. He stepped through the door and closed it behind him. Good fit. Parlor first. The Holtzes had left various pieces of furniture. Sofa, chair, cloth carpet. Large mirror still on the wall. He touched the frame of the mirror and it moved. Pulling it aside, he saw the safe box built in the wall. Marvelous!

Table, three chairs. Cabinet. Hand pump by the water pitcher. A few kettles they must not have considered worth taking. Bed frames with the rope webbing removed. They must have needed the rope. No problem. He'd need feather mattresses. Also a bureau. No doubt a lot of other things (things that Louise would be able to count off in seconds but he'd need a bit more time). He'd just have to learn. Fast.

No use to waste time in the out buildings. They were there, and that was enough.

Buster headed back, still in a good humor. That gave Stanley time to wonder how Mac had fared with his ladies, the young and the old. He'd owe him a bit, but fortunately, money was not his immediate problem. His pockets were heavy with the coins from the third wagon, and he'd just leave his other money in Mac's safe box.

Two new Colts. Guns were always valuable. Should be worth something if he had to sell one. The trusty old six shooter he wore would do him best just now. Argyle ahead, and there was just enough light to see the outlines of the buildings. Sigh! It was as though he had turned the page of a book he must read, though he dreaded it. Have courage, Stanley, he chided. You can do it.

Miz Lizzie opened her eyes to the large room with the beds. She felt well and somewhat rested. There was the pressing need for the Necessary Room. Mama had told her she must always call it that if there were menfolk around. Never say backhouse or privy.

She pulled at her thread of memory. She knew where the Necessary Room was, and when she sat up, she was amazed at the number of beds in the room with no one on them. Covers folded and pillows fluffed. Strange, but no matter. So many things were strange to her, now.

Carefully making her way to the back door, she took care of her needs and returned. James would be somewhere near. He wouldn't leave her now that he was back. Stretching out on her bed, she drew the cover over her legs and shut her eyes. She would like to remember more, but that had become so hard. When she tried to think, the thoughts thinned themselves like the lacy clouds that came before a winter 'norther.' She reached into them, but her hand came back empty. So did her mind.

It was interesting about James. She remembered well the last time she had seen him. He had a different suit, and he told her he had to go away. He needed to make things safe for her, but he would be back. James McDonald. Some of the family called him Jamie, but that didn't fit, somehow. James. Her James. He had always taken care of his little sister. Miss Lizzie, he used to call her. Her childhood playmate and big brother protector.

What was strange, though, was when they told her he couldn't ever come home, and that had to be wrong. She knew he would return. He had promised. It was not a clan fight... and they were teamed up with the McMahans. The McDonalds and McMahans often fought together to protect their lands, but not this time. This 'going away' was something else.

No one could explain where he went or why he couldn't come home. There were people to tell her what to do, and that was a comfort. She hated to be confused. They let her play with children, and rock the babies. She loved babies.

Now, after a terrible fire, James had returned. She had only stepped into the bushes to see if there were any fresh greens for the next meal. She was good at picking greens and always remembered what was tasty and nutritious. Then there was a fire.

She was scared because she didn't know what to do. But there was James. He always spoke softly to her so she could understand, and he told her what to do. That was why she let him lift her up on that horse. Mama wouldn't have let her, but James always knew what to do. If he said she must ride like a man, then that was the right thing to do. And the baby. She hadn't got to hold the baby for a long time. It was strange about that baby. When the horse juggled her, and she had to hold on, the baby held onto her. Around the neck. She couldn't see how the baby was holding on, but when she got her balance, there it was... right there in her lap, cuddly and warm.

She remembered James's baby, of course. Little Lutie. Named Betty Lou after her mother. Where was his Betty Lou? She must be near, because he wouldn't leave her. Ever!

She was still weary, and this was such a good bed. It was firm and curved like a hammock, and it didn't jiggle like the bed she had when she... what was it she had been doing...?

Memories hung like musty cobwebs in an unused room. Touch them and they go away. Then they were back again. The bed had been bumpy and jiggly, but she didn't know why. James would tell her, though. Someone said it was what they had to do, but she couldn't count on that. They told her James could not come back, but he did. He even brought baby Lutie for her to hold.

Her weary eyes closed within the bed of wrinkles beneath her brow. Her thin cheeks settled into hollows as she drifted back into sleep. Such a good bed James had provided because he cared about her.

Later she remembered waking up, but no one told her to get up so she didn't. She thought she would be hungry soon, but not bad yet. Turning on her side she set her thoughts into pictures again. A fire. Riding a horse. Her dress smelled like baby. Comforting. She sensed there were other things to give her pleasure, but she'd save them until later. James would not let the good memories float away, now that he was back with her.

He had looked so strange but handsome when he had told her goodbye. His clothes were green and fitted loosely. He had an odd-looking green hat. His belt had a strap that went over his shoulder, and his buttons were shiny metal. Betty Lou cried, but Lizzie didn't want to think about that. It hurt when someone she loved was crying.

James had hugged her and said, "Keep smiling, Miss Lizzie. I'll be back before you know it!" James never lied to her, so she knew he would be back. Just when she needed him the most, here he was! She stretched out and breathed deeply as sleep claimed her… once more.

Stanley settled himself before the meal of meat, potatoes and gravy. Steaming coffee, scalding and strong as an ox! Pie. Spicy apples and flakey crust. Mac had presented a bill that he was happy to pay. The store-keeper assured him that he had included pay to the young lady, very young lady, who had cared for the baby. Girls learned young, and this particular one would have cared for the baby for nothing.

Most of the next day was spent selecting and loading a borrowed wagon with necessities. Mac had promised to watch for one he could buy, but he could rent this one from him until that happened.

Stanley spent a bit of time looking at the Montgomery Ward catalog. He knew he'd be back to place an order soon. The girl who had cared for Lettie was also happy to outfit the old woman with necessary clothing. He was grateful. Under things for ladies were an unthinkable mystery that he was not prepared to unravel. She also advised him of things he'd need for the baby. He had the feeling he might be wanting to hire her services again when he made his catalog order.

Mac steered him to where he could buy a milk goat. Babies could not be raised properly on oatmeal alone.

Old Miz Lizzie looked a lot different in the new black bonnet and gray dress. She even hugged him for the gift and said she was so glad he was back, now. Had she thought he would abandon her in Argyle? Not a chance! They were buddies, now, and obviously needed each other. If she could be contented with the arrangement, so much the better.

They must have made quite a sight as they left with the loaded wagon. Two feather mattresses on the wagon bed that was filled with plunder. Goat tied behind, waddling around her huge udder. He'd never milked a goat, but he'd bet he could do it when Lettie started howling!

He'd practically had to lift Miz Lizzie into the wagon. Wondered what her family had done about that. Maybe a box step to take along would be good. Of course, he'd get a buggy later, but even in Argyle, some things were just naturally scarce. He hated to think how he would have managed without Mac and his store.

Well, he was now headed out to the community that its residents called Shady Ridge. Bare up, Miz Lizzie, we got us a tough row ahead of us that's gotta be hoed! But you and me... we can do it. We got each other to lean on.

He turned the team into the yard and leaped down. "We're home, Miz Lizzie," he told her brightly. The baby was asleep on the bench, so he reached for the old woman's hand and lifted her down to the ground. She made no objection. He had no way of knowing that if someone other than her brother had done that, she would have screamed for help from someone.

Picking up the baby, he led the woman to the house. Miz Lizzie did not remember the house, but if he said it was home, it likely was. There were so many things she didn't remember, and by now nothing (and everything) seemed really strange. She was used to it, as long as there was someone to tell her it was all right… or what she should do.

She looked around in the parlor. Someone had left it a bit dirty, but she could handle that. No one needed to tell her about cleaning. Very nice mirror. She looked in, and she saw an old wrinkled face peering back at her. Oh, that must be part of the family that she didn't remember. No problem there. She always got along well with old ladies.

Nice kitchen. James demonstrated the pump for her. Water! Right there in the kitchen. Nice stove. Good oven. She would enjoy cooking here. Huge kettle. Rabbit stew? "James, we could have rabbit stew!"

He smiled his wonderful smile. "Quick as I get out there with my gun, we'll have rabbit stew!"

Lizzie smoothed out the feather mattress and spread the sheets. Nice quilts. Light weight with summer coming on. Pillows. Her room and James' room. He would sleep with Lettie on his bed. That was his right, as she was his baby. However, there would be naps when she could have her in bed with her. Babies were such fun, and no one ever told her she couldn't take care of babies. They always told her she did a good job.

The kitchen. There were beans and potatoes. Side meat for the beans. 'Go fer' matches and cow pats for the stove. The big rabbit stew kettle for the beans. Sort them and put them to soak for later.

Pleasure thrills passed down her arms and back. The long ride was over. She was home, and she knew exactly what to do. Food was first. Garden out back? She couldn't be sure, but where else would it be? She found good green turnip tops from last year's crop, and picked her apron full. Wilted in the skillet with grease from the side meat. Onions? Yes, there they were.

She looked up into the sky at the drifting white clouds and contentment flowed over her, warm as melted butter. So many times she had prepared food for her brother and Betty Lou, and now she got to do it again. What more was there to wish for? Betty Lou would be along, shortly. She would be glad the meal was started.

# CHAPTER 6

Stanley (James) on the other hand was working on the puzzle of the goat. The animal was agreeable enough, but her heavy udder reached almost to the ground and he, having no stool, sat on the ground with the pan. Splat, splat! Well, it worked, but something would have to be done. Couldn't even get a bucket under her. Platform? Likely.

He brought the results of his effort into the house and rinsed one of the bottles young Miss Sally had told him would work for the baby. Poured the warm milk into the bottle and fitted on the rubber nipple. Harder than it looked, but he got it done.

All right, Miss Lettie. Let's see if you know what to do with this. When the hard nipple touched her lips, she tried to spit. Milk should come from something soft and warm. She whimpered and whined, tossing her head away.

The old woman watched for a minute, took the bottle from him and shook it, bringing a drop of milk to the tip. Gently, she touched the baby's lips and pulled the bottle away. Shook down another drop and watched as the baby sucked it in. Opening her mouth for more, she still shied away from the hard nipple, but the old woman patted her chin, gently, insistently, and Lettie finally agreed to close her mouth and suck. Her hunger helped.

Stanley held her until she had her fill and drowsed into sleep. He placed her in the middle of his bed with a feeling of accomplishment that matched his most difficult jobs.

He carried all the plunder into the house and drove the team to the barn. Good barn. It was better than he had remembered. Stored the wagon and wandered around, looking at everything. There was even a platform that would work with the goat. It had an attached ramp if he could get her to climb. Now was a good time to try.

Brought the milking pan and the goat into the barn. The animal saw the platform, let out an accusing 'blat,' and scurried up the ramp. Looking his way, she gave him an expression that said 'get with it'. Well, that settled that. The goat knew what to do.

When he took the pan of milk to the kitchen, good smells met him. Potatoes fried in onions and side meat. Wilted turnip greens. Biscuits and a warm glow coming from the stove. He couldn't resist hugging Lizzie's shoulders in appreciation as he walked by. She was certainly doing her part.

The place at the table was set for three. Lizzie put on the food and led him to the parlor. Pointing to the mirror, she told him, "She needs to come and eat. I set her a place."

While he sought for an answer that might make sense to her, she continued. "Old woman. I think she can't hear me. She moves her mouth, but I can't hear her. Tell her to come eat."

Stanley glanced toward the ceiling. Give me help! What do I say? "No, Miz Lizzie. That old woman isn't hungry. I can hear her, and that's what she says. She likes to live in that room by herself. She told us to go ahead and eat."

Lizzie looked from him to the old woman, who kept looking at her. Another strange thing, but she was used to strangeness. If James said the old woman was not hungry, she could believe him. Together they went to the kitchen and ate the greens and potatoes with browned slabs of side meat, and warm goat milk in the new drinking glasses.

Later, stretched out on the new feather mattress smoothed by Miz Lizzie, tiny Lettie beside him, Stanley Barlow took stock. He would have preferred to sink into dreamless sleep, but that was not to be. Thoughts raced in his head, overturning each other and canceling each other out like a flock of blackbirds gathering to head south. He seemed unable to separate them out. Likely he'd have to just take the thoughts as they came. Worst ones first.

The biggest and most powerful thought was what he must do about the lost grape vines. His and his brother's whole dreams and plans were wrapped in the oiled canvas bags that had created such an impressive blaze. Plans… they had dissolved into black smoke clouds and spread themselves across the prairie skies.

Forget that, Stanley, and erase the picture. What next.

Well, there were still the vines back in Ohio. The vines did well there, it was just the grapes that did not. There could be more cuttings. He could ask the new owner to... what? Make new cuttings? He had said he had no experience with grapes.

So, then what? It wouldn't hurt to ask him... what? In his mind he formed the telegram. "Could you cut branches and ship them in moist wrappings? If so, state price and time of availability."

The telegram came shooting back. "You pay labor and shipping charges I send whole vine."

Without a shred of a second thought, Stanley wired back, "Agreed. Dig up. Cut roots one foot long cut vines two feet high remove all branches. Pack canvas bags with wet newspapers. Advice when"

Answer. "Laborer says two weeks."

Response. "Agreed. Mail bill."

That taken care of, Stanley found himself with total mental freedom. Anything was now possible. He took his shovel out to the south-facing slope that he and his brother had agreed upon. He pointed the shovel into the sandy loam of the Territorial soil and lifted a full dip. With spontaneous enthusiasm he tossed the soil into the air and said, "Richard, buddy, I'll take care of it! Your dreams can come true for Lettie!"

He had forgotten exactly how many plants they had, but he knew it was more than 200. So he'd count on 250, eventually. Stepping off the rows, he counted six feet per vine. That meant 250 posts and about 4000 feet of wire. That oughtta make a dent in the coins at Mac's place! Actually, though, even taking into account the unskilled labor of digging the vines, what he would get would be far better than the cuttings he had lost. They could not help but be. Those vines should bear in two years rather than the four or five they had estimated.

Cottonwood saplings he had aplenty. Not the best, but posts could be replaced. No time to put a handle onto the ax heads he had. Back to Mac's for an ax and to order the wire. Looking around the station, he spied a stack of small boxes containing chocolates. Clutching the ax and the candy, he mounted Buster and was off, excitement and energy oozing from him.

He swept into the house. "Hey there, Miz Lizzie! Brought you somethin'."

He was obliged to submit to a hug. "Oh, thank you, James," her crackly voice breathless with excitement. She studied the box carefully. It had been a long time since she had a box of candy. She took it to her room and put it in a drawer, covering it over with some of her new stockings. No one else need know she had such a treasure. He had brought it to her! Her, alone!

Under the swing of his ax, young cottonwood saplings fell like summer rain. Most of the young trees made three posts when trimmed up. A bit short but time was also short and posts would be replaced anyway. Two weeks plus shipping time… hard to tell just when they'd be here, but he'd be ready.

Grapes did not have to be planted deep, and these would have only a foot of root, so figure… hole two feet deep with topsoil layered in? That ought to do it.

He often cast his eyes about for game. Rabbit stew, particularly. Today he bagged three. Young and tender. Louise would say they were wasted in stew. Should be fried. But what matter! One thing about Lizzie, she managed to find something to cook, but she did want eggs. Next trip in he'd order some chickens from the catalog. The small shed should make a place for them.

One thing about cutting poles, it gave a lot of time to think. And dream. And plan. And wonder if the money would hold out until the grapes came in. And where could he sell that many grapes? All the "thinks" that had been planned out with others, now dumped themselves on his head. Have to start from scratch. Alone.

The day the vines came was the day Lettie sat up alone. He came in and found her on a pallet on the floor, sitting up and gnawing on a biscuit crust.

"Teething," explained Lizzie. One thing about the old woman, she was a gal of few words. And nothing much bothered her. She moved about in the house, doing this and that, humming contentedly, or speaking softly to herself.

Stanley, by this time, had begun to feel comfortable inside the skin of James. Piecing statements together, he decided that James had been her beloved older brother who "took care of her," possibly because of her slowness. Stanley had first thought it was her age that made her seem so childlike, but now he wasn't so sure. She did, however, have trouble remembering anything recent. It was as though the fire had dropped her back into her girlhood and young years... times when she had been cared for and comfortable.

Miz Lizzie's James must have been called up to serve in the war between the states, and had not survived. They'd told her he wouldn't come home, but sure enough, he had. That was all it took to make her happy. Her only concern, it seemed, was the old woman in the other room who was never hungry. Also, when Bettie Lou would come.

The old woman in the window did, however, help Lizzie with the dusting in the parlor. She dusted the furniture on her side of the 'window.' Lizzie could tell she did a good job of the dusting, and that woman's furniture was just like hers. That made it nice. She wouldn't mind visiting with the woman, but it was the other woman's place to visit first, as she was in the house first. So Lizzie would just wait until she wanted to come for tea. Lizzie, herself, had slipped comfortably into her former self and remembered nothing of the years that had recently passed.

By September, the newly planted vines were showing good leaves, a promise of rapid growth next year. Rains had come, and the sandy soil gave them the nourishment they needed. "Look, Richard, our plan was a good one."

Then he smiled. Think of Lizzie moving back into the years she was comfortable with, and here he was, talking with his brother, gone these six months.

He had found time between the demands of the vineyard and the time required of his two women folk to plant the kitchen garden. Lizzie liked to help tend it, and she took over the harvesting and preserving. One thing about taking on a place that had been "proved up," so many necessary things were left in place, including expensive Mason jars for canning. A pair of pigs were added for the pen, and a cow joined the goat in the barn.

He now had a team of mules for the plow, another horse to help Buster with the wagon or the buggy. A collie dog helped to clear varmints from the place. Or, at least, tell someone they were there.

And Lettie was walking. She could cover a lot of ground, but Mama Lizzie was one step ahead. If she couldn't give the child her attention, she set a table leg on her dress tail and gave her toys, a favorite toy being the string of fancy and colorful buttons along with anything else that had a convenient hole for stringing. Sometimes, of an evening, Stanley would point to objects and count with numbers. Lettie would mimic the counting and make her own sounds for the numbers. Smart, he decided.

Mama Lizzie chattered to the child, and sometimes encouraged her to speak. "Mama Lizzie" and "Papa" were her first words. By Christmas she had learned a few more words, including "NO!". Stanley would never have thought the rambling old woman he had lifted to the horse's back would have such endurance. Why, she must be at least 60 years old, and she was thin as a stray cat! How did she do it?

He thought she must have stopped maturing at maybe age 12. A trip to Argyle was exciting to her, and she liked peppermint stick candy. She liked taking Lettie up and down the short main street, showing her this and that. Sometimes, young Sally would see them, and come to see how Lettie had grown. Sally had no trouble with Lizzie's age, either actual or mental.

Stanley Barlow sighed, wearily, dispiritedly. So very much to do he hardly knew what to do next. Winter was definitely coming. There was that loose board by the kitchen cabinet that let in a sharp breeze. In a month it would be a blizzard. Stanley, he told himself. Fix that board. One thing about Miz Lizzie, she never complained, just did what she thought was next go do. But he must keep her from coming down with something. She was much too valuable. Fix that board!

Nails. Where was the pile of nails he had retrieved from the third ash heap? In the shed. Somewhere. It would be nice if he were a bit more organized. On the shelf with the other retrieved objects? Hmmm, there was that can of coffee. Seemed heavy. Does coffee get heavier as it gets older?

He took down the can and shook it. No sound, but of course coffee grounds would make no sound. The lid was firmly seized up. Finally, taking his knife, he ripped through the thin metal of the lid.

No coffee. Just cloth… maybe a bag. Lifting out the cloth, which actually was a bag, he peeked in. Gold coins. Of course. He had known at the time that no one starts out on a journey the way they had with no means of support. Well, the coins were from Miz Lizzie's family, and Miz Lizzie would get the first purchase.

One of his most immediate concerns was the state of Miz Lizzie's clothing. She had nothing warm. No coat or jacket or warmer underthings. This house was sure to be drafty this winter. Maybe better next year.

He set the bag of coins aside without counting them and continued to look for the nails. It took only three of them to fasten the board against the most of the draft… more later. Right now he had a better errand.

"Miz Lizzie, we're going to Argyle. Get a blanket to wrap Lutie, and you and I are going to get jackets."

It was fascinating to watch the old woman's expression. Her faded blue eyes lit up, her smile of pleasure rearranged her facial wrinkles, and she nodded, vigorously.

Grabbing up the blanket, she followed Stanley out to the buggy that was already hitched to old Buster. Lizzie hummed merrily as they jogged along, sometimes clapping hands to the tune and encouraging the baby to do the same. Stanley was feeling charged up. One small problem was going to be taken care of, and he hoped for Sally's help. But that was not to be.

It was from Sally's mother that he learned, "Our Sally's not home. Her and her friends, they're makin' a party for their fellers. Cookin' candy and such. She ain't to be home till late in the night. Reckon I could help?"

A sigh of relief. "Oh, you could! If you have the time, that is."

The mother nodded. "I'll just take off my apron and get my shawl. By the way, my name's Helen. I'm 'specktin' you'll want to go over to Mac's." She disappeared, and in moments she was back.

On the way he explained. "I left the Miz Lizzie and the baby to go look around. She likes to do that, and she likes for people to see her with the baby."

Lowering her voice, Helen asked, "She doin' all right? I mean with the baby… and all?

Stanley was happy to tell her, "That seems to be her best thing. I'm thinkin' she must'a been tossed around within the family, helping to take care of whatever baby needed her. Very careful, she is, but I know it'll get bad when the baby gets to runnin' around. She's a good cook, though. Does well with what she has. Likes rabbit stew."

Nearer to Mac's he explained. "She's in need of winter things. A coat and a jacket and a warm shawl. Maybe dresses of thicker cloth and some warmer underthings. Like the fuzzy... I mean..." He hesitated as he felt his face getting redder and redder. How did he know what was the name of what ladies wore under their dresses?

Helen didn't bat an eye. Likely she was going to be even better help than Sally. "I believe you're thinkin'a flannel pettislips. Most older ladies set a store by them."

Stanley nodded with relief. "Get two, or maybe three. It's bound to be drafty around the floor."

"I could suggest flannel drawers. They're really warm to wear in the house under a dress. And wool stockings, too. What we're talkin' on, that's gonna be a bit'a... cash...?"

Stanley nodded. "I know but it's gotta be. Can't let her be cold, and maybe comin' down with somethin'. Need clothes for the girl, too. If I could ask you somethin', it'd be to pick out what you think is best while I do some other buyin'."

Helen smiled with pleasure. The only thing she liked better than that was buying for herself. Shopping at Mac's was a pure pleasure, now that he started handling some of the newer things.

Stanley moved into the men's section where he was much more comfortable. Heavy underwear. New overalls and jacket. Thick mackinaw jacket lined with sheepskin, with the fur still on. Gloves, for working with the grapes. Shoes and rubber boots. Wool socks. Gathered together they made quite a pile, so he paid for them and took them to the buggy.

"Uh, Miss Helen, I was thinkin' on askin' something else from you. I'll take the jacket and shawl with me, but I need for everything else to be wrapped up like presents. I think Miz Lizzie'd like presents, maybe for Christmas, bein' that it's only three weeks away. If you could do that, I'd pick 'em up the next time in town."

He was rewarded with a smile of pleasure. Wrapping presents might just figure as the third or fourth thing Helen liked doing best. When he looked over what she had picked out, he had a moment of fear. It was a hugely impressive heap.

Three dresses, thick and long sleeved. A heap of soft, gray unmentionables. Long woolen stockings, three pair, and a pair of garters. A fleecy night gown and robe. Fleecy house slippers. A wool knitted shawl with fringe on the ends. Sturdy coat with heavy lining, black and charcoal plaid, and scarf of charcoal. Fur trimmed bonnet that fastened under the chin.

A jacket that was red, and was made of thick material like canvas. Soft gray lining in the sleeves. Two coverall aprons with gathered skirts and large pockets. A package of men's hankies, red and blue plaid.

Helen was flushed and excited over her choices. "Now, I just picked up what I knew my Grandma would have liked, so if I got too much, we'll put it back. I was specktin' you'd want shoes, but you'd have to trace the bottoms of the ones she wears so I could get the size right.

"Now, I'm knowin' them's men's hankies, but my old Gran, she'd like them better'n ones for ladies. Them aprons is really important for work and keeping warm. She could do with only one and dry it over the stove, if you want. That there bonnet, that'll be somethin' she'll really like. That fur… it's soft as a baby kitten."

Nodding, he accepted her choices. "Keep both aprons." He'd have sure not known about them. "Now there's somethin' else. I've seen ladies wear hats indoors, gathered with lace or somethin' that they tuck their hair in under. She's not had one, but I think ladies like 'em."

He hardly got the description out of his mouth until his guide smiled, nodded knowingly and walked off. He followed.

"You're talkin' about dust caps. Ladies love 'em. They's winter ones and summer ones, fancy ones and plain ones. Here they are. See?" Helen popped one over her own head and turned to smile at him. Yes, that was what he wanted. "Get the one there with lace, and that pink one with flowers. And the gray one. I'll take the gray one with me."

115

Helen nodded with approval at his choices. "Now for the baby, these flannel dresses are nice, and the little pettislips with sleeves. They're nice and warm. And shoes. She'll be big enough before you know it and want to be on the floor. And if they're too big, just put on two or three pairs of stockings. They'll be warmer that way. I picked out only one coat, the way youngens grow, and a big, thick blanket to wrap up in. You got enough diapers? They don't dry too good in the winter." She indicated a package of a dozen, explaining, "Never hurts to have extra diapers. When they don't need 'em no more, they's a lot of things they're used for."

Stanley accepted her choice. "How about a bonnet? A warm one?"

Helen selected a pink one with bows. "Good thing about bonnets, they don't outgrow 'em so fast." She gathered the small things and added them to the big pile.

Stanley hesitated. "Toys? For little girls?"

With a nod, his guide was gone again, and he was obliged to follow. "If'n she was mine, I'd get a rubber baby doll. A little one she can hold easy. She'll likely gnaw off the fingers, teethin', but she'll still like it. Now here's a plush kitten. And a blanket for the doll. A tiny bottle to feed the doll. Here's colored rings some babies like to put on their arms. Now, later on, you'll need blocks and there's somethin' else you might like. Mac's started keepin' domino blocks. Later on, she'll like to build things… likely."

"Let's have all of those things, and I'll think of more, later. That should about do it for now."

Helen took out a dress for Lizzie, the fuzzy shawl and one of the aprons. Also the handkerchiefs. Then raised her eyes in question. Yes, that was what he wanted now. The rest would be wrapped.

He chose the colored rings, saving the doll for Lettie's Christmas. He took the little coat and the bonnet, along with the heavy blanket.

Now it was time to pay. The hugeness of the looming bill was countered only by the fact that he did, in fact, have enough to pay for them, and they were an absolute essential, with winter coming on. Was that a smile of satisfaction on Mac's face as he totaled up the bill?

Not so bad as Stanley had expected. He hadn't had to dip into his safe box, and still had several coins left in the bag. And his heart beat with pleasure over what he knew would be the reaction by Miz Lizzie to her 'gifts.'

Back at Helen's place, he carried the merchandise to the house. "You say Sally is partying with her boyfriend? Is marriage in the plans?"

Sad smile from Helen. "They'd like it to be, but Lonnie ain't located a solid job, yet. See, he's only eighteen, but really strong. Sometimes gets a day or two, here and there, but nothin' sure enough to take on a wife."

Stanley paused, his mind quickly turning. "Do you think he'd like a couple days at my place? Maybe more. I got more work a'breathin' down my neck than I can get done before cold sets in."

Helen nodded, asking with interest, "You got somethin' he could do? I'm thinkin' he'd go for it. If you'd tell me, I'll ask 'im then I could tell you."

Good! "Well, now what I got that needs doin' this minute is prunin' some grapevines."

"You think he'd know how?"

"I could tell 'em in fifteen minutes. Show 'im, in fact."

"Mr. Barlow, tell me this. Could I send 'im on out to your place to talk with you and see what the job is? He's just a'pinin' to get more to do, and them as have work ta be done don't always have the money ta pay to get it done." She had told herself that his man must indeed have money, as he hadn't batted an eyelash over the pile of items she had just selected.

Stanley nodded agreement. "Send 'im on out. He'd know where I am, I'm thinkin'. We'll see what happens."

Loading his purchases aboard the buggy, he found his ladies in the Sweet Shop, eying the jars of candy. The baby cooing and jabbering at the bright colors, and the old lady mentally tasting the flavor and sweetness of her childhood treat. He watched for a few moments, enjoying the picture.

"I'll take two peppermint sticks and a dozen lemon drops." Miz Lizzie smiled and crinkled her eyes in anticipation. She was so easy to please that it was fun to bring on her smiles. With his two charges aboard, he extracted a peppermint stick for Miz Lizzie and one for himself, pocketing the lemon drops. They would make a treat for Miz Lizzie while he was out.

Nearing home, he turned to Miz Lizzie, who was touching her candy stick to the baby's lips, enjoying the baby's surprised and pleased expression. "Miz Lizzie, do you like Christmas trees?"

A startled and wide-eyes look met him, and she responded, "Oh, yes. The way you used to do. You bring in the tree, and I get to trim it. The old woman in the window won't want to help, and your Betty Lou ain't come yet. James, when she gonna come?"

He was getting used to this question. "Not too long, maybe. When she gets through with what she's doin'."

"What all she doin'?"

"Tell you what, Miz Lizzie. When she gets here we'll ask her what took her so long." As usual, this answer satisfied her, buoyed up as she was over the prospect of a tree.

Reaching the house, he lifted Lettie from the seat and guided Miz Lizzie's feet onto the buggy step. Picking up the package of her things, he followed her into the house.

Opening the package, he took out Lettie's coat and bonnet. He had thought to put them on her until he saw how sticky she was. Instantly, Miz Lizzie grabbed up the garments and, holding them out in front of her, she wheeled around in a circle, chuckling with glee. "Oh, she'll be so pretty! Pretty Lutie, pretty Lutie," she sang in a song-song tune.

Stanley set Lettie on the floor with the colored rings and lifted out the overall apron. Sleeveless, but covering the whole chest and back, the apron covered her entire dress except for the sleeves. The skirt was gathered on but divided in the back. It was longer than her dress, and the huge pockets could be buttoned at the top. Absolutely a marvel of feminine usefulness. Miz Lizzie knew exactly what it was. "I always wanted one of these. They said it cost too much money. I knew you would get me one sometime!"

Still being curious about her background, he asked, "Who told you it cost too much money?"

"Oh, you know! Them I was stayin' with."

"Which ones were they?"

Miz Lizzie thought a minute. "I don't remember. It was some other time...."

He nodded. That was very true. It was some other time. He shook out the soft knitted shawl, feeling its smooth fuzziness on both sides. Which side was the right side? Maybe it didn't matter. He held it out and draped it over her bony shoulders, snugging it up under her scraggly hair. Now she was speechless. Turning to stare at him, she spread her arms and hugged his waist.

"Oh, you always was one to give the best presents! James, you gotta be hungry. Let me poke the fire and heat up the soup I got made. Hold my shawl for me so I don't get ashes on it."

Lettie squealed with pleasure, whacking her colorful celluloid hoops against the floor. Then in her exuberance she slung one across the room. Miz Lizzie calmly walked after it, picked it up, and brought it back. In a stern voice she chided, "No, Lutie. Don't throw your toys." Giving her a firm stare, she finally gave back the toy, and Lettie resumed banging against the floor.

Miz Lizzie nodded, knowingly. "Find me a string, I will, and tie them hoops together. She'll like 'em just as well." Stanley nodded. Truly a wisdom bought with experience.

Boyfriend Lonnie did not say how long he had been waiting outside, but he was there when Stanley rubbed sleep from his eyes and washed his face. He was persuaded to have oatmeal and butter biscuits before they made the trip up the hill to the vineyard.

Stanley took along the hand clippers and a sharp knife. "Now, you see how bushy these grape vines are? I gotta have 'em pruned a certain way. See this shoot? Almost big as my finger. It's gotta be cut off at ten inches." With that, he snapped the end of the branch from the trunk, and it fell to the ground.

Poor Lonnie was horrified. Didn't nobody ever cut off limbs that'd grow fruit! "But Mr. Barlow..."

Stanley was ready. "I know, Lonnie. It looks like a mistake, but these are special vines. If they aren't pruned, they go to long limbs and big leaves and not many grapes. You'll have to get used to seeing what is cut at ten inches and what is cut off at the trunk. See this one? It's just a twig like a fat toothpick. Cut it off here," and he removed the twig with the knife.

"Now, the reason you have a clipper and a knife is that the clipper makes a cleaner cut, but if you use it all day, you get a cramp so you can't work the next day. But little ones like this cut clean with a sharp knife. And don't bother to gather up the branches, yet. I'll want to see if some of them might make roots. Then you can gather them up and bring them down to the kitchen to burn."

He handed the tools to Lonnie. "Stretch your fingers out as far as you can. Look, from the tip of your thumb to your little finger is pretty much ten inches. That way you don't have to use a measure stick. Does this look like a job you want to do?"

"You mean just clip those branches off? That's all?"

"Yes, until you bring them down to the kitchen."

"Sure, man! I mean, yes, sir, I want the job. On this whole patch'a vines? I sure do! When can I start?"

"Whenever you want."

"How about now? I can get a fer piece done 'afore dinner!"

"Hmm, well, don't go too fast. I have some things to do, but I'll be back in a while to see how things are goin'."

Stanley found himself whistling as he returned to the house. Miz Lizzie's gold may get to go to a good cause. The fellow certainly was eager. How old would he be? Eighteen, she said? Already found him a girl to marry? Hmm...

Picking up a shovel, he stopped at the kitchen garden to lift out a few potatoes. That was a job that was good for thinking about the next thing he had to do. Tossing the potatoes into a bucket, he allowed to himself that bringing in the hay piles would be next.

At the end of summer, he had brought down the prairie hay with his long handled scythe and tossed it into piles. Hay that dries out in a pile instead of scattered, retains more of its nutrition, and he had two mules, three horses, a cow and a goat to feed. That meant a lot of hay. He needed to make a better way to get the hay in the loft than pitching it. That was a job that was hard on the arms. This winter he'd get at that.

Christmas tree. He needed to check on Lonnie, and the trees were nearby. He could do that now. He could hear the click of the clippers and the rustle of leaves under the whistling of the fellow.

"Hey, Mr. Barlow, I'm glad to see ya. Wondered if you wanted me to trim off these cottonwood sprouts whilst I was at it."

"Cottonwood sprouts?"

"Yeah, these here growin' on the posts. They's somethin' they put on 'em to keep 'em from sproutin', but we allers just nipped 'em off when we found 'em."

Stanley inspected the post. Sprouts. Small limbs looking like they really wanted to come on. How did he miss that? Of course, who would expect the cottonwood posts with no roots to actually grow? "Are you tellin' me that these posts make roots?"

"Shore as shootin' jackrabbits in the field. They're cottonwood, ain' they, and persimmon'll do the same thing. Cut green like you done these, they'll grow ever time. Not all of 'em, but most'll sprout limbs and roots. You know, they's those folks that'll set these close in a row to grow into a fence. Makes a good fence, chance the deer don't eat off the sprouts."

"The deer... Here...?"

"Yeah, man. You done missed it. A ten-point buck come by drivin' three does. Chargin' right through the vines. He didn't eat none, though, him havin' other thoughts on his mind."

Stanley suddenly had a couple of things on his mind. *A fence out of growing trees? A full-grown deer for Miz Lizzie's stew pot?* He had a notion she would know exactly how to fix the animal. *Smoked, maybe?*

Chopping his small hatchet through the trunk of a three foot high cedar didn't take long. A fence out of trees. Lonnie seemed to know exactly how to do it. Hmmm. What posts didn't sprout the first year could get replanted. Then a string of barbed wire. Fence should last a lifetime!

By now the loss of his brother had lessened from painful stab that left him shaken and trembling with weakness, to a dull ache that came at unexpected times. This was one of those times. It seemed most natural to talk with him, not that his brother could hear, but that he needed a response and he knew his brother so well, he knew what that response could be.

"Did you hear that, Rich? We were right about this bein' good growin' land. Even the fence posts are wantin' to grow. I'm thinkin'

121

about tryin' a fence with cottonwood stumps. What'd'ya think of that?"

Miz Lizzie watched with interest as the tree stand was nailed together and the tree was finally made to stand straight and solid. It was purely a sight of the time it took on measly little jobs. But when the tree was finally and solidly in place, she laughed and clapped her hands with enthusiasm.

"James, 'member what we liked for puttin' on a tree?"

Oops, another one of those 'remembers.' He grinned companionably and answered, "No, you tell me."

Pursing her lips in a childish way, she shook her head. "You think and remember."

"Now, Miz Lizzie, I been gone a long time. You know how long it was, and I forgot a lot'a things. You'll have to tell me, or I won't know."

That took away a bit of her joy, but she obliged. "All that store bought candy, pa'd get! Stripped canes and peppermints with holes and marsh mellors. Jelly beans and them sticky orange slices. Made that tree look good enough to eat!" She chuckled with merriment over her joke. "Next year I can have sweet gum balls dyed with poke berries. They look good, too, but we can't eat 'em."

Well, the tree would have to do for today, but candy was certainly an easy choice for later.

"James, I don't 'member this house too good. They's a lot I don't 'member, but I don't even know where to find the poke salat no more. 'Spose that old woman in the window could tell me?"

"Oh, no, let's don't bother her. I'll help you find it next year when it comes up. Maybe I'll remember where it grows."

That answer pacified her. "Oh, yes, and 'simmons, too."

Hmmm, didn't Lonnie say persimmons grew from sprouts? How long would it take?

The shorter fall day was getting dusky when Lonnie knocked on the door. "Mr. Barlow, I got me most half way through that patch, and I can get an earlier start tomorrow. Likely finish mid-afternoon. If'n you got other chores… or somethin'?"

Stanley's immediate thought was getting that hay up in the loft. "Tell you what, Lonnie. You come on out prepared to work when you get ready, and we'll talk about somethin' else needin' to be done." If he'd just get that hay up to the loft, then there would be time to pick over the limbs for cuttings. After that, Lonnie could gather the wood. Say, this might just work, long as the money held out.

There were a lot of things to do, like making a pen for the chickens so the varmints didn't get at them. If another section of the farm was plowed, he'd put in wheat. By the looks, that dirt never saw a plow. Cottonwood tree fences? That could use some thought. And he needed to trace Miz Lizzie's shoe size, but she always had them on.

Another cow? Or maybe he'd go with goats instead. A sight easier to mess with. Miz Lizzie made a right good cheese out of the goat milk. And then, some people eat goat meat. Make sausage or something.

Miz Lizzie yelled that supper was ready, and he thought he'd make a trip to the outhouse on the way. And what do you know? Right there in the dust of the path was the perfect print of Miz Lizzie's shoe. He measured with a stalk of weed. Length… Width? That should do it. At the table, he decided to get a bit of help with his decision.

"Miz Lizzie, you ever make anything out'a goat meat? Young goat like a kid, maybe?"

The old woman put down her spoon. Somewhere she must have been told not to talk with a spoon or fork in her hand. "Thing is I don't know why you don't 'member? Goat meat tastes good. Mama made sausage. I need some sage, and I know it's growin' in the garden. I looked, but it ain't where it was."

"I don't think we have any, anymore. I'll see if I can buy some."

The response was a severe reproof. "No. Folks don't buy sage. They get it from the garden. You showed me where to find it, one time. You ain't 'memberin' good."

"Well, you remember I've been away for a long time. I think I forgot what it looks like. We may not have any, anymore."

Exasperated frown. "'Course we have some. Folks ever havin' any sage, they always got sage. We just gotta find it. 'Spose somebody moved it?"

"We'll find it. What does it take to make sausage, besides sage?"

"Need a grinder. I looked all over the shed for it, and it ain't here. Someone must'a stole it."

"A grinder?"

"You know, the one that hooks on the cabinet. If I had a grinder and wheat, I'd make that cereal Mama used to make. You know, with butter and honey? I think somebody stole our bee hive, too."

With that, she picked up her spoon and began to eat her soup, crumbled liberally with leftover biscuits.

All right, so he needed to grow wheat, and the straw would be good for the animals, and for bedding for the pig. He needed to get a grinder and somehow find some sage plants. There was a fenced-in place he had thought might be a pen of some sort. He could have Lonnie spade it up for the sage plants. He really needed a lot more garden space.

Lonnie was there when Stanley went out to milk. He wouldn't come in the kitchen for tea and a biscuit, but wanted to get right with the job. The weak winter sun had disappeared when he reported back that the clipping job was done. What was next?

"Lonnie, how are you on the end of a spade? I've got a little spot here that needs turned. Got a lot of weed stems."

"I'm up with the best on a spade, Mr. Barlow. Show me where, and I'll start there in the morning."

A lot of the vegetation in the small patch was still green and spreading. Maybe he'd gather it up for the goat.

Lonnie leaned on the spade and looked down at the weeds. Reached down and examined them more closely. "Mr. Barlow, you right shore you want this here spaded up? I'd give it another thought if I was you. It takes a right smart time to get plants like these here started."

"Plants…?"

"Yes, sir, Mr. Barlow. You got a good stand'a rosemary. And this here's fennel, and you got a dill comin' up everywhere. See them flower heads? Gotta have that to make pickles. And sage, here. Most women folks think they gotta have sage."

"Sage…?"

"Yeah. It could'a been picked, but it's still good when it's wilted and dry. No tellin' what else you got comin' up in the spring. I shore would hate to be puttin' a spade in this herb garden. Real good dirt, here. Been fertilized heavy."

"Lonnie, I hate to admit it, but I know nothing about farming. I can see I'm going to need more help than I thought. So, tomorrow let's talk about puttin' those lazy mules to work. Wheat, maybe."

"Could do that. Fact is, though, it's a mite late. Folks here plant wheat of a fall to let it sprout in the winter. Makes spring graze for cows, and that don't hurt it none. We can try it, though. You got the seed? I'd think Mr. Mac still got some."

So that took care of tomorrow. Go to Argyle for wheat seed, take Miz Lizzie's shoe size to Helen and pick up his packages. And what else… oh, yeah, a grinder. But now…

"Say, Miz Lizzie, I found that sneaky old herb garden. It was hiding out behind the barn right where it was put. I'll show it to you tomorrow after I get back from Argyle. Don't be goin' out by yourself to look for it. Remember, you need to stay in the house and watch over Betty Lou's little girl."

Mr. Mac had wheat. "Ain't gonna guarantee it. Should'a been put out two months ago. You're a good customer, you can have that wheat for free. I got that grinder and the old woman shoes like you need. Anything else?"

The wheat was in a large sack, just about as heavy as a man could pick up. He gathered the wrapped packages, bright in patterned paper and ribbons. He checked around for the amount of pay a man expected for general farm labor. Lonnie hadn't said a word about money. Could be, he was a real find. Stanley kept learning how much he didn't know.

At the Sweet Shop, he bought wrapped hard candy in every shape he thought could go on a tree. It was less than two weeks until Christmas. That would make Lettie about 14 months old… maybe 15. He wished he could remember what day in October she was born. Back when she was born, birthdays were considered a woman thing. But now, two women had become HIS thing! Enough to make a fellow shake his head in dismay.

He stowed the packages in the barn loft. Picked up the shoes and the rubber boots he had bought for himself along with the hand grinder and went to the house.

125

"You found the grinder!"

"Yeah, it was wore out." Surely he was not responsible for telling almost lies to comfort an old woman.

"Had to buy a new one." He was getting good at quick thought and pretending he was James. "Got somethin' else, too. You and me, we're both needin' shoes, winter comin' on. You're getting holes in the side leather. Here's new shoes for you and some for me. We gotta lot'a work to do."

"New shoes! Another present. I'll put 'em in the drawer and keep 'em nice, like Mama said."

"No, Miz Lizzie. Mama isn't here any longer, and I'm the boss now. I tell you that you have to wear the new shoes. I don't want you to have cold feet. But you can save the old ones for the garden work next summer if you want to. Right now we're going to look at the herb garden. Grab up your shawl and come with me while Lutie's asleep."

The old woman strolled lovingly among the 'weeds,' stroking them and sniffing their scent on her hands. Many of these had leaves still green this late in the year. "The garlic gonna be around here somewhere."

Stanley knew better than to argue. If she said there should be garlic, then for certain there would be garlic somewhere. He'd bet the farm on that!

Dropping to her knees, she smoothed her hand across the dirt. Reaching for a stick, she poked it in the ground and brought up a pungent bulb. "Found 'em. Right where we put them. A smidgen of garlic goes good in beans. Ain't had none for a year."

Later that day she commented on the blackberries. "Couldn't find them old blackberry vines. You know, the ones by the fence front'a the house."

"You went lookin' for berry vines?"

Nodding, she answered, "Gonna be needin' 'em for jelly next summer."

Another problem. She seemed to be improving and remembering certain things, and that could be dangerous. Who knew what she would decide to do next? She could wander off looking for something that she thought she remembered and not find her way back. Or even remember who she was… and of course she would have Lettie with her.

# CHAPTER 7

Listen, Miz Lizzie. I gotta say somethin' important. I can't have you walkin' around lookin' for things, now that you gotta take care'a Betty Lou's baby. She's too big and heavy for you to be carryin', wanderin' around lookin' for things. Now about blackberries, you think maybe they messed 'em up when the worked on the road? We got a pretty good road, and it takes work to keep it that way.

"Besides, I know where the GOOD berries were, and they are still there. Up past where I got the Christmas tree there's that really big patch, and they like to'a ripped up my overalls to shreds with their stickers. There'll be more berries than you'll ever be able to pick."

The old eyes brightened and a smile spread. "Then you'll help like you used to!"

Stanley sighed in frustration. Tiny pieces of memory were still in her mind, and the pieces didn't really fit together. It seemed that when James married Betty Lou, they took her with them, and she must have been well treated. Then the baby came, and after that memory seemed fuzzy except for the "folks" that gave her commands and didn't let her have things she wanted. Surely they were family members and heading to some destination nearby. Why were they bringing her so far from somewhere else? Of course, he'd never really know. What she actually said was disconnected and still at the twelve-year level. A very skillful and well trained twelve, but a child, nevertheless. He had a puzzle, for certain.

Another subject. "James, 'member when you found that birdnest and put it in the Christmas tree? We put jelly beans in it and told the little'ns Jack Frost turned the eggs into candy?" She giggled with pleasure at the scene in her mind. "Then you'd lift 'em up so's they could see in the nest. 'Member that?"

Stanley struggled to be truthful and yet satisfy her questions. "Those were good times, weren't they! They made good memories."

Before those words were out of his mouth, he remembered the wren's nest on the high shelf where he had put the coffee can. Tiny and well made. He smiled to himself with satisfaction. There wouldn't be little ones to lift for a peek, but she could for certain have her nest. With jelly bean eggs.

This was a friendly place. Neighbor ladies came by with baked treats to welcome their neighbor, and were quick to size up the situation. Miz Lizzie's comments about the old woman in the window were a tip off, and her friendliness to strangers, likely assuming they were old friends, made the matter clear. The kind ladies still dropped by, occasionally, but out of kindness rather than friendliness.

And small Lettie grew. Pulling herself up by the table leg, she propelled herself across the kitchen, tumbling flat before she reached her destination. Sitting back on her plump rear, she crowed with happiness and health. Oh, Rich, buddy! You should see this youngen'a yours! You'd be so proud...!

Christmas morning he made Miz Lizzie fix breakfast and eat before checking out the wrapped packages. He had been concerned that she would notice no wrapped package for himself, so he unwrapped her heavy winter coat and hung it on a hanger over the door, alongside the new sheep fur lined mackinaw for himself. That produced a sheet of paper and ribbon to wrap his rubber boots and new plaid flannel shirts. The blue paper with gold angels was never meant to wrap work clothes, but it was the only one big enough.

Miz Lizzie spooned wheat cereal into her own mouth, then into Lettie's, with her eyes on the coat. Twelve years old, for a fact! When the baby had enough, Miz Lizzie picked off a tiny striped candy cane and put it in her chubby hand. Lettie knew what to do, just not how to do it. Poking it in her eye, then in her hair, she finally got it in her mouth.

One thing about Miz Lizzie, messes made by children didn't bother her. Here she came with the wet dishcloth and swiped the sticky face clean.

The first gift he picked off the tree was the pink, fuzzy house slippers... a pure luxury and maybe a waste of money on the hardness of life in the Territory. Maybe a bad choice. She carefully removed the paper and untied the ribbon. Opening the fancy box, she looked in at their fresh pinkness and, covering her face with her hands, she cried. Sobbed.

Lettie, sitting at her feet, pulled up with the help of Miz Lizzie's skirt and patted her on her head, whimpering. Fine Christmas! Both of his ladies were weeping at the very first present.

"Miz Lizzie, try on the slippers. Maybe they won't fit, and I'll have to throw them out!" That did the trick. She lifted her tear-wet face and smiled, hugging the footwear to her bony chest. "No! No! You can't."

Stepping out of her new shoes, she poked her feet into the fluffy softness of the slippers. In her mind she danced, but her body didn't follow well as she turned circles in the room. "Just right! They fit!"

Encouraged, she opened package after package, squealing with pleasure at each item. The box of men's hankies was held against her withered cheek while she nodded her head, excitedly. She slipped on the light weight red jacket and wore it the rest of the day.

Finally she agreed to open those for Lettie. Unwrapping the baby doll, she held it in her arms like a baby and told the girl, "Lutie? See my new baby?" Lettie saw, and grabbed the doll by the leg holding it in her own arms, feet up-head down. When she noticed the tiny rubber toes, they looked so delicious they went into her mouth. Just as Helen said they would.

Pretty little black patent leather shoes were interesting, but she didn't want them on her feet. She agreed to try on the coat, but grabbed off the bonnet and tossed it into the tree. Miz Lizzie laughed until the tears flowed again. There was just too much happiness to be contained in her tiny body.

Stanley finally had to pull himself away to do the chores. The complaining cow didn't care if it was Christmas. He slipped on the new, warm jacket, and his last look saw Miz Lizzie in the big rocker with a peppermint stick in her hand. She took a lick and Lettie took a lick, rocking and licking contentedly. Oh, Richard, you'd never believe this scene!

The day after Christmas, Lonnie was there as early as usual. This time he allowed himself to be lured into the kitchen for a cup of steaming tea.

"Mr. Barlow, over yesterday with my folks and Sally's folks, some stuff was said. I'm shakey to be so bold, but I got reasons. My Sally, she just turned 16, and she's sufferin' for a house'a her own. She loves me, but fellow's are flockin' after her like possums in a 'simmon tree.

"My Pa, he had a idea. It's seemin' like you think I work good, and that'd be true. Farmin' in the Territory ain't somethin' you been doin', and there ain't hardly much that goes on, by way'a farmin', that I can't handle.

"Fact is, I got three older brothers good as me, and they just about sucked up all the duties on Pa's farm, and they shore don't need my help. Here's what they was sayin'.

"Seems you may be needin' help off and on, that I can give. If I was to live out here close, I'd be handy anytime you needed somethin' done. There's that cleared patch up past the grape garden. Good place for a helper's cabin.

"My Sally, what she wants is two things. One is a cabin. Two rooms'd be enough for a while. The other thing is a punched well like you got. If I was to have dimension lumber, I could put up a cabin. My brothers and pa, and Sally's pa, they'd help, and it'd be up in less'n a week."

Lonnie's calloused hands were shaking with... fear? He wrapped them both around the hot mug holding the tea, and took a long drink. Seeming to be partly revived, he continued.

"I'm just eighteen, but Sally's the onliest girl I ever wanted. Thing is, there's too many others as wants her, too. If I had the cabin, I could marry her right now, and I'd be close here for whatever you needed done. I wouldn't be expectin' that the cabin was mine. Just that I could live there so's I'd be close. Nuther thing, chance the old woman'd need help with your little girl, bein' sick or somethin', Sally'd be here. Anything she don't know, her ma does.

"I think I'm bein' too bold, no better'n you know me. Thing was, I don't have no time, other fellow's breathin' down my neck. Laid awake all night fetchin' up the courage to talk to ya'. I was thinkin' that times you didn't need me, I might find work close around here, but you'd always be first." Another long swig from the tea mug and he waited, obviously drained by his lengthy presentation and the seriousness of it.

The thoughtful hostess that Miz Lizzie was, she sensed the importance of the conversation and filled the cup to the brim once more. She would give the obviously distraught young man whatever comfort she could.

Stanley Barlow listened, his mind racing. He had long known that his project was not a one-man effort. It was not planned to be. It was as though he had been tossed into the raging Atlantic with swimming experience only in a quiet pond. He had pushed away the fear, afraid that thinking would make him be too discouraged to go on, and at this point stopping was not an option.

"Lonnie, what you're saying is very interesting. I may take a few days to make up my mind, and we'd need to do more talking, like how much land you'd need for a garden, and for your animals. You're right that I don't know much about the Territory.

"Today, I want you to walk with me around the whole section. I've actually not seen very much, being busy at the house. You might have suggestions here and there.

"Also, I'd like to see the place you think would be a good cabin sight. I want to make sure nothing disturbs that huge blackberry patch. Miz Lizzie sets a store by them. Let's finish this tea and get going. Your horse is still in saddle, and mine won't take long to get."

Given a partial answer had relaxed the younger man, and he lifted the mug and drained it. Walking and looking at land would be a relaxation to his pounding heart and racing nerves.

By the time he returned to the house, Stanley had made exciting plans for the future, with Lonnie's suggestions as the foundation. He was not ready, yet, to give permission, but he was sure that Lonnie knew it was just a matter of days, and he could tell his Sally with assurance that he could provide what she wanted.

He came inside the house with a project going in full swing. Miz Lizzie sat with elbows on the table and scissors in her hand. The colorfully printed paper that had wrapped the presents had been smoothed out… presumably with the flat iron. The wrinkled old hands were painstakingly cutting around the outlines of stars and angels, wrapped presents and bells… lots of bells, some tied with a fancy ribbon print. The paper, itself, had been glued to another paper with a mixture of egg white and flour. Very sticky.

Each trimmed design was placed flat on the table and a tiny pinhole punched at the top. She still had a long ways to go, but she turned and smiled happily at 'James.' She had wanted more decorations on the tree than the candy, and she knew how to get them. Next year she would be ready.

The box that had brought her slippers had been skillfully covered with paper printed with colored ribbon candy. It had obviously been prepared to store these treasures until next year.

Also there were strips of paper doubled over and glued so that both sides were colorful. While the paper was still soggy with the 'glue' she had wound them around a pencil and left to solidify. Carefully removing the spiral, she put it aside. Whirligigs for the tree! A suitable morning's work for a skillful twelve year old.

Admiring each finished ornament, she placed them carefully in the decorated box, arranging the spirals on top. Looking toward Stanley for his approval, he realized what part he played in the act. She had what she wanted and had saved him money! He had carefully examined a few and was lavish with praise.

Still smiling, she set on the bowls for lunch. White beans simmered with large chunks of ham. Thick onion slices on the side, served with steaming cornbread. Glasses were filled with whipped clabber milk, salted and peppered into a tasty, filling drink.

The twelve year old had amused herself with her project, but the hardened woman inside knew that food would be needed. 'James' could only shake his head in puzzlement. And wonder. Without her, his dreams could never have come true. Worth her weight in gold, and maybe more… considering how little she weighed.

It was early in the year of 1889 that the small, two roomed cabin was erected in plain view of the main house. Just up the hill from the vineyard. Close enough to signal and to hear a warning bell. Drillers with the equipment to make a punched well had settled three miles to the east in Carlile Corners. They had the well dug and cased in a week.

Sally had decided to be patient, but she intended on having a pump in the kitchen sometime. Having her own cabin and a fellow who loved her were enough right now.

By the end of the year, little Miss Lettie was dashing here and there. She had enough words to insist on what she wanted. "Papa, go!" was clearly intended to mean Stanley should take her wherever he went, milking, digging, repairing, or animal tending.

That was the year the first grapes appeared. Time to talk with his brother.

You oughtta see these vines, Richard. Course, they weren't cuttings so they came on quicker, but there's buds forming on the fruit spurs. I've got to set my mind to circulars, like you said we'd need, and get them posted by late March. Thinkin' a makin' a trip over to Oklahoma City. And the root cuttings I packed last fall… there are a lot of sprouts. We'll just have to see… It was a such comfort to talk with his brother… the only one who knew him inside and out, here in this land of strangers.

But there were fewer strangers, now. Men dropped by his house for this and that, and told him where the nearest blacksmith shop was. That was good news.

It was early last fall that he had taken one of the shiny, new Colt 45 revolvers over to Argyle. Laying the expensive weapon on Mac's counter, he saw the look of raw greed in the eyes of the shopkeeper. "I'm thinkin' on a trade, Mac. I got me a six shooter that ain't too new, and I lost my 3030 rifle in the tragedy. Need me somethin' to bring down a deer. Miz Lizzie's got her head set on jerky and sausage."

"I could trade…" Mac spoke slowly, thinking as he talked. "You can see what I got here. Some new, some used. I always buy firearms when I can. What're you wantin' for this thing?"

Stanley ignored the question. "Still thinkin'. What I get now's gotta be somethin' good, to last me a long time. Been thinkin' on lookin' in the Montgomery Ward Catalog, seein' what they got. Gonna have to make a trip over the City before too long. Could make a good deal there."

Mac listened. "Come look again. Could'a got somethin' in since you looked at 'em." Stanley followed him, companionably

133

silent. There were several serviceable weapons that would do him well. Stanley, however, knew the value of the Colt, both as a weapon and a possession. And this one had all the bells and whistles that were available, enough to make a man feel important. He did not let Mac know he had another Colt. He remained silent and thoughtful, as though he was parting with a favored possession.

Stanley let him talk for a while, then he pocketed the Colt. "I got a few chores to take care of. By the way, you carry raisins?"

Mac shook his head. "Not right now. They cost a mite, so I only bring 'em in when I have a customer that wants 'em. You want me to order a box for you?"

Stanley turned toward the door. "Order two boxes. Miz Lizzie thinks the girl oughtta have raisin cookies."

To the sweet shop for peppermint sticks and lemon drops. Tack shop for rivets to repair leather straps. Back to Mac's.

He wandered over to the children's things. Measuring the soles against a mark on his hand, he selected footwear for Lettie's lengthening feet. Mac called to him. "Friend, come over here a minute. Just 'membered somethin' after you left. Somethin' I got in a few months back. Sort'a slipped my mind."

Stanley smiled within. Just as he suspected. He was learning the ways of the Territory, and the first rule was 'make the best deal you can or you don't survive' and 'try not to take the first offer'."

Deal made. Tucked in its heavy canvas carrying case was the shiny new rifle, its varnished wood handle glowing softly. One thing Stanley knew about was guns. He had lifted the weapon and hefted it for balance. Perfect. Sighted through the cross hairs and approved. "Got ammo for this thing? Couple hundred rounds?"

"Well, the fact is…"

Stanley butted in. "Could make a trade. Make it one box'a ammo and it might save me a trip to the City till spring. Got fruit spurs formin' on my vines, and I could be lookin' for a market for grapes. Likely have to freight 'em on over, though." Stanley complemented himself. Good timing. Put no emphasis on the trade as though it was not important. Lowered the 'price' to one ammo box, and at the same time, put it in Mac's mind that there might be grapes on the market. French grapes, that is. If there was anything Mac liked, it was to be first in on any information.

Putting down the rifle, Stanley picked up the shoes and headed to the money register. Mac called after him. "Trade or not? So I can get the ammo for you."

"Yeah, why not? I do need me a rifle to get after that deer before he eats up my vines."

That happened the day before he brought down an eight-point buck that Miz Lizzie turned into a lot of tasty meals. Lonnie bagged two of the fat animals. One for himself and the other for his family to repay the labor on the cabin building.

It was in the year of 1890 that Lettie became a great concern. The old woman was just not reliably up to watching after her. The child was like quicksilver and gone in a minute while Miz Lizzie was busy with other duties. The little girl was not wicked, just inquisitive and restless. Consequently, she spent a lot of days, and some of most other days with 'Papa'. Trips to the Blacksmith shop and the mail hook were well known. The 'young fellow and the girl' were an interesting conversational tidbit.

Neighbor ladies in Shady Ridge were concerned, in between their own busy duties, about who was caring for the child.

Miz Lizzie welcomed the absence of the child for certain periods so she could do what she considered her duties. In between other pressing necessities, Stanley worried and tried to plan. Sally often came and begged to have the little girl 'just for company' insisting to Miz Lizzie that Lettie's Papa said she could go. Lettie adored Sally.

Stanley, between pressing activities, was the most concerned. He saw that he might be forced to look for help in neighboring farms. It was about this time that he heard of the school. Problem was, five was the minimum starting age, and that was the better part of a year away. It could be a very long year. He might actually have to enlist the fulltime help of Sally, as Lonnie had offered.

After one trying day, he confided to his brother. Richard, the only thing I was glad about, today, was that you and Louise did not have twins. Actually though, I think two little girls might even be easier! Old Joke! Smiling at the very thought, he sunk into needed sleep, the object of his concern snugged on the bed beside him, breathing softly.

He needed to make her a bed of her own, but he was honestly afraid to. He might sleep too soundly to hear if she slipped out of bed and disappeared. He had even thought of tying her to the bed or latching the door of her room, but that seemed just too degrading to actually do. Already all doors had a hook-and-eye catch at high level, but it would be only a matter of weeks, likely, that she'd see she could climb on a chair and reach it.

During a period of concern, he had installed a large 'dinner bell' on the side of the front porch. Miz Lizzie had instructions that if Lettie disappeared, or if she had trouble of any kind, she was to bang on the bell until either he or Miss Sally appeared. That gave him a minor feeling of relief, though a later thought told him she would never use it. That would be too much like admitting she was not up to taking care of 'Betty Lou's' little girl.

It was in September 1901 that the matter came to a head.

It was an incredibly hot summer, and the prairie grass browned to the color of a well-baked biscuit. Walking the distance between the house and the barn produced a bath of perspiration. Even the flies buzzed lazily and the cow didn't bother to switch them off her back.

The two milk goats flipped their tails and kept nibbling here and there, looking up to chew, then nibbling somewhere else. They were the first to smell smoke, and they began to bleat as though they were being murdered.

The soil of the Territory contained a variety of mineral stones ranging from granite to crystal quartz. The overhead brightness of the sun on the flat surface of silica, mica or reflective quartz, acted like a mirror, gathering and consolidating the brightness, turning it into heat.

The first tendrils of smoke appeared on the hillside not far from Lonnie's house, and a good couple hundred feet from the vineyard. A small huff of breeze flashed a grass stem into a flame. Fed by the sun-dried prairie grass, the flame burst into tongues of orange. Lifted by their own rising hot air, they pulled in the oxygen-filled breezes that fed them.

The goats were feeding close to the barn, but they lifted their heads and bleated in thundering unison. A wolf attack could not have produced more sound. Stanley, piddling at work in the shed, came to see what the problem was and caught the scent of a foreign smell.

PRAIRIE FIRE! He had heard talk of how disastrous they were. Dashing to the dinner bell, he clanged as loudly as he could, and Lonnie appeared on the hillside. Pointing to the advancing flame, Stanley set the young man into motion.

Poking Lettie into the house he called to Miz Lizzie. "Keep her in the house and don't let her out till I get back. Lock the doors and don't let her out of sight. I have to go put out a fire!" And he was gone.

Trembling, the old woman did as she was told. Somewhere in her dim memory she associated the current problem with great loss and locked all doors with their high hooks. She tied strings around the hooks so they could not be opened by small fingers. Shivering with fear, she walked from room to room and back, the almost five-year-old child following her, puzzled into silence.

Grabbing up the spade, Stanley dashed up the hill toward the flame. It was obvious that the fire would not be blown toward his own house, but there were flying sparks to be pounded out. Everywhere.

Lonnie had pretty well protected his own cabin but the fire had now spread rapidly toward the south. Above the roar Stanley directed, "LONNIE, YOU GO WARN THE NEIGHBORS. I CAN TAKE OVER HERE."

With a nod, the young man turned and ran with his best speed to the closest neighbor.

Stanley paused a moment to access the dangers. Sandy Creek meandered through his quarter section. Water level was very low, but the stream bed was wide. There would be a little water for those downstream to use. Beating against the flying sparks without water was possible on his own land, and he should start there. Lonnie could do much more with the neighbors than he.

He ran after sparks, beating them with the back of the shovel. The dry grass was short, so the fire burned it quickly and moved on. All around him the sound of dinner bells rang out, amassing

137

whatever forces were available. This battle was tantamount to a life or death struggle. Everyone knew it. Everything they owned was in danger. Animal lives at risk. Possibly human as well.

Lonnie was young and fast on his feet. Near neighbors were quickly alerted. When Stanley reached the next neighbor to the south, he heard the shouts, the ringing of bells and several half grown children were working with mops, brooms and wet towels. Enough help there so he moved on.

His heart pounded, and a painful muscle stitch attacked his side, but he couldn't stop. The heat produced by the burning grass rose up creating its own draft. Half burned seed heads and grass blades were swirled up, only to settle to the earth, most often on untouched grass ready to burst into flame.

Just ahead of him was the section-line road. Not wide, but it would be a help. Then, with a booming flash, a field haystack blazed into the sky. A scarlet-orange heap of tender-dry vegetation. A plume of the burning wheat straws shot up into the roiling dark smoke. Higher and higher toward the farm house roof shingles.

Stanley dragged himself onward. One half-grown girl was stationed on the house roof with a bucket of water and a towel. Good thinking. Another child was on the shed. Neighbors were working around the barn in an attempt to save it, and the hay stored in its loft. There seemed to be enough help there so, again, he moved on.

Directly across the street was what must be the schoolhouse. A bell was clanging loudly, and someone was furiously beating sparks in the yard. Fortunately, the children playing in the yard had kept the grass worn away, but the flying embers from the haystack were still a real threat. The dry shingles on the roof were totally exposed.

Isabel and her family had been in the midst of the bean harvest and were working about a quarter of a mile to the west. Miss Francine had just set her students to light work. It was much too hot for them to concentrate and the blank paper and crayons were saved for such a time as this. Fanning herself with a card from the math game, she stepped to the front door for a breath. Along with the breath of air came the smoke. Fear like an iron-fingered hand clutched her lungs and heart.

PRAIRIE FIRE! And here she had a room full of children she was responsible for! She looked around outside and saw no one. She drew in a breath and braced herself for attack.

"Students, listen. This is not a game, and I want you to stay in your seat unless I call your name. Eddie Brown, you run to your house and ring the dinner bell until someone comes. Keep yelling, 'Fire!! Fire!' until you see someone, and then start drawing water into the water trough.

"Mary Kate, run as fast as you can to your house and ring the bell. Be careful not to fall. Richie, go draw water and pour it in the stock tank until Eddie can help. Then you both carry it here in buckets.

"Emma, Darlene, Susan, go to the Browns and find buckets to bring water. Dip from the stock tank. I'll tell you where to put it. Find brooms and shovels and don't ask if you can use them. Just take them. Everyone else stay seated and continue to color if you want. Edith, you will watch that no one leaves the room."

Grabbing up her bonnet, a pillow and the bath towels that were handy she went to the yard to watch for sparks.

Seeing Troy across the road, she called and he came running. He was a last year's graduate student, so she felt qualified to give orders. Richie had arrived with the first water bucket. "Troy, come get this water and soak these towels to have them ready. Start looking for sparks and beat them out. If someone comes to help, show them the towels."

The flames were now visible across the road. The fire line had passed the farmhouse, and the noisy group was still trying to save to barn. Sparks still flew. "Troy, go into the schoolroom and get help to bring out a study table. You've got to get on the roof. I see sparks landing."

Troy always took orders well, and he had been one of her favorite students. He was also the one who cared for her pony and buggy during the week.

Moments later the boy was shouting at younger boys to turn the table sideways and work it through the door. He was behind them bringing a recitation bench that he knew would be needed for extra height.

Francine cast her eyes about trying to see all the places at once, and it was a dizzying attempt. The heat was unbearable, and sweat poured down from her hair into her eyes. Salty. Stinging! Blinding! She felt heat on her elbow and saw a tongue of flame climbing up the lace on her skirt. Another flame was on the delicate fabric of sleeve of her favorite shirtwaist. Flying sparks were everywhere! Slapping with her hand, she freed the blouse from the flame and began to beat on the skirt. More sparks. Help had to get here soon!

There were shouts from the direction of the Browns. Someone giving orders. A young man came tearing across the road toward her. "I think you got trouble, Miss. Got a blaze on the roof. I'm goin' up." Snatching the table from the small, struggling boys he put it against the house just as Troy emerged with a bench. "Bring it here, son, and get water!"

Darlene was there first with water, lifting it up to Troy on the table. Troy handed it on the man on the roof. The man scrambled to the gable and splashed a stream of water on the flame. Other burning straws were settling on the dry cedar shingles. A shout from the young lady, and a wet towel came sailing through the air toward him.

He snagged the soggy tool and began beating at the smoking spots on the shingles. Troy appeared with another bucket of water. The man told him, "Start at the gable and pour water on the peak, so it can run down over the shingles. Get more as fast as you can. We have to make the whole roof wet."

A sharp, clear, "Yes, Sir." Others came carrying buckets, pans, pitchers and anything that would hold water. Francine continuously circled the schoolhouse searching for sparks. The pasture haystack was burning down now, and there were not so many flying embers. Water was dripping off the roof.

Darlene and Susan were armed with wet towels, searching with her. The girls were black with flying soot and ashes. Hair straggled and pulling out of braids. Dorcas' hair of sunshine yellow was a heap of gray ash. Ribbon bows untied and straggling down their backs.

Marvin, a ten year old and one of her older boys, came to her. "Miss Francine, I looked way out in the yard, and there ain't no more sparks. I mean, there aren't any more. I looked good. Can

I do something else?" Francine looked around. "Marvin, go ask Mr. Brown. And thanks so much for helping."

Troy and the two men came down from the soaked roof and breathed a deep breath. The older man addressed her, "Miss Francine, I hate it I couldn't get here earlier. Things was perty rough over at my place, but we saved the barn. That ridge over to the west gonna stop the fire, up back'a the school. You doin' all right?"

"I'm just fine, Mr. MacGruder. I'm glad you saved your barn." The man took another look at her. She didn't look so fine.

Maybe it was nerves, but the younger man looked at Francine and couldn't hold back a smile. "I'm glad you're fine. It does look as though you had a bit of a battle for a while though."

He continued to look at her as though he enjoyed what he was seeing. Her bonnet was skewed sideways and a lock of raven black hair streamed down to her shoulders. Shorter tendrils framed her flushed and sweat-dripping face... face strained from exertion and swiped from several directions with ash. Flecks of something gray had rained down on her shoulders and on the puffed and lacy sleeve of her blouse. The other sleeve had a gaping hole and the scorched lace looped under her soot-smeared elbow. A searing red spot decorated the back of her hand.

A chunk of her rose colored skirt was burned, revealing a white pettislip beneath. The lacy hem of the skirt below the hole had raveled out and now stretched out behind her. It was any wonder she hadn't tripped herself. Her shoes, fastened with pearl buttons, were soggy from the water and spotted from ash and embers. They'd never look the same again.

A window behind her opened and a voice asked, "Miss Francine, can the youngens come out now? They're gettin' mighty restless."

"Yes, Edith. They can come out. Just tell them be careful." Who cared now if they got dirty, she reasoned. At least, they're not burned.

"Miss Francine? You must be the teacher. I've been wanting to stop by with a couple'a questions. I'm thinkin', though, that this may not be the time. Seems like you had enough questions for today."

The smeared and tattered lady looked at him with raised eyebrows. "Mr....?" she began with a cool voice.

"Oh, where are my manners! I'm Stanley Barlow, and I'm down by the creek on Ridge Road. I have a little girl that'll be needin' schoolin' soon. I was wonderin' your starting age."

Small hesitation. "Why don't we talk about that later, maybe tomorrow? I'm sure I know how I look right now and truthfully, you don't look much better. You look like you been at it a while."

He nodded with an amused smile. "Well said! We'll do just that." He made motions to tip his hat, the one he wasn't wearing. "Tomorrow it is."

He turned to go, and realized he was only a mile from home, but it still seemed like an endless journey. He limped on, wearily and totally footsore.

He beat on the door and waited till Miz Lizzie untied the string from the hook. The first thing he wanted was a cool drink and a wet washcloth over his steaming face.

When he returned to the parlor, he saw Miz Lizzie sitting on the floor, perched on a cushion from the sofa. Knees giving out on her? In front of her sat Lettie, squirming this way and that to examine all the dominos spread out on the floor in front of her. A favorite game. She and Mama Lizzie contested to see who could be first to sort out blocks from one to nine. One-blank was a favored first piece. This time Lettie had it.

While he watched, the child found two blanks for her row, but Miz Lizzie had to use two-five. Lettie quickly sorted out three-two and fitted it with the two beside her one. Next a three from the five-three block and a four from the four-one. Then it got harder.

She seemed stumped, and Mama Lizzie whispered, "Count one, two, three. You can do it." She did and was rewarded by a smile and a hug from her competitor.

Richard, I'd give a gold piece if you could be standing here lookin' at this instead'a me... just for a minute. I've got to get your little girl in school. I'm workin' on it.

When Lettie completed a column of all nine spots, she shouted, "I win! I got the 'fine.'"

Mama Lizzie reminded her in a soft voice, "Not fine, sweetie. It's a nine."

"But you always say 'fine' when I get the last one?"

"I know. I'll have to start saying nine. How about a story?"

Leaving the dominos on the floor, they snuggled into the rocker, side by side. "Three bears!" shouted the child, so the story started, "Once upon a time…"

Stanley turned his attention to the old woman. Her grizzled hair was now a silver white. He hadn't noticed. Also, if it was possible, there were even more wrinkles, almost hiding her eyes. She had lost a tooth… amazing that it was only one, at her age. It had begun to hurt her, so she had pulled it with the pliers. Then it didn't hurt any more.

It was hard to estimate her weight, huddled inside the voluminous dress, but she couldn't weigh more than eighty pounds. He sighed with sadness. How much longer could she go on? And she never, ever complained. Had she learned, somewhere, that no one cared about how she felt?

Her memory seemed to have dulled after James had gone. There was the huge gap until the tragedy on the road. What had happened to Betty Lou? They'd surely never know, and that was best. If she started to remember, it might be too painful. He sincerely wanted nothing to enlighten her that he was not actually her brother. Also, that she was bent and wrinkled. Precarious, the situation was. Surely, day school for Lettie would help.

Stanley left them and went to the kitchen. Sitting at the table, he dropped his face into his hands in weary discouragement. A small rock had gotten in his shoe, and he had been too distracted to take it out. Now his sock was bloody. And he had a hole. He felt like he had a ton of wheat straw inside his shirt. Itchy!

A gentle tap on the door. "Mr. Barlow? I'm back. Just wanted to say no house burned. Over back'a us they lost a shed, and a sheep got a burned place on her back. It won't kill her, though. I'm headed up the hill to get cleaned up. I'll be back in the morning."

"Thanks, Lonnie. Time to take a rest."

Miz Lizzie had come in the kitchen. He heard the sizzle of something in a skillet and caught an aroma of bacon and onions.

Baked potatoes came out of the oven. Likely could'a baked 'em on the shed roof, he told himself.

He washed again to get cooled off, and when he got back to the table there was fried cabbage and onions, baked potato with melted goat cheese, fall lettuce with bacon. Pudding she had put in a jar and lowered in a pail of water to keep cool. Sure couldn't fault Miz Lizzie on her cooking!

Something had to be done to make life easier on her… but what? Other than Lettie's acceptance in school, nothing came to mind.

He settled his eyes on the child. Whatever gave him the responsibility of the two girls, one twelve and the other under five? What mistake was he about to make? Sturdy, bright eyed, rosy cheeked little girl… Hair a shiny dark color long enough to turn up at her shoulders. Cut in the front in a ragged way possibly meant to be bangs. Dark brows and lashes. Talks all the time. What was normal for a child almost five? How could he be expected to know… he had no experience with girls of any age?

For example, the teacher. Reason should have told him she was worried, exhausted and knew that she did not look the way she would have preferred, and here he was, trying to talk business. And he, himself, looking like a tramp, and a dirty one at that. He must learn to do better. Too many things piled in on him too fast. No excuses.

He couldn't ask Sally or her mother about every little question of his life. He must stand on his own feet. A good start had been the bed for Lettie. It wasn't really a bed, just a platform with a feather pad, but she thought it was a bed and was excited to have a small bed of her own. That was one nice thing about his 'girls'. It took so little to please them, but one was growing up and the other growing… old? …senile? A long sigh.

He had stopped by the place where the Dutch family lived… Van Pelt, was it? He'd heard they made good furniture, and that would beat ordering it out from the catalog. A bed, a chest, and maybe a small rocker for Lettie's room. He could have picked up the chest and rocker now, but the only bed they had finished was a short one. It would fit her now, but not in another eight or ten years. The new one would be ready by Christmas, and it would make a very good present for her.

He had looked at other little girls, and a lot of them had something tied on their heads that was bouncy and colorful and looked like a big ribbon bow. He thought they looked really good, but how did they stay right on top of their heads while they jumped and played? Apparently Miz Lizzie didn't know, or she would have said something. Who could he ask? Maybe he'd bother Sally with it. If Lettie was going to attend school, she needed to look as good as the other little girls.

Finally, with a sigh, he decided to permit himself to quit worrying and get some sleep. Across the room, on the platform, the girl slept peacefully. Pink summer nightie, arms stretched wide, dark hair fanned out on the white pillow. Nodding to himself, he decided to leave the platform in his room until the new furniture came.

His other big problem was Miz Lizzie, and he was just too exhausted after the fire to even think about it. Maybe he'd have more time for her later.

He was hardly asleep when the other fire launched an attack his dreams. Blazes reaching into the sky and he, astride the horse, was pounding the prairie to reach them. The horse ran and ran but seemed to make no headway, and the strange part of it was that the other part of himself knew it would be hopeless when he got there, but he just couldn't keep from hurrying. Weird and frustrating, and he tried to wake himself. Couldn't.

The rooster woke him, and he was just as tired as before he went to sleep. Fire fighting day and night was exhausting. Field work. Lonnie was pulling a thing called a harrow over the planted wheat to keep the crows from getting the seeds. It seemed that the forked contraption buried the seed just the right depth.

Stanley remembered he needed to separate the sow into the small pen before she farrowed. Easier to move her without being concerned with the piglets, and mama sows were so touchy. They grunted with such anger, they might just take off a hand. He'd do that today.

Also, he had to compose a letter to some place in Oklahoma City called 'Jackrabbit Canning Company.' Mac had told him they might be a market for his grapes, as there was talk they were thinking of a brewery, or a wine making place… or something. Stanley had been putting it off. That was supposed to be Louise's job. She'd know exactly what to say. No Louise. No help. He could only do his best. The few grapes last year went well in the local towns, but next year's crop looked big. Really big!

How would he ever be able to transport a crop of ripe grapes twenty miles in a juggling wagon? Whatever had he been thinking of? If he and Richard had ever considered marketing, he couldn't remember it. They couldn't get past the growing. Well, a letter was a start.

He needed to decide where he wanted the persimmon fence. Lonnie said another month would be the time to transplant the saplings.

Did he have enough hay for all his animals? And fuel for the winter? And where was a bull? Oh, yes… the fellows that made furniture had a good-looking animal. He'd have to make an arrangement for when the time came.

With a groan he swung his feet over the edge of the bed. He was getting nowhere lying there worrying. Besides, he smelled bacon and coffee.

And he needed to be at the school, fairly clean and decent looking, at the time school let out. About four, he thought. He hoped he could make a better impression than he had yesterday.

Lonnie rapped on the door and pushed it open. "Mr. Barlow? That there sow, she's done farrowed. Got herself 13 squealers, and she's got 12 faucets. Put the runt in a box, I did, and moved the rest into the small pen. Figurin' to take the little feller on up to Sally. She likes jobs like this and could be she'll keep 'im alive. I'm headin' on out with the mules, now."

Stanley had the presence of mind to respond, "Thanks, Lonnie." That took care of one of his jobs. Nothing seemed to get ahead of Lonnie.

The letter. When it was put together the best he could, he could take it either three miles to the Corners, or five miles to Argyle. Argyle won. He'd ask Sally's ma about the thing little girls wore on their heads. His little girl was going to have whatever other little girls had.

# CHAPTER 8

Francine heated water to bathe and wash her hair. Again. Still had ashes in it. So embarrassing to be looking the way she did yesterday, but she had to save the school. Didn't she?

And that four year old from down Ridge Road. Did she have room for her? Ticking off the beginners, she came up with five, plus the little Kiowa girl brought in by her grandmother.

Poor old woman, such a struggle with the 'newcomer' words. "Little girl, Nellie," she had said. "Wants school." She pointed to herself. Obviously it was she that wanted school for the girl. How was it that it was the grandparents who were most concerned that their child get 'newcomer' words? Like Old Gray Owl's granddaughter, Lily, and her brother's grandsons.

The woman had pointed to her mouth and nodded deeply. "Say words and know books. She come?"

Francine had asked, "How old is the girl?"

The woman lifted a spread hand. Five fingers. Then another one. Maybe almost six.

Francine had considered. "We can try for five days." Lifting her one spread fingered hand. "See how it goes and if she wants to stay."

"She stay," the grandmother had nodded, emphatically. "Now I pay." She produced a handful of coins. "You take..."

"We can wait for five days and see. Then you would pay Mrs. Brown next door." Francine indicated the house just west of the school.

"I pay now. Nellie Spotted Pony come next day." Smiling a toothless grin and ducking her head out of respect, she said "I go now."

Francine had watched her leave. What courage! It seemed clear that her family was not particularly in favor of what she did or they would have come with her. At her age, trying to communicate with a language as confusing as English must take a real conviction. It could be hoped that Nellie was as determined.

The next day the little girl came and waved her grandmother goodbye. Combed hair in braids tied with pink string. Faded pink dress and sandals made from kind of animal skin. Eyes black as cinders and shiny as new grapes. Mouth soberly held in a firm line but a face that moved from side to side, missing nothing. She did not join in the play, but watched with interest. Looked hopeful.

She fingered the slate on the table before her, and even picked up the chalk, watching the others. No marks, but she seemed to be thinking it over. Francine had told Isabel to let her take her time. And this was another day.

Too tired to think. Lifting her window high, the teacher let in a fresh draft of air with the heavy smell of burned… world…? Black and powdery. But it didn't burn the play equipment, and no sparks burned through the roof shingles. She tipped her face upward. A 'Thank You' because the school was spared! There must certainly have been a lot of help from above as nothing but a haystack and a shed was lost.

Too bad about the shirtwaist, it had been one of her favorites. The material was light and cool and perfect for summer. Ruined. All her careful stitches… gone. Well, maybe not. If she'd take it over to the Corners to Pat and Bridie, maybe they had some of the same fabric and could replace the sleeve. Or make her another one. They were very skillful and becoming known all over. Even making hats now, and she had bought two for herself. Maybe she'd see if they had thin fabric in another color and would make two shirtwaists. She could use one in light green.

Hair dried and braided for the night, she realized how tired she was. Totally gone was all her energy. Couldn't even think anymore.

Too tired even to thumb through her favorite poem book. Blowing out the flame in her cut glass lamp she stretched out on the cool sheets. Crickets in the remaining trees screeched their song, and she went to sleep.

Young bodies revive fast. Francine was out of bed before the roosters, and leaned out her window. Still a scorched smell, but the air was a lot fresher. Nature was very efficient in cleaning up messes.

Green skirt with white dots. White shirtwaist with a cool wide neck line. Inset strip of lace in the sleeve added to its cool comfort. Shoes were a wreck, but she had a spare pair. It wouldn't do to be without a spare for who knew when they would break a heel? Decorative combs with small green sets held hair into the large roll she had pinned to the top of her head.

Put on hot water for her boiled eggs and she now smelled ham. Time to go for her breakfast. Coffee with jelly biscuit would be for later. Another day. It was going on the third week of the school year, and the beginners were still confused but were eager to try. This would be the time to watch little Nellie....

At the perfect time, Old Grandmother Spotted Pony poked her charge through the door, smiled and waved, and was gone. Nellie took the seat assigned to her yesterday. Isabel smiled and greeted her, and busied herself with the flash cards she would start with.

One thing fed into the next, and the day was over. Little Nellie had made an "A" out of chalk on the slate, and had looked up for approval. Isabel was quick to give it. She loved being called Miss Isabel. The fourteen year old loved for Margie to be occupied, so she would get to teach. Margie, a married lady now, was not as regular as before, but still as enthusiastic.

At four o'clock, the students filtered out, and Francine settled down at her desk, resting a chin in her hands and elbows on the desk. A favored thinking position. Nellie was going to make it... she was sure of that now.

Someone appeared in the open door. Oh, the pa about his little girl, the four year old. It must be him, though it didn't look like it. Clean straw hat and boots. Waist pants with belt and shiny buckle. Plaid shirt with sleeves rolled up. No soot streaks on his face. No burn marks on his hands, at least that she could see.

He walked confidently toward her. "Miss Francine, you got an apology comin'. No way I should'a tried to talk business, the shape we were both in. I hope you won't hold it against me. I've no excuse for it."

Francine smiled her acceptance and indicated the recitation bench as a seat. He took it.

"My little girl, she's to be five in October, and I'm not sure just which day. When she was born, I wasn't thinkin' of it being my job to remember, but I found out I was mistaken. Her pa was my brother, and he died in a robbery on the way out here, along with her mother. She was a baby at the time, and I've had her every day since." He paused and glanced around the room. Then continued.

"There was another wagon taken at the same time, and an old woman was missed by the flame. We come on together, best we could do. I don't know who she is, and she's been confused for the last four years. Thing is, though, don't know what I'd'a done without her. Seemed certain she was used to babies, and she's been the nearest to a ma that my little girl ever had.

"Her name's Violette, French pronunciation, but we call her Lettie. The old woman calls her "Lutie" and thinks her mother was named Betty Lou. She thinks I'm her older brother named James. Seemed best not to try to straighten her out. Even if I knew what the straight of it was.

"Fact is, though, she's gettin' to where Lettie is too quick for her, and I can't be with them all the time and still make a living. Don't mean to be tellin' you my troubles, but thought it might be a help, in case you could see your way clear...."

Francine nodded and cut in, "Outgoing, is she? Not afraid of strangers? Plays well?"

"I think she'd like to play, but all she'd got is the old woman. They do the best they can, the two of 'em. Outgoing, I'd have to say yes."

"I'd like to see her first, before I agree. Would that be all right?"

At his nod, she went to the door and called out. "Troy? Could you hitch me up? I have to make a little trip." To Stanley she said, "He won't be very long."

Ten minutes later the chocolate pony was in front of the school, juggling his harness and switching the ever present flies. They set out, Stanley Barlow on his horse and the small buggy following. He was wishing he had said something to warn Miz Lizzie, but what would he have said? Best that he just spring it on her, chips would fall wherever.

150

The pony pulled the buggy into the drive beside the house. Stanley remembered to offer his arm to her as a gesture, though it was obvious she didn't need it. Together they walked into the house.

His 'girls' were in the parlor playing their "guess where I am" game, but it stopped as he stepped through the parlor door instead of the kitchen as usual. The little girl stared with great interest at the lady beside her 'father,' but Miz Lizzie's eyes flew open in an instant of unbelievability. Hurrying toward Francine, she threw her bony arms around her in a welcoming hug.

"Come, Lutie." She called to the child. "It's your mama that's come home. It's our own Betty Lou! Come see your mama!"

The willing child came running with a joyful squeal. A mama seemed to be a good thing, and if this one was to be hers, she'd gladly take it.

Turned into a horrified statue was Stanley. Of all the things that he could have imagined, this was the least likely. Speechless. He might never think of another word to say. This unfortunate young lady would for certain think he had lost his mind or had drawn him into a trap. He just stood and stared.

The little girl hugged Francine just above her knees because Mama Lizzie's hug was around her waist. The green polka-dotted skirt was gathered and bunched into loving arms and adoring eyes looked up into her face.

Francine, the composed, put one arm around the old woman and patted the child with the other hand. Smiling, she told them, "I'm so glad to be here. I've been missing you a lot. And such a sweet little girl! Lettie, sweetie, have you been a good girl for your papa?"

"Yes, yes, yes!" screamed the child. "I'm a good girl. I love you Mama Betty Lou. I can show you my new doll! Come with me."

Miz Lizzie took the girl's arm. "Wait, Lutie. Your mama, she'll be hungry, and I got food ready. Show your toys after she eats. Folks comin' in, they're always hungry so we'll eat."

Stanley, still wordless, stood aside and watched, for surely this was a dream (nightmare?) or maybe a playact he had gotten into, accidentally. Miz Lizzie scurried into the kitchen, guiding the child by the arm.

"Lutie, you set on another plate. I didn't know this was the day you would come or I would have had your place set. I'll know next time. I hope you still like my dumplings. We got a good garden. Tomatoes purty as a picture…" It was evident that it was Miz Lizzie's nerves that made her chatter, but it was plain that she intended for Francine (Betty Lou) to eat with them. There seemed no way to stop her, at least that Stanley saw.

Finally seated, Miz Lizzie bowed her head and the others followed. "I'm glad You finally answered, God. I was gettin' purely tired'a waitin'. I thank You anyway, and I'm glad she's still purty as she always was. Amen, till next time." Lifting her chin and smiling all around, she handed the bowl of light, steamy chicken dumplings to Betty Lou (Francine.)

Unable to wait any longer, she demanded, softly, "Why was you gone so long and us waitin' every day?"

Startled, Stanley found a few words. "I told you, Miz Lizzie. She had things she had to do. She may have to go and work some more before she finishes them."

Francine came to the rescue. "Sometimes folks do a lot of work they don't like, and it takes a long time." What was the name he said she called him? James? "You see, James was right. I will have to go back after supper. The dumplings are delicious, I believe I'll have some more. Miz Lizzie, you've been so good to take care of Lutie. She's grown up into a very pretty girl."

The old woman smiled her wrinkles into a different pattern. It was so good to be appreciated. If Betty Lou had to go away again, at least she got to see her for a minute. She'd try to be patient.

The used plates were removed, and a platter with half a chocolate cake appeared. The old woman lifted Lettie's cake onto the saucer and spread it generously with butter. Looking at Francine, she apologized, "I'd let you do that, but I didn't know if you knew she liked butter on her cake. Did I do all right?"

Francine smiled broadly. "You did exactly right. If I knew about the butter, I've forgotten. You remember I've been away for a long time."

Relieved, the woman instructed, "Now, Betty Lou, you and James go to the parlor while I wash up. If you got'a go back, I know you got things to say." Her bony-fingered hand shooed them from the room.

Lettie grabbed her hand. "You come see my toys first, Mama Betty Lou." It seemed the toy box was in the parlor, and she set all her toys in a row as her 'parents' watched.

Francine stole a look at Stanley. He was as white as a ghost. She could not hold back a grin. "It's all right," she whispered. "But one thing for sure, that little girl is ready for school, and she can start tomorrow if you want. We need to have a story for her as to who I am and why I can't stay. You'll be able to handle Miz Lizzie. You've obviously been doing it for years."

With that, she knelt down and examined the doll, stuffed bear, four books, and the box with the toy dishes. When they were all examined, the child looked at Francine. "You're so beautiful! Mama Lizzie told me you were, but I couldn't think about it."

Francine eased down to the floor, and the little girl climbed into her lap and wrapped her arms around her neck. Leaning her head over to Francine's shoulder, she sighed a long breath of contentment. Francine glanced at Stanley. Her look said this might be harder than they imagined. Her sympathy went out to the man who was going to have to pick up the pieces, and he seemed to have a lot of trouble with words.

"You know, James, I'm thinking this little girl might like a ride in my toy buggy, so she can see where I have to stay. And we need to tell her how my name had to change to Miss Francine. Unless you have a better idea."

He had no ideas at all. If he had no words, certainly had no ideas. He did find the strength to nod.

In the buggy, Lettie leaned back against the leather cushion and smiled a wide smile while staring at her 'mama.' Not a word. Just that look of quiet contentment.

Wide eyed, she was led into the school room and allowed to examine the small benches, the many books, and the slates. She looked at the bed, opened the closet to examine Francine's clothes, smiled and pointed at the cut glass lamp on its shelf. While Stanley looked on, Francine lifted the girl to her bed and put her arm around her. "Lutie, honey, there's things your papa and I have to tell you, and you might not like some of them, but sometimes we don't get what we like.

"I have to stay here and live in this little room because I'm a teacher, and a lot of boys and girls come here to learn a lot of things. Your papa says you can come and learn with them if you want to, and you and I can see each other every school day. I have to tell you something, else, though. I know Mama Lizzie told you that my name is Betty Lou, but now it's Francine. The boys and girls call me Miss Francine, and if you come to school, you'll have to do it, too."

The bright intelligent eyes followed her expression. "Miss... Francine?"

"That's right," she encouraged.

"I can come see you every day? And look at the books?"

"Yes, and you can see some of the books. I'll show you which ones, and you'll meet a nice lady named Miss Margie, or another one called Miss Isabel. But there's a secret we have to remember. Do you know what a secret is? It's when you know something that you can't say to anyone, even if you want to. Our secret will be that you can't call me mama while you're at school. Can you remember that?"

A reluctant nod by Lettie. Strange... she had a mama she couldn't tell anyone about. "But I can see the books?"

"Yes, and you can play domino games with the teacher."

"DOMINOS!" she screamed. "One, two, three, four, five, six, seven, eight, and fine. I mean, nine! Mama Lizzie says it's nine and not fine, but she says fine, and we laugh."

Eyes wide with interest, Francine told her, "Such a smart little girl. You can count to nine, and I didn't know that. You're going to have such a lot of fun when you come to school. Now, there's one more thing. You can't come into this little room when other children are here because they can't. It's all right when it's just you and me but not when there are other children. Do you understand?"

A quick nod. "When can I come? Tomorrow, the next day?"

"When your papa says so. He'll talk with you about that." As least she hoped he would, anyway. He seemed to still be short of words.

At the door, Lettie hugged her again, and Stanley picked her up and sat her on the horse. She held to his belt with one hand and waved with the other, as long as she could see her new mama.

Francine went to her desk, her favorite thinking place. Elbows on desk, chin in hands she mulled over the evening. She had the sensation of having swam into water so deep she couldn't touch the bottom, and though she was still staying above the water, she was apprehensive. She hoped she had said enough in Stanley's hearing that he could build a story that worked.

It was not a half an hour later that he was back. Alone. Dejected, and with no spring in his step, he came through the open door. Big sigh.

"I can't tell you how sorry I am about this evening, and I wouldn't have had this happen for anything. I appreciate your words to Lettie, and how you went along with Miz Lizzie. I'm so sorry."

Francine indicated the recitation bench and he sat down. "You didn't do anything wrong. How could you have known, and you certainly didn't expect to have a child, actually a baby, and a woman who couldn't grow up. I think you did a marvelously fantastic thing for the both of them, and what would either of them have done without you? Incidentally, do I really look like Lettie's mother?"

Stanley nodded. "Actually, you do, but it's not the 'Betty Lou' that Miz Lizzie knows. I don't know what Betty Lou looked like, but you surely fooled the old woman."

Finally assured, he brought up the subject of the tuition. She assured him, "Just two dollars a month, and you pay Mrs. Brown, next door. It seemed best she handle it, at least at first and the fact that the school is on her land."

Then he was gone, and she resumed her thinking. Whatever happens, it is going to be an interesting year. Bright little girl. Isabel is going to have such fun with her, times she gets to be the helper and gets to be here. With canning season over, her mother would be trying to let her be here as much as she could.

Such a lovely name. Violette Barlow. Seems a waste to call her Lettie. She has a face perfect for a top curl or braid with a big red ribbon… or even white. She could use a bigger girl's dress style, too.

Then she caught herself. Shut up, Francine. She is not actually your little girl! What a thought!

With a smile at herself, Francine heated water for her evening bath and went to bed early. Exhausted. It had been a really big week. The bed seemed so inviting, and the birds were back in the trees, whistling and chirping. It was so nice to go to sleep with a concert in the trees outside her window.

Stanley brought Lettie early. Enough time for Francine to reinforce the rules and show her where she would sit. Moments later the door opened, and Nellie Spotted Pony was pushed through by the firm and loving hand of her grandmother. With a smile and a wave, grandma was gone.

The two girls took a look at each other and smiled. Coming toward each other, they hugged like old friends and crawled over the attached bench to sit at the table, side by side.

Francine was too far away to actually hear what was said, but it was clear that Nellie now felt free to say her first words spoken to another person at the school, and Lettie must have understood them, because she chattered back, and was seemingly understood. Well, one hurdle passed. Francine had never ceased to be fascinated at the interaction of children.

One thing for sure, Isabel would have a fun day today as Margie was still needed elsewhere. She was certainly excited to have two new students to add to her five. Seven! The perfect number!

This happened to be the day to introduce dominos. Isabel was to spread them on the table and see what the children did with them. Then she would point out that the white ones had one dot (one finger) and the yellow ones had two dots (one, two fingers). Then she would wait to see if anyone wanted to know about the red, green, purple, pink, orange, lavender, and blue ones.

She emptied them on the table and began to turn them so that all pieces had their colored number sides up. Instantly, Lettie drew in a joyous breath and squealed, "DOMINOS!"

Miss Francine moved closer to the table to be handy if Isabel had any difficulty, and she saw the small hands hurriedly helping Isabel with the turnings. "I love domino game," she explained to the class in general.

When they were all righted, she sorted through with her fingers and found the one-blank. From there she went to the two, three and on to nine, then leaning back with a wide smile she looked around at her seatmates. Nellie, eyes dancing with excitement stared at her new friend, and then down at the line of the tiny blocks. Such fun. Her nimble fingers found the one-one and put it before her. Then a glance at Lettie's creation, and she found the two-four, and as the class, including Isabel, stared in fascination, she finished the row, ignoring the various colors but concentrating on the number of dots.

Isabel, realizing something exciting had happened, called, "Miss Francine? Would you like to come and see what we've made?"

Francine stepped over to the table, attempting to be nonchalant. "Look class. There are a lot of games to play with dominoes, and this is one of them. In fact, this is one of the first ones. Now is the time for all of you to make the number row like Lettie and Nellie, and Miss Isabel will help you with their names." Quietly, she stepped away, back to where level two was practice reading.

She had worked out a way to practice read that seemed to work well for her. All children watched as one after the other read the next word of the printed story. This way there were no wandering eyes, as everyone had to watch the print to be ready and know when they were next up.

Also, if someone was not sure of a particular word, it was most often that the person who was to read that word knew it, pronounced it, and then it was known by all. Later, she would graduate them to taking turn-about on a whole sentence. First of all, she didn't want to embarrass anyone if she could help it, and this had worked well for her. First, create in the student a 'history of success.' That was what Miss Josie had said was important.

Behind her, she could hear young voices repeating numbers. Mostly, they waited for Lettie to say the word, and then they repeated it together. A small smile crept across Francine's face. Someone had been working with small Lettie, and if she were to guess, she would have said it was Miz Lizzie.

At recess, both Lettie and Nellie remained seated, at first, not being sure what to do. Then they crawled back over their benches, clasp hands, and left, skipping down the front steps together. At noon, they took their lunches outside, sat on the grass under a tree, carefully selecting one that had not experienced the fire, and ate, trading this and that and chattering quietly.

The first activity after lunch was chalk drawing. Isabel took a slate and gave them ideas. Stick figures, ruffled flowers, simple butterflies, houses with chimneys. They were busily at work with their choice of example. All but Nellie. She took the chalk, made a few experimental marks, wiped them clean with her eraser cloth, then set to work.

An oval shape, like a large "U." Small ovals for eyes... well placed, and a nose. She stared carefully at Isabel, tipping her head for better perspective, then creating a mouth. All around the head she drew spiraling ringlets. A critical examination showed her that she needed to make arching eyebrows, which she did. After adding a few more well-placed ringlets, she worked her way back over the bench, walked to her teacher, and handed it to her. Picking up Isabel's hand, she placed it against her cheek, turned and took her seat, folding her hands before her.

By now she had the attention of the whole class. Their teacher smiled and told them, "Everyone is doing a good job. Keep working and finish your drawing." Leaving her seat, she went to the slates and produced a new one for Nellie. Pointing to the 'tree' on the slate to her right, she said, "I believe you have time to make a tree. This is a very good one."

Nellie looked at the 'tree,' than at Isabel, then back at the 'tree.' If that was what teacher wanted, she could certainly do that. Glancing toward her right side, then back, she copied the tree, leaning and lopsided exactly the same way the small boy had drawn it.

Isabel watched with interest. Taking up the finished drawings in the order the children sat, she put them together in the same order, and returned. Holding up her hand with outstretched fingers, she told them, "First we'll count numbers, and then letters. Remember, we start with one for the little finger on the end."

Most of the class did well, with Lettie leading them. "Now the letters." Lettie's face fell, and she bit her lower lip in confusion. The teacher rescued her. "I'll say them with you and you help me on the ones you know. Remember, the thumb is "A."

Isabel went over the five letters several times, then asked, "Who would like to try them by themselves?" Lettie's hand shot up. Of course. Nellie watched, then raised her hand.

"All right. Two girls will start together. Lettie and Nellie, you may begin." Together they named their thumb and fingers with the appropriate letters, and smiled at each other with comradely satisfaction. The others followed.

Then Isabel passed out new slates and made a row of the first five letters of the alphabet. "I'm going to let each of you try to make the row of letters, and then we'll say their names again." Small fingers struggled with the chalk, but made a recognizable copy. Almost.

At the correct time, Grandma Spotted Pony arrived for her charge. She sought out Francine and nodded, smiling. "For Nellie. She laughs happy," and she pointed toward the two giggling girls. Then lifting Francine's hand, she placed it against her face, briefly, then turned, took Nellie's hand and left. Later Francine had considered, once more, the courage and difficulty of trying to communicate such a complicated language at her advanced age.

Francine and Isabel studied the chalk drawings, especially the one of "Isabel." For such an unwieldy medium as a piece of chalk, she had done amazingly well. Also, she had copied the tree carefully, putting in every "mistake." Skill and obedience. Whereas, Lettie had played the domino game with skill and exuberance.

At length, Francine decided the grandmothers had a lot to do with both skills. Miz Lizzie would, of course, know counting, and a fair amount of reading, but have little artistic talent. She was undoubtedly attempting to amuse rather than teach, so it was a noisy game. Grandma Spotted Pony, however, was undoubtedly an artist of sorts, and designs being valued by her people, she would try to pass them on. Apparently she had succeeded.

It was about two weeks later that she again approached Francine. "More," she said, holding a hand above Nellie's head, then lowering it about a foot. Nodding, she explained. "Boy... for... next days?" So Nellie had a little brother, and they would get him next year, or maybe later. Good news for the children and thanks for the old woman.

159

Francine nodded and smiled. "We'll look for him next year. We will be happy to see the boy." With a nod of understanding, the woman was gone. As always, as soon as she delivered her message, she was gone. Apparently she hadn't yet learned about 'goodbye,' but Nellie would teach her. Of that, Francine had no doubt!

It was a month or so later that Miz Lizzie demanded to know where Lutie was being taken each day and coming home with all kinds of new ideas. It became necessary, for her peace of mind, that Stanley take her to the schoolhouse one day when he went to pick her up.

In a tour of the schoolhouse, the old eyes critically examined every foot of the classroom, the softness of her bed, the apparent efficiency of the tiny kerosene stove, and the darling cut glass lamp on her shelf. She opened the closet doors and glanced over the quantity of her clothes… finally pronouncing everything satisfactory.

Then, eyes boring into Stanley's face, she pointed out, "Iffen she was always this close, it'd seem like she could be brought home for a good supper. Look at 'er, she's skinny." Then turning to Francine, she wondered, "You 'member how you liked the way I cooked meatloaf with sausage and sun dried tomatoes? I'll make that for you tomorrow and James'll bring you home. I know you gotta stay here, and they gotta call you a different name, but that don't mean you can't come and eat somethin' you always liked. You comin' tomorrow, sure."

With that, she headed back to the buggy that had brought her, and Stanley and Lettie obediently followed. With a tolerant smile, Francine closed the schoolroom door. Actually, sausage meatloaf with sun dried tomatoes sounded very good. Mrs. Brown made it quite often.

Then a few days later Patricia O'Day and Bridgit O'Grady came to Shady Ridge on 'business.' Having a supply of hats and fancy hankies, it seemed time to go on the road. In addition, they had a lot of skirts and a few shirtwaists, as well as camisoles with lace straps.

They had posted a notice above the mail hooks and had sent some of their hand-printed flyers for her to send home with each family. Giving them a week's notice, it might be possible for a number of ladies from Shady Ridge to find time to see something they could like.

Mr. O'Day hitched his team and pulled the wagon they were using as a stock room over to the brush-shaded arbor and parked it. The girls would be staying with Francine for the night, and he would come the next day to fetch them home.

It was to be a much thought-about experiment. Skirts with adjustable waists and shirtwaists of two sizes would fit so many of the women, and the loose-fitting camisoles were even more interchangeable in size. Hats and hankies would fit anyone.

The girls arrived early, and the number of grown up ladies close to the school playground came to examine the merchandise. This activity interested the students, but they were WARNED that they MUST NOT go there, but stay in the yard.

Francine had begged supper and breakfast for the girls, insisting she wanted to pay extra but Mrs. Brown wouldn't hear of it. "Food don't cost nothin', youngen! You know that. I'm just bein' that glad you got your friends over. Now that you done it, you'll have to do it more often. We don't want you gettin' lonely for your Corners friends."

Happy as Francine was to have her friends, getting lonely was an absurd suggestion. How could one get lonely with a job they loved, children every day, hundreds of books, Margie Farmer as a friend, and Isabel Brown as a worshiping follower? How, indeed! In addition to that, she had a copy book with blank pages just waiting for the next rhyme. Food was prepared and served to her, and her washing would be done if Francine would just let her. What was there to be lonely about, but it was fun to have her schoolmates for a day.

Pat and Bridie were in the class behind her at Prairie Academy, and less than a year younger. Why, Bridie's mother had had been the one who had taught Francine to sew. Now, though, it was more fun to buy something that Bridie or Pat had made. They were both skilled in making patterns fit different shaped people. A wonderful skill that Francine had not acquired.

When school closed for the day, the girls came to the schoolhouse. Together they spread quilts on a bare place on the classroom floor and dragged the feather ticking from her narrow bed to use as a pillow. They hardly needed a bed, though, as they turned the night into a slumber party.

After the supper of fried chicken and apple cake, they sat at the little schoolhouse tables that gave them such memories, and chattered, usually all at the same time. Later, they popped tubs of popcorn and sat cross-legged on the quilt giggling over things they both remembered and catching up on gossip.

It was Pat who brought up the subject. "I'm hearin' you got yourself a boyfriend and he's got a little girl that calls you 'mama.'"

"Boyfriend? What'd'ya mean! He's a full grown man over twenty years old and got more to do than a puppy followin' four youngens! Why, he hasn't even time to sneeze if he caught a cold. Likely too busy to even catch a cold in the first place."

Bridie looked at Pat with a smirk. "And you noticed she didn't say she didn't even like him... or that he didn't act like he likes her."

Pat responded, "That's right. And I think he takes her home to have supper at his house sometimes."

With exaggerated crossness, Francine told them, "I see you've been talkin' to my sister. Ever since Rosie started seein' that soldier, she thinks the whole world should fall in love. What's funny though, well, I don't mean 'funny' funny, but when the robbers burned his wagon on the way out here, only he and the baby, and an old woman that can't remember anything weren't killed. Poor old woman, she thinks Stanley is her big brother from when they were kids, and that I am the little girl's mother. She's nice, though, and she's taken good care of little Violette for almost five years. You'd have to admit that's a strange set of events."

"Yeah, but he'd like to be your boyfriend, wouldn't he?"

"Now, how would I know that?"

"FRANCINE! You don't expect us to believe that do you? A girl ALWAYS knows things like that!"

Francine lifted her chin in mock irritation. "Then I must not be a girl. I don't know any such thing! But I do know one thing, though. I know that the two of you have your eyes set on two of the best lookin' Kiowa boys in the territory."

With a toss of the head, Bridie retorted. "I don't see a way we could keep from havin' our eyes on 'em. They're always underfoot any time Raymond doesn't have 'em on the road pullin' this or diggin' with that."

Pat added, "And there they are, right across the road. We do get our mail better, now. Ray sends one of the boys to Argyle just about every day over somethin' they need to buy, or somethin' he thinks might be comin' in on the mail."

Then Francine. "What do you think of those mammoth horses Raymond likes so much? They must eat as much as an elephant."

"Oh, that's the good part! Eatin' makes big pats. Horse pats burn as good as cowpats, and the fellows are always bringing some over for the Cookie Jar and the McLaughlin girls. Our little shop is so tiny, it doesn't take much to heat it, but we never have to look for cowpats."

Francine reminded them, "I don't either. I get a bushel every month from every student... and more if I need it. I don't even have to poke the things in the stove. One of the boy's mother told him not to let the teacher mess up her pretty clothes with stoking the stove. How lucky is that, I ask you?"

It was amazing that there were enough words to last the night, but there almost were. It was well past midnight when they finally went to sleep. After all, they all three had work to do the next day.

And the next day for the seamstresses was a busy one. Their success put a whole new look on their efforts... there must be more of these trips, and they must, somehow, figure out how to do it. No problem, though for a couple of Irish girls. A problem known was a problem solved.

Francine had looked over their stock of fabric and settled on a print of very fine, delicate weave, just perfect for work in an Oklahoma summer. Or even late fall. It had softly shaped leaf prints in shades of light green. Tucked among the leaves were clusters of flowers, tangerine to pink, shaped much like lilac clusters.

"Here's what I need," she told them. "Make a skirt with a lot of gathers and a ruffle of the same material and lace above the hem. Then I want a shirtwaist made like the one that got burned. All right? And there's no really big hurry, only I'm eager to get it."

Pat looked at Bridie, nodding, knowingly.

Bridie looked at Pat, "She really means 'get with it' because she's got an important date coming up."

A deep sigh from Francine. "Will you be so kind as to tell me who the date is with?" She was getting tired of this subject, but the two girls still giggled, annoyingly.

Back to work with a classroom full of students. Something she knew more about than boyfriends. It seemed as though the eligible fellows in Shady Ridge considered her unapproachable. Oh, well, what did she care?

There was Nellie. She wished sincerely that she could let her take a book home, especially on a weekend. She couldn't, because she had made a rule that first level students were not old enough to take care of the valuable, expensive books. Mentioning this at home, she picked up on her mother's beginning sentence.

"Fancy, don't you have some…?"

Butting in excitedly as she finished her mother's thought, "I have books! There's all those we had when we were little. I'll get one."

Back at school, she wrapped the somewhat shopworn book to hide the cover, and when Grandma Spotted Pony pushed Nellie through the door, Francine slipped out on the steps. "Wait, please. I have something for Nellie, but I want you to take it home for her. This is a gift. She must say nothing about it to the other children. Do you understand?"

Firm lips and quick nod. Grandma reached with both hands as though the gift was a valuable gem, though she had no idea what was in the package. Turning quickly, she hurried away.

Francine watched the departing back, and wished she could get drawing paper and pencils to the girl as easily. She'd just have to give that some thought.

Things were easier with Lettie. After learning that Francine (Betty Lou) was so close, Miz Lizzie insisted on regular visits. On one trip Francine handed Stanley a tablet and two pencils, explaining that she wanted Lettie to develop the habit of homework.

"I need you to give her one sheet every day that it's possible, and let her write or draw on it. She can practice what we did at school, copy letters from one of her story books or even draw pictures. But she only gets one sheet, and she must bring it to me. That will make her think about what she wants on it. If she happens to skip a day, she can't have two sheets to make up for it.

"In class, I issue the paper only for special things because I want them to realize it's special. Now, I'm not meaning to put more work on you, but if I gave it to Miz Lizzie, if Lettie wanted a dozen sheets, she'd give it to her, I'm afraid. Am I being a problem?"

How did he tell Francine that she was, indeed, a problem to him, but not about the paper. He'd like very much to see her alone sometime and maybe decide whether he had a chance. She was bound to know how scarce and valuable girls were, and by sixteen they could easily be married. He'd learned that she came to Shady Ridge at hardly fourteen, and that was three years ago. That made her about seventeen, if his math was still good.

That meant one thing. Time was short and rapidly getting shorter, and if he meant to say something, he'd better figure a way to do it. He remembered Lonnie's fever to acquire the 'cabin of her own' that his Sally wanted, or she would throw him over for someone who would get it for her. At least, that was what the boy had thought, and he was certainly not dumb.

Stanley was still considering that when an answer came from the Jackrabbit Canning Company. "AM INTEREST IN GRAPES. LETTER FOLLOWS."

Hmmm… well, that was encouraging. The letter was even more encouraging.

"…Yes, we would be interested in buying the grapes. You said French grapes, do you have a way to prove it? That would give us something to advertise. The main Oklahoma grape is the purple, thick-skinned Concord. How is yours different?

"Consider this. We're thinking you might be about twenty-five miles from us, and that's a fair trip to bring fruit. As we would be using it for jelly, the condition of the fruit is not such a concern as the effects of weather on transport, therefore we would insist that our own wagons, with containers and driver be at your field on harvest day, and travel immediately, through the night, to bring them here.

"In view of this, we suggest you set a price range per pound at your field, so we may figure our costs. We will have our own scales for weighing, but you are free to weigh them also. All we want is fairness.

"We're thinking… hoping, actually… that this works out for both of us, and if it takes more than one transportation vehicle, we can manage that. As it is, we are in possession of canning facilities and have suffered a drop in customers as there is more individual hunting of the rabbits, and of their availability in the local markets. We'd like to hear from you as soon as possible, as we want to advertise and reconfigure our equipment for a different product.

"Thanking you, we are……."

Three times he read the letter, and it said the same thing every time. It was now his turn. He had been ready for failure… ready to be turned down at the first place he had contacted, but he had hardly thought of success. That would happen now. Seemingly.

Watching the pattern of the moonlight on his bedcovers, he thought, figured and tried to plan. Here was just one more thing in which he was in over his head, so to speak. He heard the flap of rooster wings as the impatient foul beat the long white feathers that lifted him to his crowing post. Stanley, he chided himself. You dummy, you! Here's an answer to two of your problems.

Letter in hand, he went to collect Lettie and Francine after school. Miz Lizzie had insisted he bring her to eat, so she could try the jelly roll cake made with the new grape jelly. As the old woman was putting the finishing touches on the meal, a duty in which she would accept no help, Stanley handed Francine the letter.

Only a bit surprised, she read it and looked up, questioningly.

"I need help. I suspect it's obvious that I've not had a lot of schooling, and didn't pay a great deal of attention to what I did have. I knew I'd be prunin' vines and pickin' grapes if my pa had his way, and he usually did. That didn't work out as you can see.

"What I did was write these folks over in Oklahoma City lookin' for a market, and it could be I found one before I was ready to figure out how to take it. I've never in my life written a business letter, and if I did, my writing is impossible to read. The thing is, I'm lookin' for help." Figuring he'd said enough to be either good or bad, he'd just shut up and let her tell him which it was.

# CHAPTER 9

Y̶ou want help with a letter, is that right?" At his nod, she continued, "Have you figured out what you want to say?"

"Yes, sort of, but I'm not quite sure how to say it." May as well be brutally honest.

"Give me a sheet of paper from Lettie's tablet and tell me what you want to say. Miss Josie had us doing a lot of this sort of writing while we were in school. I'll take it with me and put it on the white paper I have at school."

Good. One problem down, and he'd take care of the other one when he picked up the finished letter.

The jelly roll cake came in thick slices with even thicker whipped cream on top. Francine savored every bite. "Sta.., James, you need to find out exactly how Miss Lizzie made this, and send the recipe along to the company. Any other recipe she has should go as well. Couldn't hurt anything, you know. Truth be told, I'd think the jelly she makes might be better than what the canning company could make, and you might just give them some hints on that, too."

The old woman was not exactly sure what was being said, but she was certain it was about her, and it seemed to be good. She had a lot of practice trying to figure out what 'grownups' were meaning in their words, and most often she was right. She left her chair and stood behind Francine, hugged her and kissed her forehead. Then she began to clear away the dishes, another duty in which she would accept no help. It could not be said that she did not carry her own weight.

He spent an apprehensive day. Stanley was reasonably sure how it would go with the letter, but the other matter was perhaps even more important. It could go either way. The good part of it was, there was to be a musical party, likely the last in the year, to be given by the group put together by Bob Farmer, the fellow who married Margie Van Pelt.

The brush arbor on the Brown place was a perfect location for outdoor activities, and with November already here, the pleasant fall weather would soon be gone… or at least unpredictable.

Now, how did he ask to take a lady to an activity that was practically in her yard, like she couldn't just toss on her shawl and stroll over there? Couldn't she just open her east window and hear it practically as well as if she sat on the hard log benches? And would it not be presumptuous for him to think she did not see enough of him and his girls every day?

But one thing for certain, he had to speak up because when would he get a better chance than this? He had to somehow put himself out of his agony, because if she said "no," then he'd better get busy somewhere else. Available girls were like ice cream on a summer day, they didn't last long. It had not been his intention to stay single so long, but with his brother gone, the baby, and the dream of a vineyard that he was not willing to give up, when had he the chance to do anything? Ah shucks! He was forced to chide himself. You know perfectly well it is your own cowardliness, so get over it!

He read the letter, and then, stalling for time, he read it again. Beautiful script in black ink on white paper. No ink spots. Tiny circles dotted each 'i.' Words put together so easily understood. Those folks were likely to think he had a secretary when they read this.

Francine watched, studying his face as he read… and re-read the letter. "Is it all right?"

"Better than all right. You're not likely to know what this is worth to me, but there's one more thing I need to ask you?"

"Forget to say something you intended to say?"

"Nope. Didn't forget. Just didn't have the courage to say the words. I 'spect you know there'll be a music party over at the arbor next week. Could be the last of the year. I was wonderin' if you'd go over there with me?"

Hesitation. Tilted head inspection. "Stanley, are you asking me for a date?"

"Well, I was… I'll have my ladies with me, and you know how they are about you. They'd really like it if…"

"Stanley, I don't hear Miz Lizzie and Lettie asking me to go to the musical."

With a grin, and a slight blush, which embarrassed him mightily, he admitted, "You caught me! I was just hidin' behind them. Fact is, I don't understand ladies of any age."

Returning the inspection! "Stanley, don't let that bother you. Everyone knows that even ladies don't understand ladies, and that's a fact. It's just that they don't admit it."

Interestingly, the new dress came over from the Corners the same day as the party. Pat and Bridie had attached it to the mail hook, and one of the Brown nephews had brought it on. Lovely! They had pleated the skirt, and then gathered the pleats, a trick that worked well on fine-weave fabric. That process made the gathers flow more smoothly over the hips, and the heavy lace on the hem ruffle also helped it to hang straight.

Shirtwaist, perfect! Once those girls had the measurements, they could make anything fit wonderfully. Francine had to smile as she discovered the small hanky made of the same fabric, securely pinned in her pocket. A two-word note was attached, "Good Luck!" was all it said. She could only shake her head in mock dismay.

Stanley, riding on cloud nine, decided to make a day of it. Sally, when she went to see her mother over the weekend, was commissioned to buy a new bonnet for Miz Lizzie. Certainly, he did not understand women, but he could not help having heard how special it was to have a new bonnet.

"Make it a pretty one, a color that'll go with her gray dress, and maybe has trimming… or something?"

"Don't worry, I'll find a good one!" Sally loved shopping.

The bonnet was made of gray felt with a shining ribbon of very light blue. Rose shaped flowers were made from the same ribbon and attached to the right side of the crown. The tie strings were made of lace, and meant to hang down and not be tied. But that was not all.

A shawl, crocheted from sparkly thread with tiny blue roses tucked in here and there. Too thin to be worn for warmth, but just perfect for a fall evening on elderly shoulders. Stanley was speechless as Sally explained her purchase.

"If I took on too much, I can take back that shawl, but when I saw it, I knew it was just for Miz Lizzie, knowin' how you feel about her. I got a good price, too, 'cause I argued with the store, pointin' out that it was too purty for the prairie. Most ladies buy a shawl for keepin' warm, so that'n didn't get bought for a long time.

"Then after I talked 'em down, I had 'em to add the ribbon and roses on the bonnet. Done a good job, didn't they?"

"Wonderful! And I'll keep the shawl."

However, it was touch and go on the shawl. Miz Lizzie said mama wouldn't want her to wear something like that "on account'a it bein' so fancy, folk'd say I was tryin' to be better'n I was. She'd be sayin' I was dressin' like a fancy woman."

With his best firm voice, he reminded her that he was now boss, and she must wear what HE told her to wear because mama wasn't here anymore. She finally relented and he draped it around her shoulders and settled the bonnet on her head. She did look better than usual, and it was likely her mama would have had words to say. He didn't care. "One thing, though, you gotta shine up your shoes and wear a pettislip that don't let your legs get cold. You'll be settin' outside on a log that's got no back. We can take a cushion if you want to, but you'll like the music."

She relented, finally, when Lutie hugged her and told her she was "beautiful."

Heart pounding, he left the "girls" in the buggy and walked up the schoolhouse steps. Francine had removed the note and put it in the desk drawer, but the hankie stayed in the pocket. The swing of the skirt was perfect, striking an appropriate nine inches from her shoe tops. Hair piled high and set in "sausage" curls, fitted this way and that over the crown of her head, stragglers being held up with combs with shiny green trimming. Truly, her best summer outfit.

Stanley drew in a startled breath at the vision she presented, but managed to offer her his arm, in the polite fashion of courting a lady, even though the "lady" might have been shucking corn, swinging the scythe, rubbing clothes on the washboard or on her knees on the floor with lye soap suds earlier in the day.

At the arbor, he seated Miz Lizzie, himself, then Lettie, with Francine on the end with the best view. The little girl glanced both ways, extracted herself from where she was put, and took the end position. The sights were interesting for a while, but she soon drooped over with her sleeping head in Francine's lap. Miz Lizzie gave signs of dismay, surely the child would ruin Betty Lou's beautiful dress, but she said nothing.

The jug player couldn't have been better! How did he do it? Maybe weighing at least three hundred pounds had something to do with it, but he knew just how to fit his blasts among the strains of the violins and other "instruments." Needless to say, no one was disappointed with the evening.

Stanley carried the sleeping girl to the buggy, putting her in the back, settled Francine in the middle, and Miz Lizzie on the outside. He was clearly staking his claim on his 'wife,' and Miz Lizzie covered her mouth with her hand to hide the happy smile. Surely she would come home soon to where she belonged.

Neither Stanley nor Francine had much sleep that night. Both felt that a bridge had been crossed, and as all paths lead in the same direction, they had only to play out their parts. Scary... as it was.

Christmas was next. Francine had decided on the traditional Christmas play, the one originated in Bethlehem so long ago. Carlotta was persuaded to come and teach the children "Oh, Little Town of Bethlehem," "Away in a manger," and "Hark the Herald Angels Sing." Isabel, being a quick study, picked the tunes up and was able to finish their practice.

Francine pictured all of the first class seated on the recitation bench that was covered with a white sheet. They would be shrouded in white to make the angels. What a laugh! Not an angel among them!

As the shepherds, and not the wisemen, were the ones to visit the stable at the first Christmas, she concentrated there. Mary and Joseph, of course, would make their journey up the center of the room, be turned away from the crowded inn, and finally settle in the stable.

A pulled curtain would allow them to put the "baby" in the manger. The rest of the children would be clothed in 'shepherd' clothing. One other addition. Lettie, the forward and confident, was to be the angel to bring the message to "Mary," as she was small enough to stand on the recitation bench cloud.

She was rapidly learning letter sounds, but not fast enough for her. She was forever asking what this or that word was, consequently she was learning a mixture of phonics and sight reading. Also her memory was impressive.

"Now, Lettie, you're going to pretend to be an angel."

"What's an angel?"

"They're the messengers of God, and they live in heaven. Remember the story how God had something to say to a lady named Mary, and He sent an angel with the message. I'll help you learn want to say."

"I need a message paper so I can get it right."

"You won't need a paper. You'll learn the message in your head so you won't need to read it."

"I NEED A MESSAGE PAPER!"

"We'll talk about it. Here's what you'll say, "I'm an angel come from God with a message for you. You'll have a baby boy, and His name will be Jesus, and He will be a very special baby.""

The girl nodded rapidly. "You can put the words on my message paper."

Francine looked up in exasperation, and Isabel shrugged. "I'll make it." Whereupon she printed the words on a sheet of paper and handed it to Lettie.

The confident child held the paper out in front of her and spoke from her marvelous memory, "I am an angel come from God with a message for you. You'll have a baby boy, and His name will be Jesus. He's a very special baby."

Holding tight to the paper she decided, "I'll need bird wings so I can get down from heaven without falling. Wings with feathers."

Francine nodded. "We'll talk about it, later."

"While we're making my wings?"

Confidence and ability in children were not always comfortable for those in charge. It was too late to change her part, and she would insist on wings until she got them. Maybe cardboard? Or something? Anyway...

As it turned out, a pair of cardboard wings were finally constructed that might actually last throughout the performance. Miz Lizzie opened her sack of feathers, those taken from every chicken that they had eaten, and selected them, one by one, gluing them in layers over the cardboard.

Actually, they looked rather good. She sincerely hoped the other small "angels" didn't demand the same, but they seemed satisfied that she was the one that had to come from heaven, so it was right she had wings so she wouldn't fall.

The Christmas audience was assembled, mainly families of students. They were perched on tables, seated on benches, and some were on the floor. The curtain was closed, hiding the mysterious sounds behind it, and the viewers waited with bated expectation.

Slowly it parted. Seated on a green blanket on the floor was 'Mary' bowed in an attitude of contemplation. The curtain closed to the sound of disappointed sighs, but immediately reopened. Standing on the 'cloud' consisting of a white sheet over the recitation bench stood an 'angel' clutching a sheet of paper fashioned into a scroll.

At a whispered cue of 'now' from the back drape, and the angel lifted the message to eye level and read, "I'm an angel come from God with a message for you. You'll have a baby boy, and His name will be Jesus. He will be a very special baby."

After a respectable pause, the angel looked up toward the classroom ceiling and asked, "Did I say that right, God?"

Smiles, and then appreciated titter of laughter, finally applause. The angel must have gotten a message from God that she was correct, because small Lettie flexed her 'wings' and smiled at the room full of people as the curtain was drawn.

With a beginning like that, what could possibly go wrong, and nothing did. Mary had slipped out the back door of Francine's apartment and joined with Joseph who was waiting, shivering, on the front steps. Sedately they traveled down among the seated audience, approaching the 'inn' which was currently in a large, cardboard packing crate (courtesy of Mac's store in Argyle).

The innkeeper silently pointed the couple toward the back curtain, and they tiredly continued their journey. Curtain closed, then reopened and revealed the packing crate which had turned, miraculously, into a stable. Mary and Joseph were seated in the stable surrounded by sheep, indicated by the ears strapped to their heads, and gray cloth draped over their shoulders.

Behind the stable stood the recitation bench cloud full of angels lined up, draped in white, and the angel on the end had been robbed of her wings so she would 'match' the others. A much taller angel with golden hair led them in singing "Hark the Herald Angels sing." The larger angel had rebelled on being draped in a sheet, but had settled for Miss Josie's white fleece robe.

On the second verse of the song, wonderfully remembered by three of the cloud angels, a back curtain parted to admit shepherds complete with robes and shepherd crooks.

When the shepherds had found a place to seat themselves among the fuzzy eared sheep, the song changed to "Away in the Manger."

After a pause, during which only a few of the sheep and shepherds turned to locate their own particular part of the audience, and wave a bit, the angel's song changed to "Oh, Little Town of Bethlehem." The second verse was performed as a solo by the golden haired angel, with the curtain closing. Then the song was finished.

Golden haired Carlotta, stepped through the curtain and thanked the audience. Applause seemed to vibrate the rafters as the characters skinned off their costumes in Francine's apartment, and streamed out to be congratulated. Cookies and tea for everyone.

Stanley recovered his own small special angel, who looked him sternly in the eyes and demanded, "Did I do good?"

The spring term proceeded with its usual number of starts and stops. Most of the beginners were reading fluently at the first McGuffy reader level, and Lettie and Nellie were working into the second book.

Nellie continued to draw pictures on every scrap of paper or flat surface she met. After a battle with her knowledge of fairness, Francine finally decided on how she could give a boost to Nellie's talent. Ordering a package of 100 sheets of white paper, she put it and a handful of sharpened pencils in a bag. Along with the paper, she put in a foot square mirror and a small hand mirror. Following Nellie and her grandmother out of the schoolyard, she gave the package to grandma, and a message to Nellie.

"Nellie, honey, I want you to do something for me if you will. I'm giving you some paper and pencils, and I want you to draw for

174

me a picture of your grandmother and one of you. Two pictures. Right? I want you to do your best, so I'm sending a lot of paper and a mirror so you can see yourself really well. Can you do that for me?"

Nellie, with shining eyes and deep nods, decided that she could do that.

"Now, you don't have to hurry. I will wait until you get the picture finished. Also, I don't want you to tell anyone because I didn't have paper and mirrors for everyone. Can you remember that?"

More nods.

That was on a Friday, and Monday morning the girl shyly handed Francine a rolled up tube of paper. Taking the gift to her apartment, she opened the sheets on her bed. Staring back at her was a sober mouthed, piercing eyed Kiowa lady, every wrinkle in place. Also staring at her was the face of Nellie, eyes brightly opened, one braid over her shoulder and the half-smile of interest she so often exhibited.

How... How... How does she do this? On the heels of that thought came the voice of Miss Josie, "Francine... How... How... How do you just write down descriptive words that rhyme and have the correct meter?" Well, she knew about the words, but these pictures...? She'd have to devise a way for Nellie to draw a companion picture of Lettie, her inseparable friend.

It was Wednesday that Nellie slipped her another gift of a paper roll. Opening it, she saw the mischievous dimples of Violette Barlow staring back at her, eyes sparkling dark and slightly tilted... just enough.

Francine disobeyed another rule of teachers. Motioning Nellie into her apartment, she hugged her, smiling her thanks. Nodding, the girl, without a word and just the interested half-smile, turned and walked away. Immediately, though, she stepped back.

"My Grandma say to bring back paper and mirror. I say I ask you first. Miss Francine say gift. Grandma say gift too much for my pictures." She waited, staring soberly up at her teacher.

"No, Sweetheart. Your gift of the pictures is much more valuable to me than the paper and the mirrors. If Grandma wants to hear me say it, I will."

Quick, satisfied nod and she was gone to her class. Over the next weeks Francine received many gifts of pictures. A deer, a skunk, several wild flowers, a grove of trees, all looking natural enough to slip right off the paper.

The wedding of the grape farmer and the teacher was to be in June on a Sunday that the circuit rider preacher would be in Shady Ridge. Her friends wanted to know what he said when he proposed, but after a bit of thought, she decided that he hadn't actually said anything. It was just that they had both known without words.

The interesting part was when Stanley (James) tried to explain the up-coming wedding to Miz Lizzie. Betty Lou would be coming home, but why was a wedding happening? They were already married. Sure, she had been gone a long time, and had to change her name (still a puzzle), but why was there a wedding?

Stanley scraped his brain and finally plunged in. "Miz Lizzie, you do remember that wedding, don't you?"

"Course I do. Wasn't I standin' right there 'tween mama and papa? Mama was almost cryin' over th' bad trouble just happenin', but Betty Lou said it was all right?"

"I've forgotten about the bad trouble. What was it that happened?"

"You're funnin' me. You couldn't forget if you wanted to. You just wanted to marry Betty Lou right then."

Another tactic. "Did mama want us to wait?"

"No, but she cried. Don't you remember? I don't know why Betty Lou wants to do it again. Lettie's five years old now, and what's she gonna think?"

New idea! "Miz Lizzie, do you remember what Betty Lou was wearing when she got married?"

Smiles wreathed her old face. "Course I do. I couldn't forget. It was her pink Sunday dress and roses in her hair. She was so beautiful I like to'a cried with happiness that she would be my sister. Almost."

New idea worked! "There wasn't money for a beautiful white dress for her then, but now I can buy whatever dress she wants to get married in. There'll be music and a lot of people there. It'll be a party for everyone. Do you think she should have what she wants?"

Nods. Doubtful expression. This seemed to be another of those grownup things she didn't understand but decided to accept. Someday she would know more, and then she wouldn't be so puzzled trying to remember what she thought she should know... what other people seemed to think she should know. Someday, when she was older...

The weather was beautiful on that second Sunday in June. It was one of those perfect days that the Oklahoma Territory tucked in amongst its frisky winds, sudden temperature changes, and showers that came out of nowhere.

It seemed that at least half of the Corners had arrived and were gathered in the arbor. Miss Josie was there along with her four sons, two sets of twin boys, and she was progressing well on her next... surely not more twins. Isabel insisted on staying in the schoolroom to help Francine dress. The girl would allow no other person this privilege.

The filmy, snow white dress. Polished leather, pearl button shoes brushed to perfection, pearl necklace from her mother, dating back in the days before they had come to the territory. White gloves ordered for the occasion held a bouquet of bridal wreath spray.

Her tiny buggy with Chock was hitched. The driver of her 'chariot' was Troy Cameron, who had sprouted into a tall, broad shouldered, laughing young man, highly honored by this privilege. He and Chock had spent a lot of hours together, and never had the pony been brushed this thoroughly.

Barely visible from the arbor, he escorted his teacher to her chariot, assisting with the billowing skirt that had suddenly come alive in the soft June breeze. All eyes turned to the buggy as it approached. On the arm of her special pupil, she descended and walked with him down to the front of the arbor. The preacher in his best-brushed coat and pants, waited. On one side of him stood her parents, and on the other side were Rosalie and Raymond, her sister and brother. In front stood Stanley. The fascinated Miz Lizzie, and Lettie had the best view of everyone, seated there on the front log bench.

A few words and it was over. Violins in the hands of Margie and Bob Farmer started softly, but moved quickly into bouncy, joyful tunes. Hugs. Best wishes. The Irish girls, the McLaughlin sisters, Carmelita and Carlotta, Miss Josie and Isabel… surrounding her… laughing and teasing. "A mama she is… already!" they observed, as little Miss Lettie came in for her share of the fun.

But the six year old soon lost interest and sneaked off to play with Nellie.

Miz Lizzie had to admit in her twelve-year-old mind, that this might just have been worth waiting for. She stood back away from the crowd that surrounded her 'childhood friend' and watched, treasuring the pictures of Francine… her friends all around her in their lovely dresses… all happy for her.

Miz Lizzie was patient, for she knew her time was coming. She hadn't understood why James was gone so long, why Betty Lou was not with him when he came for her, why she had to live in the school house for so long, and certainly, why she had changed her name. All of these things she put into the part of her mind that told her she would understand them better, later. When she was older…

So far, people were still telling her what to do so she would know. James had always been good about that. She had duties that she could do well and be praised for them. She was patient, and she could wait her turn, as she always had, only this time it was different.

This time her beloved 'sister' would be coming home with her. She would be leaving all the people who were gathered around her, and James would be taking her home, just as he should do. When that happened, she would know everything she needed to know, and she could take care of Betty Lou and little Lutie. Yes, she could wait because everything would be clear… very soon.

And it was. After the laughing, the cookie eating, the waved goodbyes… James brought the big buggy up close and seated his bride on the seat beside him. Miz Lizzie and the sleepy Lutie were put on the second seat. The horses were turned toward home.

The old face smiled, contentedly. It had happened the way she thought it would… the way she hoped it would, and now her family was together again.

# EPILOGUE

*(Researched and written by historian
Merytaten Franchesca Angelique Evangeline Cullen Carpenter)*

I really hated to stop right after the wedding, but it was such fun writing about Stanley and Francine that it would have run on for the next 1000 pages, and this Chronology is not about individual people. It is about the Territory of Oklahoma and how it shaped the people who shaped the land.

Me? I'm Merytaten Cullen Carpenter, my mother's fifth child. Josephine Wheeler from New York is my mother, and she has assigned this project to me. I suppose I should be flattered! One should be flattered when assigned a project by her mother.

Miss Francine was one of my mother's first pupils when she originated the Prairie Academy in her living room. Her oldest class was a special pleasure to her, four girls of eleven and twelve whose only brush with school was what some adult had time to tell them. They could read… somewhat. They could write… but not well.

She taught them for two years, stuffing them with everything she thought they could hold, then held them another year for practice teaching the younger children coming up behind them. She took the four girls to Oklahoma City to test for Teaching Certification and all four excelled.

As you likely know by now, two of the girls took over her classes while she had babies, and one of them went to the next town. That one was Francine. I used to call her Aunt Francine even though she wasn't. I guess I wanted her to be an aunt because I loved her so much. She was still teaching after I was grown, because she could not bear the thought of stopping.

Her little stepdaughter, Violette was a special joy to her, even though she produced three daughters of her own. They were Josephine Margaretta (Rita), Olivia Miranda (Livie), and Khristina Lucille (Lucy).

Violette was different, to say the least. No one was going to put her in a box! Starting with the Christmas play when she was a "messenger from God," she was a ham... the center of a drama, usually of her own making. She did what she wanted to do, and didn't blame anyone if it didn't turn out like she wanted. She and Nellie (Nelda) Spotted Pony were thick as pea soup from the moment they saw each other.

Lettie was made out of music. She sang, she played the violin that she had teased Miss Margie to teach her at age twelve. She saw an accordion being played by a circuit rider preacher, and demanded to have one. But there was no one to teach her.

No matter. She printed a notice for Mac's store in Argyle, and another one for the mail hooks in the Corners. When Eve Adams, a former classmate who taught at a school three miles south, saw the note, she answered it that there was a woman there in Enterprise who had an accordion and would 'get her started'. Lettie teased her "papa" Stanley until he either took or found transportation for lessons.

That was when they remembered the tiny buggy Francine had rode to school from Corners, and Lettie was put on her own. After that, she was like a balloon cut loose!

Not satisfied with the accordion, then called a lap organ, she insisted on and got an actual organ from Oklahoma City. She could play anything she had ever heard, and taught herself to read music. At age fifteen she was giving lessons to anyone who could convince their parents to get them an instrument.

Nellie Spotted Pony was the satellite to Violette's planet, and they created their own orbit. Nellie could draw and sketch from the time she could walk, but she got so much better that she was in great demand to sketch portraits and portray the bride and groom in a wedding.

Sweet natured Nellie would have been glad to do it for free if Lettie would permit it, which she wouldn't. Lettie timed her friend's work period, and multiplied by the going wage of a working man. Then she added the cost of the materials and doubled the amount. That was the cost of work done by Nelda Pony, and Lettie was ruthless in extracting it for her. The "Spotted" in Spotted Pony became her middle name, and not often used.

Nellie's younger brother, Bart, (their grandmother saw the name on a soup can and liked it) could also draw, but his best skill was making jewelry. Locally mined silver… with the local turquoise or other polished stones. Lettie looked through magazines sent by Josie's Aunt Sharon in New York. She found a company with instruction booklets and ordered the one on Jewelry making.

When it came, she didn't even open it, but handed it to Bart and said he was to learn everything in it. She talked him out of an especially lovely piece and sent it to Aunt Sharon. After that, any piece of his work which he signed as "A Spotted Horse," that he sent to Aunt Sharon, was quickly acknowledged with a check. With those checks he could buy better materials and get a few tools he needed.

To my knowledge, Bart has never willingly done another thing in his life except make jewelry. When Nellie drew a picture of some of the pieces and sent it to New York, orders came back for this or that particular piece, but Bart didn't like that as well as just making what he felt like. On any particular day. If he was "supposed" to do it, it was a job, and he didn't like jobs.

When she was eighteen, Violette rented a house on State Highway about a mile and a half each way between Shady Ridge and Corners. A fair amount of traffic plowed its way through the ruts of the dirt roadbed of State Highway, and many saw the sign that said GALLERY GIFTS.

Somehow, the traffic and Aunt Sharon (from New York) made a good living for Nellie and her brother, and Lettie tossed off music lessons when she felt like it. She seemed to be a very good teacher. You'd actually think she was Francine's blood daughter.

Speaking of blood daughters, by the time Francine's three daughters were looking for male company, their father's vineyard had grown to the point he was accepting local pickers for the grapes. The jelly company in Oklahoma City was doing so well, it took everything that Stanley grew.

He let his hired man, Lonnie, and his brothers have the job of picking the first "picking" for the canning company, but the second picking… not so large, was let out on "shares." For every three baskets they picked for sale, they could pick one basket for themselves. This kept up a good feeling with the neighbors as the "French" grapes were something of a trend-setter and consequently more valuable than the native fruit. Just like Miss Josie's New York education was desired above others on the territory.

Well, Francine's daughters attracted a lot of attention among the young male harvesters. When the girl's father saw this, he fired any young man who did not work well because he had begun to think his future sons in law would be selected from among the pickers.

He was right. By the time the fellows joined the family as sons in law, the vineyard had expanded to need all three of the fellows as supervisors, and his quarter section of land made plenty of room for a house and garden for each of them.

Francine taught all of her daughters, also her sons in law, but there were no "teachers" among them. They contented themselves with producing grandchildren for her.

Isabel Brown, however, was her shining success. As time went on, the little schoolhouse became too crowded, so Stanley began to step off a portion of his land that faced onto Ridge Road for a bigger school building. It had two large rooms with archway doors between that were closed with heavy tapestry hangings.

Isabel taught the first three grades, and she was extraordinarily successful with smaller children, while Francine, favoring the older ones, taught what would be fourth to the seventh. More money being available on the territory, and Isabel needing a salary, the tuition was gradually raised to $2.00 per student per month. They never lacked for students, which showed that the price of education makes its own place.

Another thing that was really cool was the woodwork shop over on Sandy Creek and State Road. The settler, Jacob Van Pelt, was from Holland and had been trained in woodworking... a skill he passed to his brother-in-law, who married Margie Van Pelt. Remember, she was the one with the limp that Bob Farmer said was a plus, as she would never ask him to dance with her... and he hated to dance. Four left feet, remember?

Anyway, the fellow, Jacob, had two little boys after the two girls. The girls had been named Edith and Susan, easy for Americans to pronounce. Some Dutch names were practically impossible. But then when the little boys were born, the first was named Dirk, and the next one was Henrick. Their mama said if Americans couldn't pronounce those names, they were in trouble, and a bit of trouble never hurt anyone.

Then Margie had a little boy she named Robbie. They had some very nice white oak trees down by Sandy Creek, and the lumber from them was made into strong, beautiful furniture. Beds, stools, chairs and tables. They even had the machine that made the round pattern on the spreaders for chair legs.

The best thing they had, though was the huge, squarish bureaus with deep, wide drawers. The frontier ladies just loved them because they held so much stuff. Mr. Van Pelt even started ordering mirror glass, two feet square, and he put the glass in a frame that matched the bureaus with a bracket for hanging on the wall.

Folks asked them why they didn't set up a shop on the road, and the stubborn Dutchmen replied that if folks couldn't walk back to his shed to look at the stock, they didn't deserve it.

Besides, everything sold just about as fast as it got made, because most of the time they were special orders. The little boys at five and six were learning to "sand" the boards. By the time they were in their teens, they could make anything they wanted to.

It was about three years after Francine married that Miz Lizzie began to take a "turn" as the locals said. There were times that she would put on the bonnet with the blue roses and toss the shawl around her shoulders. Then go out and sit in the porch swing, moving slowly back and forth.

At first Francine and Stanley were concerned, thinking she thought they were going to go somewhere and would be disappointed, but that didn't seem to be it. She just sat... contented like, and they decided she was just reliving the pleasure she had when she went to the musical and the wedding. It was like she was playing the scenes through her memory and enjoying them again. After all, who knew what was actually going on in her mind?

They never did learn what terrible thing happened long ago that still bothered her. It might have been nothing, just something built up in her twelve-year-old mind.

When the Oklahoma wind was brisk, she sat inside the house in her rocker, moving slowly back and forth. Then, after a while, she

EPILOGUE

would take off the bonnet and put it in its box and fold her shawl inside a towel to keep it from getting snagged, and put it in her drawer.

She still cooked and cleaned, which seemed to be her particular pleasure, though she had a little trouble getting some heavy things to stay on the clothesline.

She still liked making jelly and blackberry was her favorite. She boiled down the juice until it was as rich flavored as candy. She was giddy with pleasure that the jelly was a favorite of Francine's (Betty Lou's), who enjoyed a jelly biscuit with her coffee after breakfast.

One fall day she counted the jars of jelly she had left and thought she should make more. She mustn't run out of Betty Lou's favorite.

She took her bonnet from its box and settled it onto her scraggly, snow-white hair and draped the shawl over her shoulders. She picked up her berry picking pail and set out to the patch that was about an eighth of a mile away.

As she closed the door behind her, she knew there was something she was forgetting, something about going to pick berries, but there was no one at home to ask, so she started out.

When nothing was started for supper, the family began looking for her. She was not at any of her usual haunts or favorites places, like her herb garden. After a bit, they called in the neighbors, and finally the whole town was looking for the twelve year old in the seventy (?) year old body.

Special attention was paid to the creek, but it had nothing but fish and frogs. Finally, they met back at the house to plot another course. She had to be somewhere nearby… her feet couldn't carry her very far.

While sitting and standing in the kitchen with cups of coffee, Sally, wife of the hired man, set down her coffee and yelled, "I KNOW where she is!"

"Where?" everyone wondered.

"Come and see," she told them and took off running up the side of the hill, past the first vineyard. And there, sitting on the ground beneath the dried and low hanging berry vines of last summer's crop sat the old lady, leaning against a fence post. The berry bucket was between her knees and her hands folded in her lap. Her head, wearing the blue trimmed bonnet, was bent forward.

Sally threw herself to the ground beside her, picked up a cold stiff hand, and let her tears flow. Over the years they had become close, Sally, the old woman and the little girl. Two of the men took Sally's arms and lifted her away so they could pick up the old woman, but Sally wailed in agonized sorrow all the way back to the house.

Miz Lizzie was "laid out" on her bed. Hair was combed, body was washed, and her best dress was put on her. The near neighbor commented, "I'd be of a mind to let this bonnet and shawl be put away with her, but it is such a thing of beauty and she loved it so much, I think it should be kept for that little girl she kept alive. There'll be a time when she'll treasure it the way she treasured the old lady."

One of the wonderful women in attendance reached into the drawer nearby where she knew Miz Lizzie would keep her snow white hankies, and shook out a filmy, lace-trimmed "Sunday" one. The aroma of rose petals filled the room. She bent and tucked the white scrap of fabric under the swollen knuckles of the old woman's gnarled hands as they were crossed over her chest. She instinctively knew that no "lady" would go anywhere without a clean hankie. It just wasn't done.

Nods of agreement. The bonnet was brushed and boxed, the shawl was folded and wrapped. When they were handed the shawl to ten-year-old Lettie, she hugged the package and soaked it with her tears, rocking back and forth in the rocker she had shared with Mama Lizzie.

(Ten years later, at her age twenty, she put on the hat and draped the shawl over her shoulders, demanding that Nellie draw her. That picture stayed on the wall wherever Violette lived at any particular time.)

The preacher was due in three days, so they closed her in her room, on the bed where she had spent her last years. Activity in the house came to a screeching halt, and the neighbors came with food and cookies for the two oldest of Francine's girls (the third was still cradled within her).

School was halted out of respect.

The grave was dug up on the side of the hill by the blackberry patch. As it turned out, Stanley later fenced off a chunk of land for that purpose, and there are a number of graves there now.

The funeral was held in the old schoolhouse. The preacher began:

"This funeral is not for Miz Lizzie. She doesn't need it and would not enjoy it. It's for us. From what I hear, this lady lived her life to the fullest with every facility she had. She made the most of her life, finding pleasure in service.

"There is so much we can't know, but in the years we've known her, she has possibly saved the life of a baby, and made it possible for the baby's uncle to be among us. He has been a blessing to many.

"This lady is now in a place of rest. Very likely she can use it. From what I hear, she never complained, did what she could, tried to understand what was continuously beyond her. She spent her last hours waiting for the blackberries to blossom and ripen so there would be a supply of favorite jelly for someone she adored. It was cold and windy on the hill, but that didn't matter when she busied herself with a job she felt she needed to do.

"We are here to perform the last act we can do for Miz Lizzie McMurty, but it is an act we perform for ourselves. Her Maker would not depend on mere mortals to take care of her. His own angels have long since carried her away on snowy wings. She will not be tired; she will not be cold. She will not feel inadequate as she must have at times, and she will not be puzzled by things she could not understand. She will not even miss her family, including the little girl she loved. If she missed them, she would be sorrowful, and we are assured that there is no sorrow where she is.

"There will, however, be gladness when at last she sees them again. The Bible tells us that. She would want us to rejoice with her, hard as that will be for her family, but I have asked our local violin musicians to play "In the Sweet Bye and Bye" as we all pass by for a chance to see her for the last time. Will you all stand."

The strains of the violins muffled the footsteps as the mourners passed by the pine box and then on to the outside, dispersing themselves to their homes. The pain in Stanley's heart was equal to that he had felt on the prairie as he had viewed his brother and sister-in-law. His own mother had not evoked such painful tears. Be strong, Stanley, he chided himself. Life goes on, and no one will call you James again. He had added about ten years to her life, but she had added immeasurably more to his and Violette's.

Sally had remained behind the others and stood with the family. Sobbing painfully, she stood within the arms of Francine and Stanley as they shared grief. Young Lettie wedged herself into the center of their arms. Lonnie, with furrowed brow, stood aside in agonized concern for his Sally in her "condition."

Gently extracting her, he tucked her into the buggy and headed down Ridge Road, with Stanley not far behind. Francine's parents were waiting at the house with Rita, age almost three and Livie, coming up on seventeen months. They would be taken to the Corners by their grandparents just as soon as the older folks were assured that Francine was "holding up." They left with sad eyes.

Lonnie took Stanley aside. "I'm knowin' you'll want to be on the site for the buryin'. Wanted to say, I'll stay with the girls and try and get 'em to eat somethin'. That'd be a help." With an appreciative nod, Stanley slipped through the door.

He did not, however, escape Lettie's watchful eyes. Easing through the door after him, she announced, "I'm goin' with you."

"No, honey you mustn't. Stay and eat, so you'll feel better."

"No, Papa. Ain't nothin' that'd make me feel better. Mama Lizzie was mine, too. I'm goin' all the way I can, far as she goes, I go. Papa, she was the one that kept us together. You'd had to put me somewhere, but she was there, and she held me all the way to Argyle." A sniffle and a meaningful hiccough. "She held me all the way and her being scared spitless the whole time." Lettie knew her 'Mama Lizzie' very well.

Put that way, Stanley understood. What happened to his charming, chubby toddler? Here was his niece, sapling thin and just as wiry... her dark eyes piercing as arrows. Yes, she had the right and possibly the duty to attend the last journey of the only real mother her young life had known.

Together they stood, tears flowing, as the four strong neighbors lowered her into the ground, allowed slack in the ropes so the hooks would release and settle her on the dirt. Terrible sound! Final sound! Final burst of tears as they headed back down the hill.

Isabel Brown, who had moved into the apartment Francine had vacated, packed necessities in her suitcase and walked the mile down Ridge Road. She marched into the house without an explanation, went into Miz Lizzie's old room. She yanked off the bedding, spread a clean sheet. Fluffed the pillows in their fresh cases and spread a quilt. She was here to stay for a few days and 'help out,' and there would be no discussion of the matter. Perhaps she could do for Miss Francine some of what the beloved teacher had done for her.

Years later, Violette told me that moment as a ten year old was like a 'period, paragraph' of her life. She learned to battle the moods of the wood-burning stove and managed to turn out food, still edible. She appropriated her own mug and drank the steaming bitterish brew called coffee, to exaggerate her grownup-ness.

She rubbed the soiled clothing on the washboard twice before she thumbed through the catalog at Argyle, locating the washtub on legs with a lever to turn the agitator. Not easy to operate, but at least there was no bending. Or rubbing. She was fascinated with the tiny oil burning stove in Francine's apartment at the school, and found a much larger version. Not only would it provide instant flame that could be adjusted, it also eliminated much of the need for cowpats. Oil was easily available at Argyle stored in five gallon cans. The convenience was worth putting up with the fumes until the flame turned blue.

She picked the blackberries growing by Mama Lizzie's grave, tears streaming down her face. She boiled them as she had seen the old woman do, she strained them and reduced the juice to a candy-like flavor. It was possible, now, to buy a package of powder that made the juice jell, so she didn't have to use apples for pectin. She knew to put the strained-out berries in the cheesecloth bag and squeeze, to increase the flavor in the jam that would be mixed with grated pears for extra sweetness.

She and her beloved "new" mama worked together to learn to do a bit of what Miz Lizzie did so well. More than once, they had been forced to go to Mrs. Brown to help them out of a mess. Stanley

JOANN KLUSMEYER

was so busy, fortunately, that he hardly noticed the change in food quality, but it improved steadily.

There were times now, especially during very bad weather, that Nellie stayed over with Lettie, and she was a wealth of information. While she was there, and before the memory softened, she drew a portrait of the old woman, true as always to wrinkles, eye slant and mouth shape. She dressed her portrait in her bonnet and shawl, and handed the finished product to her best friend.

Lettie took one look, picked up Nellie's hand to place against her face, and then slid the picture under the underwear in her drawer. Later, she would show it to Francine and Papa, but for now it was hers… alone. When she framed the two pictures Nellie had drawn of them both at age 5 and 6, she slid the one of Mama Lizzie behind her own.

Then the two pictures of little girls were hung in the "gallery" where she gave music lessons, and where Nellie's drawings were displayed for sale along with the native jewelry created by her brother. An increasing market had developed for Bart's jewelry, sporting the engraved symbol of "A Spotted Pony."

It was about then that I, Miss Josie's daughter, was given a sad mission by Violette. "If you're still here," she told me, "when I have to leave this earth, I want you to see that this picture of Mama Lizzie goes in the box with me."

The horror of her words was so great that I gasped, "Oh, please don't talk like that!"

She took me by the shoulders and looked darts into my eyes. "If I don't tell you, then you won't know. I will do many things for you, but you must do this one thing for me. Promise?" What else could I do but nod my head?

Enough of this for now. More later. I'm assigned to explain how Shady Ridge was shaped during those first years of the 1900's. When Miss Josie assigns a project, it WILL be done!

Children were growing up. The quarter section that their parents had either bought or proved out was ample room for new homes and the gardens that went with them. All along State Highway houses sprung up at the daring distance of only a hundred feet apart.

189

Much of the time, the land was cut up with the help of a surveyor, providing portions for grownup children.

It was good, in most ways. Family was close if needed, and that need almost always happened. There were also feuds and disagreements among siblings and a patch of the "old home place" would be sold to a "stranger" from Oklahoma City, or even as far away as Arkansas or Kansas.

The community to the west that occupied the less desirable land also increased in population. The Spotted Pony family, along with Brown Bear, Black Hawk, Fire Eagle, and their close kin managed somehow to produce a living. The names were also changing. In addition to each child having his own picture name, they were given names that would be understood by the newcomers.

It made families more consolidated, such as the Spotted Pony family who had a cluster of cousins and in laws who found their separate occupations and worked together. Houses became more comfortable as negotiable coins took the place of "trade items."

Their young men were proved to be good workers, wanting the newcomer money to get newcomer luxuries. Nellie's success made a great impression on other mothers and grandmothers of her tribe, and they wanted their girls to have the same opportunities. Skills traded for coins.

The schoolhouse in the Brown's yard took on another life after the new school was built. Isabel still occupied the apartment, which eased the space strain on the other members of her family, but the classroom stayed open.

The circuit rider preachers greatly appreciated the comfort of the closed-in building, especially during winter and also on rainy days. In addition, it was available for any sort of "town meeting" and even musical parties if the weather forced them from the arbor.

Isabel Brown, of course, worked with Francine in the new school down on Ridge Road, but Laura Black Bird, one grade below Isabel, had attempted her own project up over the "ridge" and seemed to be having a fair amount of success. Such bravery and dedication for one who had been permitted only sporadic attendance! More about Linda later.

State Highway had an increase in traffic as the west became more settled. Single riders, wagons and even the horseless contraptions created up north by a man named Ford, plied the rutted roads. Some purists turned up their noses at the "horseless carriage," but most owners preferred the name "tin Lizzie."

The first ones seen in Shady Ridge had no roof, but soon a sun shade of sorts appeared, fashioned after the "surrey with the fringe on top." Then, later, it had sides and doors that closed. First the Model "A" and then the "T." The most fun was the little two seated model with a "rumble seat" instead of a boot in the back. Very popular with younger people.

One hang-up on the popularity of the tin lizzie was the availability of gasoline. Even after a tank was put in at Mac's store, and another one at the Corners, it was still safer to carry a "gas can" of one's own even though there was the danger of its catching on fire from spontaneous combustion.

But there was always the trusty horse. It was a common sight to see two of the four footers hitched to one of the four wheelers, hauling it to a gas pump. Or thumping it along with a flat tire. Or pulling it from the depth of the muddy ruts that the machines made of the unstable dirt roads.

The bystanders laughed as the horse was drafted to pull the car, but those who laughed soon found themselves wanting one. One the first Model "T" Fords in Shady Ridge was owned by Troy Cameron, one of the far-thinkers.

The young man could plainly see that, with the frequency of breakdowns, there would be a very good market, also profit, for the person who could repair the engines. About a hundred feet east of where he had corralled Miss Francine's little pony, he opened a shed that was stocked with the most often broken bits of the tin lizzie.

TROY'S FIXIT got a lot of business, and he even began to stock several cans of the gasoline, the liquid so often depleted on the country roads. Charged a sensibly high price for it, too. One thing about school and Troy… he learned to add, and multiply whenever possible. In addition to repair of the cars, he also continued to board a few horses, as he had for Miss Francine.

The Garcia family opened a sandwich shop for those stranded in the country and found themselves hungry. It also became popular with the locals, especially young men. The Garcia girls had a passing parade of young men to admire them, but Papa Garcia had a sharp eye and a shotgun over his door.

He was not adverse, however, to the money, and during the summer he strung kerosene lanterns in the trees and benches under them. To the men of the neighborhood, he insisted that it "beat working."

Francine, who was born and grew up in the Corners, was, however, a true daughter of Shady Ridge. Through the school, she had access to and knowledge of nearly every family in the extended community. She took an active interest in the maturing of each child, advising when asked, helping when possible. Year after year she turned another eight or ten young people into the town, educated, confident, and full of ideas.

Many of them were forced to leave Shady Ridge to a bigger place to live their dream, but others found their own small nook within the cluster of houses. The three mile stretch between the Corners and Shady Ridge became prime business property.

It was on this thoroughfare that Lettie set up her own business. An abandoned house was rented, and THE GALLERY became a landmark. Crocheted lace collars and cuffs, pens, ink, and paper. Pencils by the box. Cards of safety pins. Side combs to hold up straying locks (especially since the onset of the "tin lizzie" and its windy speed, zooming down the road occasionally up to 20 dangerous miles an hour. There were those who speculated that the speed might shorten a person's life, and as many as 40 miles an hour would render the passengers without enough breath to breathe.)

The Gallery offered any small item the girls thought might sell, and changed them often enough for curious folks to stop in just to see, and maybe buy the beautiful sketches and paintings, or the Spotted Pony jewelry.

Violette's music lessons required no advertisement. She had as many students as she wanted, and if they did not show immediate progress, they were released, in favor of the next in line. Also that girl did not plan on working every minute of her life. Laughter and fun were as necessary to her as her breath.

Eventually the owner of the quarter section across the road surveyed his land into plots facing State Road. He created enough plots for six businesses, The Gallery being the first. Then came a tack and saddle shop, followed rapidly by others.

Wesley Palmer lived way east of the Corners, but he had a new tin lizzie and decided to try it out on State Highway. He whizzed past the Owens, on to the Wilsons and pulled into the Corners for a cup of coffee at the Cookie Jar. Thus fortified, he had the courage to head to the west past Canfield Dirt Works and onward, just to see what was there.

What he saw was the Gallery. He stopped, having not much else to do. His cotton plants had not yet poked through the soil, and they wouldn't, until a shower of rain encouraged them.

In a holiday mood, he looked around and saw Miss Nellie Spotted Pony at her easel. Paint dabbled smock on her shoulders and a long handled brush in her hand. Face sober in concentration on the canvas before her. The sun coming through the window onto her face, the color of ripened stalks of wheat. In the euphoria of his tin lizzie purchase, he thought he also deserved this girl as well.

Now, Wesley was a persistent young man, but his cotton patch grew, was harvested, and the ground turned under before he got Nellie. Her price was the insistence that her art came first before ANYTHING else, and Wesley had no power to resist her. They were married the next spring in a double wedding with Violette and young Bertrand François who had become Randall France before he stepped off the boat.

The young Frenchman knew exactly where he was headed at the time he had boarded the ship in Amsterdam. He would go to the new lands and head west out to the prairies to invest all he had been able to save on as large a patch of land as his savings would buy. It was his dream to grow sheep, the long-haired kind whose wool brought a premium price. He was considerably older than he had intended to be at this time in his life, but he had found money harder to accumulate than he had anticipated.

With blind luck, he stumbled into a half section just outside a small settled community. It fitted within his budget because the access 'road' had not yet been cut, much less built, and, at present, being hardly more than a trail. The besotted young man hardly saw this important deterrent. Fencing he could afford and water ran through both quarter sections. He put up a fairly comfortable 'shepherd's shack' on the land and then paused to figure how he would get his animals on the land and care for them, as there was not even a graded trail where the road would eventually be and the little stream with no bridge crossed it twice.

Walking the perimeter while he thought, he was inordinately pleased to see that his neighbors on the back side and both ends of his land had put up a very serviceable fence. A bit of reinforcement on his side would hold in the sheep. They were docile, after all, being sheep!

He could scarcely afford to create a road down the raw land, crossing the stream twice. Hardly even a wagon trail… and that would not service the fifty sheep he wished to start with. While ambling down the back edge, a half mile stretch, he looked over the fence into a cotton patch. The owner of the cotton patch had created a road, of sorts, all the way around his quarter section for hauling away the harvested cotton.

Hmmm, all that separated him from the road was a section of barbed wire, three strands high. Maybe…?

The owner of the cotton patch stroked his chin and considered. "What I'd need from you, man, is a good gate, and another strand of wire to make sure your bleaters don't get through. I hear they like cotton plant leaves. Also, when the road has to be upgraded, you'll pay a one third share. There's a fellow over east a mile or so, and he has road equipment. I use him."

Randal thought only a minute and saw that his only way out was a good one, so he agreed. That was when Wesley Palmer, owner of the new tin lizzie, offered his hand to Randal France, who just became the part owner of a road that made his sheep ranch possible.

Wesley eyed the new neighbor up and down and deemed his appearance presentable, so he invited, "Man, if you got the time, we could amble over across the road to an art shop where they have good coffee. Drop a five center in the jug and drink all you want. We likely need to put some kind of a paper to what we just agreed, but all in good time."

That was how Violette Barlow met Randal France, thereby making it possible to have a double wedding the following spring.

Randal had come up against an unexpected problem. When he became situated, he had looked around for companionship. Having passed age thirty was a problem, because the ladies near his age were on their second or third child. And why would the eighteen to twenty year olds take a glance at an old guy of thirty three? Grating problem, it was, but there were others even more immediate.

One thing the French shepherd had not considered was that he was providing many good meals of mutton to the local coyotes and wolves. What he had saved on the road was spent on shepherd shacks, sheep dogs and young or very old men as guards. The cost of guns, a number of kerosene lanterns and a pittance salary licked up the last pennies he had brought with him.

He had paid the five center and agreed that the coffee was uncommonly good, when his eyes fell onto the delight of his life. She was twenty one and an impossible vision. A butterfly... hummingbird? Maybe a field of daisies rippling in the wind? Poetry he did not know he knew, suddenly invaded his soul. This creature couldn't possibly look twice at him, but he had reckoned without Miss Violette.

Just before her third glance, she knew this person was something she would have, and the vestige remainder of his French accent was, if anything, charming. Mr. Randal France chased her until she caught him, and he never did know the difference.

He had no money left, but that was no problem to Violette. No matter, they could just live in the gallery apartment. He moved in with his bride just as her partner had moved in with her groom near the cotton patch.

The people of the prairie carved the land, the land shaped the people and Shady Ridge had continued to grow. Slowly, of course. Words were slow at seeping in from the outside and the business of everyday life was all-consuming.

This would change.

Of course, clever young men began to play with crystal radio sets, windmills appeared to suck up water for people, and cattle and the central government designated a few mail routes. The first one in the vicinity of Shady Ridge was one of the coveted star routes, long and twisted, reaching as many of the small towns as possible in the shortest distance of miles and time.

State Highway was one of those routes chosen, and the path came through Argyle south to the Corners. Any regulation mailbox along the way was serviced, and small towns were designated to receive mail for their community. Mrs. Brown permitted her nephew, who was actually claimed as her own, to use the schoolhouse. Pigeon-hole cubbies were arranged, and the mail sorted into families and stuffed in the box. When a family member came by, they would pick up the lot. For the most part it worked satisfactorily.

Then there came more rumors of disquiet in Europe. Aggressive behavior on the part of Germany. Imagine that! At first it was just something to discuss when all other subjects had been covered.

News outlets began to send out their papers to the routes on subscription, and the matter of the aggressive behavior became more pertinent... largely by old men who had nothing better to do than read the papers. The Kansas City Star was a favorite.

It seemed that England had alliances with some of the European states and could be called into the war in an emergency. Imagine that as well! A great lot of Shady Ridge people had ties to England or the European states involved.

A sad state of affairs, for a fact, and if it doesn't rain soon, the popcorn is going to pop right there on the stalk and already the peanuts were roasting themselves in the hot sand. Disagreements across the ocean were of fleeting interest.

An interesting story was unearthed by someone in the white-haired, bearded group. The sons of those rich dudes in Britain bought those ridiculous flying machines for their sons... likely to keep them out of mischief. The thing was, those flying machines were going to be used in the war for something or other. The picture showed the machine made of what looked like sticks and canvas, likely stuck together with glue. That thing on the front looked like the blades on the new water-drawing windmills. Can you beat that? Entirely too much to get a fellow's mind around!

Weeks later, it looked like those brainless sons wanted to fly those machines over to Europe to drop explosives, but their government wasn't too hot on the idea. Seems they wanted those rich fellows to stay home and teach farmer's sons how to fly them. Didn't want them rich kids to get themselves killed because they were the only ones who knew how to keep the dinky little motors running. They figured out there wasn't no place to pull over and park up there in the sky, and there weren't any flying horses to come to the rescue.

And do you think those snap beans will ever come on… if we don't get a rain soon?

Then there were words about America going to help Britain. Couldn't be true, of course. And then there came the notice for young fellows eighteen and over to come and tell the government where they were, just in case the world needed them to straighten out the mess.

That was when Shady Ridge came alive. Miss Francine wore a continued look of concern. In her ordered life, here was something she could not comprehend, and for sure it would affect her students, those current and also those of years ago.

Manuel and Troy were the first. An evil little card telling them to register because their country might, sometime in the future, need them. Why? The trouble was a long way away, and it certainly didn't affect the price of horse feed.

Then the village back west began to get notices. The area of the ridge had begun to be called Westridge. It consisted of a spread of rough land that had escaped the 'land run' because it was inhabited by its original owners. Most of the boys had been past school age when Miss Francine opened the school, but she had taught younger siblings.

Mitch Tall Tree was the first to actually go, then Pete Gray Wolf. His sister, Beverly Gray Wolf, had been a charming girl and a hard-working student. Then Troy Cameron told them goodbye.

There was a lot of talk about those from the Corners and from down south at Enterprise that had to go. John Black Hawk walked away from his home instead of going in to Oklahoma City to register. As far as anyone knew, the unfortunate boy just disappeared from the face of the earth. But he didn't go to war.

Then there were the Fire Eagle boys. Their mother had wanted the best for them, so when they were expected, she asked the preacher what were the best names in the Bible for boys, and, seeking a good answer for her, he decided one couldn't go wrong with Matthew, Mark, Luke, and John.

John did not appear in the Fire Eagle family, but Matthew, Mark, and Luke were barely a year apart. They had created their own reputation as they tore down the rutted roads on the fastest horses available, walked away with every prize in shooting contests, always winning first, second, and third. A lot of their spending money was earned by bringing down a six-point buck and selling it in town. They passed by the eight- and ten-point animals as they were too heavy to bring into town on horseback.

They all three took after their Papa Fire Eagle who cleared six foot two and carried a well-placed 240 pounds. His slimmer sons would get there when they were papa's age. Their younger sister, Elizabeth, could turn any head at any time.

These brothers were inordinately interested in those canvas-covered contraptions that flew like a bird. Why, they'd likely give their eyeteeth to get into... say! It just might be possible!

Then when the Brown Bear twins, Harley and Harold, received their notices, the Fire Eagle brothers went along with them to register. Maybe they could talk someone into letting them ride in one of them flying machines. Or even drive it through the clouds themselves!

Francine stared in dismay as the eight, nine, and ten year olds with toy guns were banging at each other, laughing joyfully. What was the town coming to? Then it got even closer to home when Bart Spotted Pony was called up. Bart, the sunny tempered free spirit, doing what was required without complaint. Except for his tanned skin, he could have reminded her even more of her brother, Raymond. Seeming never to put forth much effort, still turning in carefully completed lessons, and reciting without hesitation or a stutter.

There was that thing called boot camp that all the boys went through to make sure they were fit to fight for freedom of people they had never met. The laughing music parties at the brush arbor were now only a quiet gathering of the girls, who could sadly compare portions of letters and wonder when the boys would be back. The few fellows who were still at home knew it was only a matter of time.

Then they were given "induction leaves," whatever that was. They had a month to say their goodbyes and have their duffels packed. Bart, the easy-going free spirit was packed off to Britain and settled into a dungeon with deciphering equipment, trying to break the enemy's code and learn what they planned on doing before they did it. The tests he had taken said he would be good at it because of his education.

He wrote home, but his letters did not indicate exactly where he was, and if he said anything questionable, the words were stamped out with black ink patches. And there was really not much to say, anyway. But his sister faithfully wrote long, newsy letters, even if she had to make up a few things. Lettie, now called Violette, always put in a note.

The Black Bear twins were separated. After their driving tests, Harold was sent to France, and Harley was attached to a headquarters agency ferrying high officials around. The trick was to somehow keep the "brass" alive to continue the war, and who knew how many German spies were among them?

The Fire Eagle brothers got what they wanted. No one yet had been able to deny them anything if they ganged up with a united front. Certainly, the United States Government was no match for them. They were put through every test known, and a few that were made up, and then transferred over to the Royal Air Force in England. Number 100 Squadron, Royal Flying Corps, was sent, en masse, to France to engage in night bombing missions.

Sure enough, on closer inspection, the flying machines actually WERE made out of broomsticks and canvas, or so their letters home insisted. Not a problem, though, because it just added to the challenge. Their letters did not mention, however, that Luke came in at dawn, one morning, with his engine pounding like a jackhammer, and a third of his left wing shot off. His tail-gunner was left hanging onto a flap of canvass, almost, and was a quivering mass of nerves and allowed a week off to 'get his head together' then sent out again.

Luke was issued another plane and took off at dusk, sighting by the moonlight shining off the river and estimating where he was by his air speed and the uplift of draft on the winds. Armed with that information he had reached an ammunition factory. Circling the target twice, to let the gunner be certain, he dived to within 50 feet of the top of the building and let it go. When the building exploded, the air turbulence flipped the plane over, and Luke coaxed the coughing engine back into life and followed the river toward home base.

He was two miles from the base in the early morning light when the engine sipped its last drop of fuel. Luke edged the machine over toward a cow pasture and glided down onto the grass, nosing into a haystack to keep from hitting the curious black and white cow.

All the damage was a bent propeller. The two airmen walked the final two miles and a flat-bed truck went after the wounded canvas bird. Luke and his gunner checked out another plane, ate a hearty lunch and grabbed a nap. They already had their orders for the next night.

Matthew wished it had been him, but he was given the job of transporting important people from Dover, in England, over to the French base. His ability to fly low and dodge trouble made him a valuable asset and generals often wished they could clone Matthew Fire Eagle.

It was a night with bright moonlight that he pealed off the white cliffs of Dover and ducked as low as possible to avoid detection. Half way across the channel, an enemy appeared out of nowhere. Matthew sensed the flame of the ammo before he saw it and ducked even lower managing to get off a shot of his own as he pulled up out of the dive. An explosion behind him rocked the air waves, flinging him down against the water. The impact unseated his passengers, but the straining engine managed to lift the aircraft out of the briny. It limped on at an angle and the shaken passengers had to hold to the sides of the aircraft to keep from sliding from their bench seats.

Daylight revealed a bent tail fin and a clump of seaweed clinging to the raw rigging of the broken frame where the covering had been torn away. Being taught to be polite, Airman Fire Eagle apologized, "I had to fire off somethin', sir, or he'd'a had us for sure."

The generals looked at each other and decided this man was wasted on shuttle runs, and that night he joined his brother on the bomb missions. It was Matthew, actually, who flew low over the lakes that furnished water power to the factories. He learned to drop his load and pull up just before hitting the dam itself. The released bomb skipped across the water like the stones the boys used to skip on the water of Sandy Creek.

The skipping bomb then landed against the dam wall and blew, and by that time Matthew and his bombardier were high enough that the air turbulence only gave them a forward boost. That kind of flying was hard on the small engines, and they had to be changed out often. It seemed worth the trouble, however, to the heads that made the decisions.

Mark got himself in an air battle with two of the enemy. He was dipping and twisting away from them, knowing he was getting farther and farther from base. He managed to bring down one of them in flames, and send the other back home streaming fuel, before he, himself, had to ditch in a field. A snowy field, a good foot deep in the white freezing stuff.

It was a fact that the decision makers tried to keep the men from frostbite by requiring them to take extra wool socks and wear them under their shirts, just like the marching foot shoulders. They had orders to change out often, putting on the dry socks and tucking the cold, moist ones back into their shirt.

The airmen tended to laugh at this precaution, but Mark was thankful as he trudged in the direction his compass said was his base. It was then that he saw the child (age 5?) huddled against a bush, shivering and pale. He didn't learn much about the child, due to the language barrier, but one thing he knew. The little fellow was going to lose both feet and maybe his life if something wasn't done.

He took off the child's ragged shoes and socks that contained embedded frost crystals and put them inside his shirt. Taking his warm, dry socks and slipping them on the small feet, he hoisted the child into his arms and under his coat.

He didn't know how many miles he walked in the snow, but he and the child were pretty well done in before they came across a patrol that spoke his own language! He was not only fed, but they insisted they could spare a vehicle to get him to his own people!

He never knew what happened to the child, but he wagered the little fellow had had a story to tell when he found someone who could understand him. He might have been speaking German, for all Mark knew, but what did it matter? He was a kid.

Mark was checked in with the medics, where he lost a toe on one foot and three on the other. Luckily it was not his big toe, or he would not have been able to talk the decision makers to letting him go up again. The decision had not been hard. Fighting flyers like Mark Fire Eagle were not found in every cabbage patch!

The letters back to Shady Ridge were cheery and never a word of what it was really like. The Fire Eagle boys could never really come home, though. Once they had experienced the skies, who could expect them to come down?

Miss Francine went through her days wanting to know everything and not wanting to hear a thing. These were her boys the Government was using, and she had plans for them. And her plans did not include being in danger in a foreign land.

Troy wrote back that he was in communications and in charge of the preparation for advance offensive. Stringing wires and poles and hooking up something or other. Technical, of course. (Francine remembered the crystal radio set he had put together so he could hear the news of the war.)

Her heart ached with every bit of news, and it ached when there was no news. One of the Black Bear twins would not be coming home. Papa Black Bear walked into the woods and sat down on a log, refusing to eat or drink. What good was his life now? Nothing Mama Black Bear could do would bring him back, so she put on her shawl and came to the woods with him, sitting on the same log. Before the day was over, Amy Black Bear combed her hair and tied on a ribbon. She put on her best dress and Sunday shoes and came after them.

To her questioning father she said, "Do I look all right? I don't want to be dirty and not have my hair combed when they find me dead."

"Dead?"

"For sure, Papa. Without you and mama, I don't want to live. This way they'll find us all three and get the funeral over. It don't matter that Harley's gonna be comin' home sometime. He'll likely be glad to have us out of the way."

Papa Black Bear stared at his daughter, heaved himself to his feet, held his hand to his wife, and told her, "You win. We'll go do what we have to do. That's what Harold did."

It was when Troy's parents received the folded flag, the purple heart and the silver star for bravery that Miss Francine almost lost it entirely. Troy had been in charge of a contingent that had been sent behind enemy lines to set up a receiver for communication. He had set up the equipment and was preparing to leave when they were surprised and outnumbered.

He had ordered his men into the nearby waterway with orders to swim under water while he became a decoy. The volley of shots from the communication shack convinced the enemy that the whole group was holed up there. He held them off for a day before he was taken out, and the enemy had been amazed when it was only one lone man. Disgusted, they marched on, decrying the waste of good ammunition.

Troy's men recited the incident with tears in their eyes and lumps in their throats. The same men came back with reinforcements and retrieved their leader. The value of the installation was inestimable, but to Shady Ridge, so was Troy. Francine remembered the care he took of her pony and buggy, and the strong arm he had offered when he brought her the last few feet from the schoolhouse to the arbor where she was married.

Her agony was so great that she could only pour out her distress in poetry. Her humor, her happiness, her joy and her sorrow… all had been poured into her words. This terrible loss was no different. She opened her composition book and wrote:

THEY'RE GONE

*They're really gone.*
*Like dew upon the grass, at dawn.*

*We can't believe they've gone away…*
*Just little boys, called from their play.*
*Just little boys,*
*Who played with friends, their dogs, their toys*
*Now weary feet march foreign soil*
*Where cannons roar and smoke clouds roil.*
*Just letters now.*
*Hurried words they snatched somehow.*
*The teasing play of teenage years…*
*…Girls left with promises… and tears.*
*They lived next door.*
*Now wake up on a distant shore.*
*Country lads, with faces fresh and clean*
*Now wear their suits of mottled green.*
*Troop ships dock.*
*Down the planks their young feet walk,*
*To where their great-grandmothers stood,*
*And waved to sons, and wished them good.*
*The farmer's son*
*Will drive a tank with turret gun*
*His sister's hand now guides the plow,*
*Food must be grown… someway… somehow.*
*With back-pack load,*
*On land their great-grandfathers hoed.*
*Their hobnail boots create a trail*
*Through frigid peaks and misty vale.*
*And on they tread*
*With blistered feet like molten lead.*
*Hedge rows in France and ruins in Rome.*
*And thoughts of all they'd left at home.*

*Fresh dug foxholes.*
*Protective band of barbed wire rolls.*
*With bullets whining overhead*
*Their orders come to march ahead.*
*Hedge rows in France.*

*Move up. Fall back and take a stance.*
*Through the Balkans, deep with snow,*
*And ferry boats through Danube's flow.*
*And on to Rome.*
*Erase nostalgic thought of home.*
*While structures of an ancient race*
*Lie broken… crumbling in their place.*
*A burning thirst.*
*Fires rage and gun shells burst.*
*Rockets flash and fiery tracers run.*
*White crosses, glistening the sun.*

*The tall ships stand*
*At anchor on some distant land.*
*They carry tall, strong sons away*
*And grandsons back some future day.*
*Wars are not won.*
*They only rage and roar till done.*
*Till one side falls in a ruined heap,*
*With children left alone, to weep.*
*The truth is this, as years go by*
*Old men make wars and young men die.*
*And women, left at home, still cry*
*And wonder why!*

Now somewhat relieved, Miss Francine was able to go on with her life, her teaching and her three teenage daughters. Life was full because she made it so but the loss of Troy and others created a hole that was impossible to fill.

The twins of her second class, Donald and Dorcas McGregor were next to feel the breath of war on their necks. Donald had hardly registered when he was invited to join up. Dorcas was at loose ends for a while, and when her twin came home for his boot camp furlough, he had orders for France. He and a Corners boy would be leaving on the same ship.

It seemed that a medical receiving station was in desperate need of assistance and a number of "able bodies" were loaned to the English contingent, duties as assigned when they got there.

Dorcas wrote to the authorities in Oklahoma City. Where could she learn basic nursing, specializing in midwifery? Her horrified parents were petrified to let their daughter go to the big city for the necessary three months of the course.

The close school friend of Dorcas' was the answer. She was the sister of Mitch Tall Tree, who was already in the Russian steppes, having answered the call. She, also, would like the medical course and what's more, Mary Ellen Tall Tree could be given the course without a fee.

Mary Ellen's family were willing to let her go… after all, the girl had to do something since she seemed reluctant to get married. The problem? Why would she be accepted with no fee while Dorcas must pay? They didn't like the answer. Papa Tall Tree made the decision. "My daughter will take the course, and she will pay the fee, just like any other citizen of her country."

In the midst of surprise, her fee was accepted and the two school friends shared a room, donned their white head scarf, dress, hose and shoes and worked almost as hard as they had for Miss Francine. Knowing no one in the city to take up their time, they were desperate to learn everything available and get back home. After all, their brothers were expected to do that.

The friend from the Corners, because of his higher education, was given the rank of Captain, and set in position of making the quick decision as the stretchers and walking wounded were brought in.

Donald was an "able body" and was at first disappointed with his assignment, but he soon graduated from bed pans to bandage application. He was schooled in pain altering drugs and the fanatic cleanliness that seemed to help avoid infection. There was the plus that the job was safe, but there was also embarrassment that he was not sent to the front. As others were. He ended up, finally, in a convalescent station where the wounded were either patched up and sent back into the battle, or put on a ship and sent home.

His work, however, was heavy and tiring, and the hours were impossibly long. Many things could be postponed, but the attention to the sick and wounded could not wait. Worse, by far, were the times he helped to stow the injured into the hospital ship. Broken bodies, blinded eyes, scarred faces. He lifted his end of the stretcher and tried to avert his eyes. The day was too long for him to become emotionally overcome… so he must be brave.

He got letters from his twin and was encouraged as she and Mary Ellen were being taught by their instructors on how to stay strong. They passed the instruction along. He was to separate himself from the "condition of patient," assuring himself that the fault was not his, and the patient was fortunate to have his services. He must remember that "he was the best that was available for the patient at that moment, and, because of him, the patient may live." It helped Donald… a little.

Mitch Tall Tree still sent letters home, and that meant a momentary relief… knowing he had been alive and possibly well, about three weeks ago when the letter was written. They mustn't think about how well he was at this moment.

Donald arose to the rank of Sergeant and his sister and Mary Ellen Tall Tree received their "cap" saying they were "practical nurses." That title was good enough for them, until better could be done. Later in the year, they rented the building vacated by Nellie and Violette. Their sign said, NURSING AND CONVALESCENT CARE, also trained midwifery. It amazed them at how readily they were accepted as knowledgeable and capable. Just little girls, but they were the best to be had at the moment.

It was in this way that Shaping of Shady Ridge continued. Shaping always meant changes, and changes were not always comfortable. Parts were whittled away, and the severing was painful. Sometimes they turned the world upside down.

In due course after the marriage of Violette Barlow to the recently docked Frenchman, Randal France, she became pregnant. Happily… joyously pregnant! Hardly ever was a baby so anticipated as this one. Violette was a special person.

Violette brought joy. Those of every age were noticed by her, and she was the glue that held a group together. You felt that she was glad you were there, and would be devastated if you were not. She erased shyness, disregarded all deficiencies and made the day joyous. Now she would have a child!

She had pulled Nellie from her natural tendency to hold back, and by that, Violette gave the world beautiful sketches and paintings. She adored her new husband and made a place for him in her town and her life, as he had left his own behind. He smiled at his new situation. His (almost) mother-in-law was only a year younger than he, and the (almost) father in law was a fellow Frenchman. The red grapes tasted the same when hot from the Oklahoma sun, the way he had enjoyed them in the old country. He was lonely no more!

Truly, the new husband knew what she did for him, and he would have breathed for her if he could have. He insisted that they move back into the gallery apartment to get away from the "dust" of the sheep.

Groups of ladies discussed the pregnancy from every angle. Days were counted.

The older ladies stood ready to be called in for help, and it was decried that Dorcas and Mary Ellen had not yet earned their "caps." They could possibly be of help, and wouldn't it be good to have a "laying-in hospital" in their town!

It was during her eight and a half month that a storm hit. The "old wives" tales said that babies preferred to be born in a storm, and that must have happened to Violette.

When the violent pains began and poor Randal was alone, he was desperate for an idea. For help! Stay with her, not knowing what to do, or leaving her alone, harnessing a horse, and going… where? In a jitter he went from room to room begging the walls for an answer.

Should there be such pain so suddenly? How could anything so wickedly painful be natural for a woman to experience? Why did he let her become pregnant? He stared at the ceiling, begging for an answer.

Then she quieted. The pain must have let up! He rushed back into the room as he heard his daughter sound her indignation at the current treatment. Excitedly, thankfully, he grabbed his wife's hands, but they hung limp in his grip. In horror, he felt her neck. No pulse… no breath. His head became empty of feeling and the room began to spin.

"You will not faint!" he shouted at himself as his daughter wailed. Drawing strength from somewhere, he pushed on her chest as though she was breathing, not knowing why he did it, but knowing within himself that it was useless effort. The thunder rolled, and the rain beat down on the shingles of the gallery, but that that was nothing to what went on inside him.

Something told him he must do something for the child, and he had a ghost of an idea that the "cord must be cut, but not before it was tied." With shaking hands he tied what he thought was the cord and bravely severed the child. Bundling her into a nearby blanket, he put her on the floor, ignoring her screams. Grabbing his rain slicker, he caught the mane of the horse and turned the harried animal out into the raging storm.

The closest neighbor was Nellie, herself, and the horse sloshed through the bar ditches full of water. Randall slid off the horse at the front door, and the frightened beast tore off up the road, riderless.

"She what…?" Nellie demanded with horror. "And she's…? WESLEY! Grab a horse and go to the Corners. Bring someone back. And bring a horse for Randal and me. We're goin' to Lettie."

Speed was actually not of value, as Violette was truly gone, and her daughter had momentarily satisfied her hunger with her fist. By the bedside, friend and husband stood, holding to each other in their helpless agony as the night went on.

Wesley brought Mrs. Wilson and Mrs. Canfield, the two closest ladies. Sam Canfield saddled a horse and headed to Shady Ridge over the softening dirt road. Horse could break a leg in this mud, but he was merciless to the animal.

The thunder and lightning were letting up as Francine and Stanley made their way to the gallery.

By morning most of the two towns were aware of the tragedy of the night. It couldn't happen to a lady barely over 21 and "healthy as a horse." What a shame Dorcas and Mary Ellen were not here, though what they could have done was still a mystery. Work was suspended as they agonized over the plight of the child and her father, though most of the agony was for themselves. This just could not have happened. She could not be gone.

But she was. It was the next day that Miss Josie's daughter, then age 12, became startlingly in memory of a shake on her shoulders and a direct order given. "If anything happens to me, and you're still here…"

Trembling fear passed from her neck down her arms. She couldn't do what she promised, she actually couldn't. Why, she couldn't even swallow past the lump in her throat! But she had to, because if she didn't, somehow Violette would know, and that would be more than she could bear. Violette, her idol… her friend… the one who could always understand. The girl must somehow do what she had been assigned to do.

The Gallery was milling alive with people, and the twelve-year-old girl had time to remove the framed picture from the wall. Violette's young face peered out at her, and the eyes told her that what was to be done must be done quickly. Turning the picture over, she slid her fingers under the backing and withdrew the picture of a wrinkled, firm-lipped old woman dressed in the gray bonnet trimmed with blue roses. Every part of the picture was done from the photographic memory of Nellie. The shawl over the bony shoulders showed every small blue flower that decorated it.

The girl found a bag used by customers to collect their purchases, and she tucked the picture inside. No one was around to wonder. The girl went to the bedroom of the apartment and tested a few drawers until she found the actual scarf and the bonnet, tightly stuffed with paper to keep its shape. They just fit in the bag.

She took the bag to the back door, where the rain had made puddles of mud. Reaching high onto a shelf, she put the bag where tools and work clothes were piled. She'd get it later. Wiping all expression from her face, she moved away from the shelf. She could do this, and she knew what it was she must do and how to do it. She had known it the instant her fingers had touched the picture frame.

By the end of the day, the roads had firmed up, the way the sandy parts of Oklahoma did, and Violette began her last ride to the home of the only parents she knew.

Julie Canfield, Francine's mother, appropriated the baby as the distraught father was less than able to make a decision past his next breath. If Julie needed any help, there were fifty women who would give it, but they knew that Julie as the closest, almost relative, it was her right and duty to give immediate care to the little girl. Rosalind. The whole town knew what the name would be if the baby was a girl.

The Van Pelt family provided a box of choice white oak. Other neighbors combined their shovels to remove the soil that would cover her. The four feet by eight feet shape was placed closely beside the last resting place of Mama Lizzie. Hardened and weather-toughened men knew that their eyes streamed tears and they didn't care.

The minister, so distraught that he hardy pronounced his words, did the best he could to give a bit of graveside comfort. In time, and in groups and pairs, most of the people left. The four who would lower the box, the minister and the immediate family stood by, and Miss Josie's only daughter stood quietly among them. Who would notice whither a quiet twelve-year-old girl had business there or not? Or care if they did?

The box lid would be opened one last time and each of those remaining would have a chance for one last look. The girl had picked a small nosegay of wild flowers growing nearby, and she held these in her hand, hiding the folded paper in her palm. The picture had been folded and refolded into a wad hardly an inch big, and held tightly intact.

When it was her turn to view, she stepped close, placed the pinch of flowers in the cold hand, and tucked the folded picture of Miz Lizzie under the cuff of the sleeve of her beautiful rose crepe dress. Firming her chin with determination, she turned and walked away. She had done it. She could cry later.

A thought. Miss Violette and her Mama Lizzie, who had become a family at one time, left together as was fitting.

Then there was only Francine, held in the embrace of Stanley, Francine's father and mother, the minister, the diggers and the girl, Miss Josie's twelve-year-old daughter.

Thoughts chased each other in the girl's head. One thing she would do for Miss Violette that she had not been asked to do. There would be time that little Miss Rosalind France would be given the framed picture of her mother, and also the bonnet and shawl. Of this last thing, I, Miss Josie's daughter, was determined to do. I knew Miss Violette would expect me to do it, or she would not have shaken my shoulders to make herself understood.

Francine stood firm-chinned and dry eyed as the men waited to lower the box. "Honey," her mother begged. "You can't do this. You have to let her go, and you haven't done that. Papa and I will take you over there, and you must tell her goodbye. I know you don't want to, but it has to be done."

"No, Mama, I can't do it! I'm not ready! She was mine and she had no right to be taken away!"

"Yes, darling, you're ready now." Gently she was moved forward until she stood by the box. Young Randal, the distraught husband stood on the other side. Francine reached her hand toward the young man, and he grasped it as though it was the lifeline to save him from drowning. Leaning forward, he pulled her toward him, and their tears flowed. Bowing double over the girl they loved, their tears soaked into the pink crepe dress and the flowers, and possibly the picture, but there was no one to care.

At length, they were able to leave and the grave was shaped over. Neighbors were at Francine's house tending tiny Rosalind, and when they handed her to Francine, they left. With a question in her eyes, Julia Canfield offered to take the baby, but Francine, with a shake of her head, only folded her arms closer around the tiny mite.

Randal noted the exchange and approved. It would be a long time before anything would seem normal, and he was grateful to his "mother-in-law," the only family he had this side of the ocean. It was insisted he stay at the house for a while, leaving only to tend the sheep. He had not the strength refuse, or even think past the next moment. Sometimes the sheep were all he could think of, and the tiny mite of a girl was almost unreal.

The devastated man was finally able to tear himself away from the sheep. Caring for the animals had gone far toward bringing him back to life, and eventually he was able to take himself to the blacksmith shop at the Corners and sit among understanding men who had all undergone trouble of some sort.

A year and a half later, he met and married a lady near his own age who had apparently been waiting for him. Being a sensible person, he accepted healing when possible, and the new couple leaned on each other and cared for the baby until they had children together.

The shaping of anything requires movement. Dorcas and Mary Ellen set up their business in a way they would never have considered, only a year ago. Donald came back, and was so touched by his sister's action, and his own new inclination, took a medical course that qualified him to give emergency assistance... the thing he had been doing for the last year.

Mitch Tall Tree, Mary Ellen's brother, came back though not unscarred. A bullet had caught him just above a cheek bone, traveled into his hair line and exited, leaving a deep furrow of splintered bone and torn flesh. The best that could be done for him at the site had left a red furrow over his lower forehead and ear. The gray-beards of Westridge gouged elbows and remember Mitch's grandpappy who had a scar they swore looked exactly the same. Said he got it when he stole the girlfriend of the fellow who was expert at slinging a hatchet. At least, that's what they said.

Working so closely, Donald McGregor and Mary Ellen Tall Tree renewed their friendship. After all, he had seen a lot of her when she visited his sister.

Mitch came home, laughing away his unique marking, and set eyes on Dorcas. Also, he had seen a lot of her when she had visited his sister.

By the time the date for the double wedding was set, Mitch had secured a wagon and strong team, and freighted cotton from the Corners through the community of Lokeba, just past Enterprise, and on to the gin in Eakley. It was a two day round trip, and before the year was out, he would have another wagon and a hired driver. There was good money in hauling.

Donald, his wife, and his sister were so incredibly busy at the clinic that they wondered how all the work got done before they had qualified? Maybe it didn't.

Their double wedding was an excuse for a week of festivities in both towns. It almost seemed that it was a tether than drew together the two communities, now that there were a lot of the tin lizzies that made it so easy to "get around."

The shaping of Shady Ridge continued. Josie's daughter, who had been commissioned to write these words, fought with her thoughts for an ending of this segment. Shaping could go on forever, but there were times that it progressed more rapidly. When was there a place to stop? The world kept turning. And turning.

Young men left to help shape the whole world, and some came back. Some were forever represented by white crosses on the land that was the former homeland of many of them. Shaping continued.

Looking deep into the kneading and twisting, the pulling and pushing, it was clear that Miss Josie was the beginning. It was Miss Josie Wheeler, who had to leave New York through the death of parents in a fire, who became the first motivation behind the shaping. Her Prairie Academy produced the intelligence and perseverance. While insisting she was not a teacher, she produced the teachers and gave students a peek into the future and what it could hold.

Miss Josie lived to see the cluster of houses called Carlile Corners become a three mile stretch of businesses and homes often called Shady Corners, Oklahoma Territory. It sucked in the communities of Enterprise, Sentinel Rock, and Westridge, and everyone was happy with the additions. Later, in 1906, it became a state.

A midnight fire one Christmas in New York City gave a number of small schools and an emergency hospital to the raw frontier of the United States. It was a part of the shaping. The shaping that was repeated with variation over the whole territory.

But there was more.

Who would have thought that the French sheepherder would have pulled his head out of the shadows of his pasture long enough to actually notice the dedicated and serenely attractive Isabel, or that the school teacher, who saw her life's dream taking place, would clearly see Mr. Randal France. They had lived in close proximity for almost two years, but they did not actually SEE each other. Time was required to pass.

The occasion of their SEEING each other was when he had come to the house of his (almost) mother-in-law to play with his daughter.

They met accidentally in the schoolyard after the students had gone, and each of the adults had finished their day of work. These two adults who had seen each other many times, now actually saw each other. The timing must have been perfect, and their eyes must have been opened. Miss Francine could not have been happier.

As a matter of fact, she might have danced at their wedding, though dancing was not her thing. Actually, she was very busy during the ceremony, counting the rosy pink year and a half old toes of tiny Rosalind (her almost granddaughter) and making her giggle.

Sometimes things came out even and loose ends were tied up in a tidy fashion! At other times the ends were spread out like the strings of a mop. As Shady Ridge was being shaped, a lot of the same thing went on in the Corners, just a small piece to the east.

A lot of it found its way into the account of COOKIES, HATS AND HANKIES, the next book of this chronology. If this title sounds like a dress-up tea party, the sound would be in error. It tells of businesses that became the bands to tie a community together… it sent its people away to settle a war across the ocean, and bring them back again. It gave what it had… and accepted what was returned to it.

Some strings were tied together, and some were raveled apart and broken. And the shaping continued.

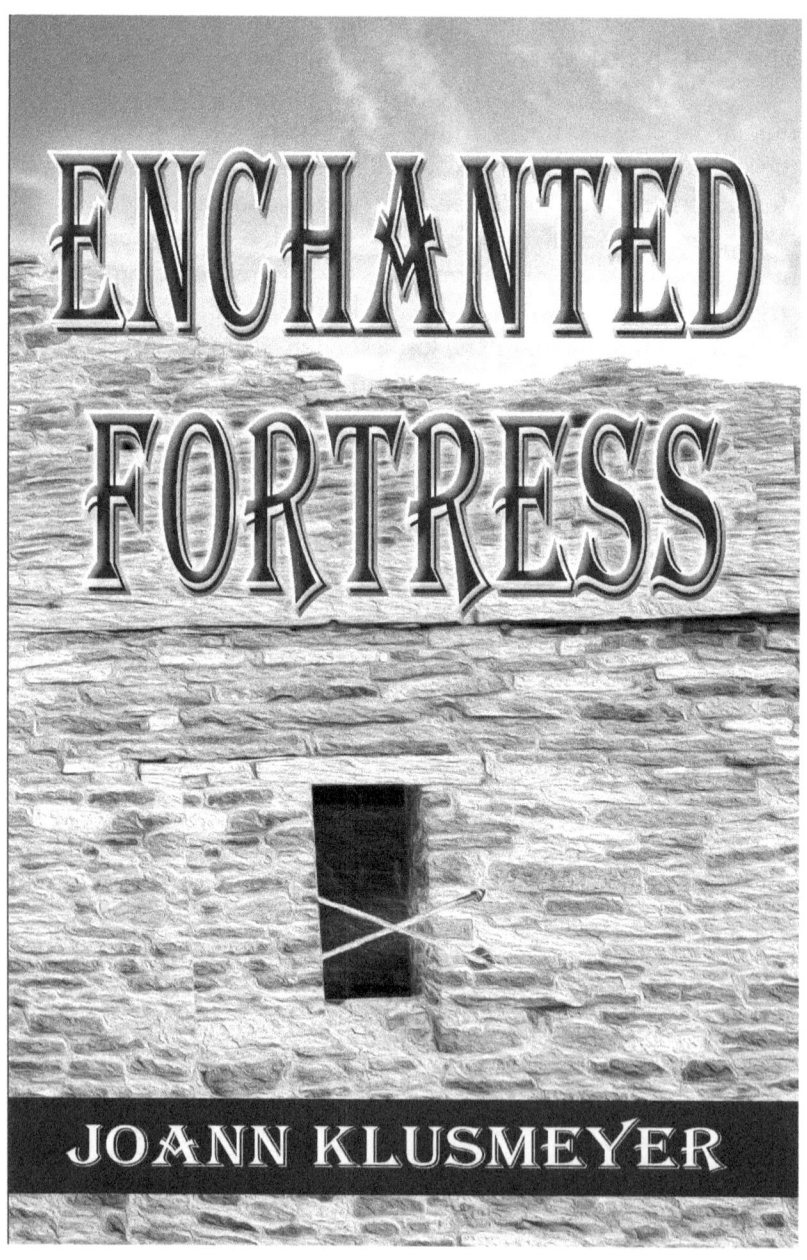

# THE ENCHANTED FORTRESS

Never, in his whole 13 years of life, had Kevin been so puzzled as he had been in the weeks since his summer vacation. What had happened to him was truly unbelievable, and there was no one to help him figure it out. He had told no one and that was because no one would believe him, even if he told them everything.

He, himself, would not believe him, except that he could see in his mind the beautifully made Ute Indian bow and arrow, and the decorated deerskin jacket with decorative stitching on the back of it and fringes on the sleeves. There they were, and it was impossible for him to explain how he got them.

And this is the way his vacation went. Kevin Montgomery leaned back against the soft upholstery of the rear seat of the family station wagon. Farms and fences sailed past outside his window, and the silver Airstream camp trailer followed obediently behind him. Kevin dozed in relaxed boredom, and the comic book slid from his hand. He might have gone to sleep, but as the highway turned, the position of the Airstream camper they pulled shifted and the afternoon sun shone against its silver surface. The reflected glare struck Kevin full in the face and his eyes popped open.

"How much farther, Dad?" he asked.

Mr. Montgomery sighed. "Now, son, I told you not more than an hour ago. We won't get to Jacob Lake Lodge before dark. We won't go on to our own campsite until morning. For a boy who didn't want to come, you sure are in a hurry to get there."

"Yeah," Kevin responded. To himself, he added that walking around in the forest alone was surely better than riding in the car alone, watching the mountains and sky go past the window, or reading the comic books for the umpteenth time. He should have remembered to go to the library before he left home to get an armload of good books.

That camp was bound to be the center of Dullsville without his best friend, Justin. Dad had promised that there would be time to do things together, just himself and Kevin, but Kevin knew how that went. When Dad got busy, his 'minutes' were hours and his 'hours' were days. If Dad said he had only a few days' work on the book he was writing, then he was sure to be busy the entire three weeks.

Kevin glanced toward his mother. She looked very tired and she hadn't said a dozen words since lunch. She had been in the hospital for a very serious operation, and the plan was that she would rest in camp while his dad finished his book. Kevin and his best pal, Justin, were going to have fun exploring.

*Justin, you traitor, you,* Kevin silently scolded the absent Justin. *Some pal you are! You don't even know when to get the measles. Everyone else knows you get the measles when you're six or seven, or even younger. Not when you're twelve, going on thirteen.* Kevin's mind also scolded Justin for his thoughtlessness but ignored the fact that his friend had been looking forward to the trip as much as Kevin had.

So he sighed and leaned back. The sun was getting lower. His stomach rumbled with emptiness. It would be useless to ask Dad to stop somewhere for a hamburger. The tiny Utah towns were far apart and he knew his parents would try to make it to the Jacob Lake Lodge Restaurant.

Oh, well. There was a banana left over but one end was squashed. There were three broken cookies. That should save him from starvation.

The mashed banana made a strong smell in the car.

"Eating, son?" his mother asked. "If you could just wait, there will be good food at Jacob Lake."

Before Kevin could swallow ("Don't ever talk with your mouth full, son.") his dad spoke up. "Let him eat, honey. Boys have strange taste buds and it'll give him something to do."

"You're right, of course," his mother agreed.

Relieved of the necessity to answer, Kevin watched the trees and mountains and munched the cookies and the banana. They didn't last long. He rolled down the window three inches and slipped out the smelly banana peeling.

"Kevin, did you throw something out the window? You know not to litter the highway."

Before he could explain, his mother came to his defense. "It was just the banana peeling, Max, and it smelled so bad!"

Kevin quickly added, "And it's biodegradable. The birds and ants will eat it up."

"Well, don't throw out the cookie wrapper."

"I wasn't going to, Dad."

Mom, again. "He wasn't, Max. He already put in into the litter bag."

"All right, just see that you don't"

Kevin sighed. Man, oh man, when would they quit treating him like a bump on a log? A stupid bump that never learned anything and couldn't even talk for himself! One good thing about having Justin along: his parents didn't treat him like a baby. Or rather, a baby moron!

More trees and mountains went by and the shadows fell across the road. There, in a clearing, was a flock of wild turkeys, scratching and pecking. They were so perfectly blended with the color of the grass that when they stopped still, they couldn't be seen. Wouldn't that be neat, to be invisible? Of course, that was almost what happened to him around his parents. Sometimes they talked about him and answered for him like he wasn't even there, and they told him the same thing a hundred times. At least.

Man, was this ever going to be a long three weeks. He eased his hand into the food chest to make sure nothing was left. He felt around carefully and drew out three grapes and the wet label off the bologna package. Two of the grapes were good, but the third one was questionable. He ate it, anyway.

"Look at the deer, son," his dad called to him.

Up ahead, three does and two fawns ran across the road. Behind them came the buck, leaping all the way across the road in a single bound. Kevin knew what his dad was going to say next, so he beat him to it.

"Those are mule deer. They have big ears like a mule."

"That's right, son. How did you know that?"

"You told me." Kevin wanted to add, "A hundred times at least," but he didn't.

"Oh," his dad said.

The deer family scampered into the thick shadows of the pine forest, and the highway began to climb into the mountains. A few logging trucks came rumbling down out of the mountain with their load of logs for the lumber mill.

They were now entering the Kiabab Forest. Kevin watched the trees for a glimpse of the Kiabab squirrel with the grey body and the white tail. He had heard that this forest was the only place in the world this little squirrel had been found. Darkness was falling fast.

He slipped his hand quietly into the food chest.

"Just a few more minutes, son, and we'll be there," advised his mother.

Kevin leaned back. They always knew what he was going to do. It wasn't fair. There were two of them and only one of him. Why did he have to be an only child, anyway?

The highway leveled suddenly and there were lights up ahead. Jacob Lake Lodge. The flashing signs said, "Welcome! Welcome! Welcome!" It was about time!

Dad turned off the highway and looked for number eleven hookup. There it was. Skillfully, he backed the Airstream camper into its slot. He stepped out and walked around and released it from the station wagon. Kevin had jumped out of the wagon and had found the electric hookup. It was good to feel the tingle in his feet after sitting so long. He shoved the large electric cord into the socket of the campsite electric meter. He heard the air conditioner motor kick in.

"Kevin!" called his dad.

Kevin ran around the Airstream. "What, Dad?"

"Son, go plug in the trailer so it can get cooled off while we eat."

"I already did it, Dad."

"You what?"

"I already did it."

"Oh. Then get in and let's drive over to the lodge for dinner."

The smell of meat and coffee and fruit pies met them at the restaurant door. Everything should go better now.

Two hours later, they were back in the camper and in their beds.

The sound of birds in the trees woke Kevin early the next morning. He slipped quietly out of his bunk in the tiny bedroom and reached for his bow and arrow. He could explore this campsite this morning because later they would go on down into the forest where they would stay for the rest of the time.

Outside the door he came face to face with a huge sign that said, "Positively no firearms, noisemakers or archery equipment."

"Well, of all the..." Kevin muttered and took his bow back to the trailer.

Dad was up. "Don't go away, Son. We'll be leaving in a few minutes."

Kevin sighed. That meant "hours." He sat down on a log beside an ant hill. He put a broken piece of leaf in the ant trail and without hesitation, several ants climbed onto it.

He moved the leaf a foot away and the ants began going in circles. *That's me*, he thought. *Dullsville, Dullsville! Nothing exciting ever happens. I just go around in circles.*

But this time it really was just a few minutes until they hooked up the trailer hitch and unplugged the cord. They nosed the station wagon into the dense trees of the forest and headed down a narrow road. The trees on either side of the road locked their branches overhead. It was like riding through a leafy tunnel. The chirps of the birds and the flutter of wings were the only sounds.

A sign beside the road advised, "Firearms and archery permitted. Bag limit on game strictly enforced."

Shucks, he wouldn't actually kill anything. He just wanted to get in some target practice.

They turned from the narrow road to a trail that wound among the pine trees. Finally, they were at Number Twelve Beaver Road.

The campsite had a cabin with two sides open. It had a table with benches and a grill. There were two lounge chairs and an electric plug. Just outside the cabin was a water faucet sticking up out of the ground.

"Perfect," said his dad.

"It should be fine," agreed his mom.

Kevin didn't say anything. Maybe the next camp on down the road had someone he could play with. Then again, if he target practiced for three solid weeks, he should be very, very good. You had to look at the bright side and try to make the best of a situation.

Kevin plugged the electricity into the trailer and checked the water faucet. It worked. He hoped someone would fix breakfast soon. His stomach wouldn't stop rumbling.

Mom moved a cushion to one of the lounge chairs and Dad lit the grill. He tossed thick slices of ham in a skillet and then he fried eggs in the sizzling grease. He warmed the giant buns they had bought from the restaurant. One thing about Dad, he was a good cook! And he was fast!

Dad didn't make you sit down at the table, use a napkin or put lettuce in your sandwich.

"Sit down while you eat, Kevin," Mom instructed.

"Aw, honey, let him go. It's his vacation, too, and you should be resting, not worrying about him."

"I guess you're right."

"Sure I am. We'll make it, won't we, Son?"

"Sure, Dad."

But before he had hardly eaten his sandwich, the quiet of the campsite was filled with the tippity-tapping of Dad's laptop. Kevin sighed and picked up his bow and arrow.

"Don't get lost, Son," Mom told him.

That was rather silly. She always said that, like he might, on purpose, decide to get lost, just to see what it was like. No one got lost on purpose, so why did she keep telling him that? But he didn't argue.

"I won't, Mom. See ya," and he was out of sight in the trees.

Kevin sniffed the air. It smelled like vacation. Damp dirt, tree leaves, flowers and the faint smell of a distant skunk.

He followed a path down the hill to a brook that whispered through the polished rocks. Tiny fish flashed silver in the sunshine. A mossy backed snapping turtle lowered himself into the water, instantly looking like a mossy rock.

Kevin walked across the brook on a worn log and started up the hill.

There, in a small clearing was a pile of stones and the remains of a large stone building. He examined it carefully. The walls were very thick. Actually, it was two walls thick, with small stones tossed between the two walls.

There were windows but they were very tiny, not more than six inches wide and a foot high. Strange!

Part of the wall had toppled over and the rocks lay in a pile of rubble. The house must have been very large, judging from the length of the walls, but there were no rooms partitioned off. Just a big auditorium. Of course, it was not easy to see much through the tiny window.

The stones of the wall were wet from the dew and some were smooth and flat. They would be perfect for practice. He put the suction tip on his arrow and backed away.

He took his stance and pointed his arrow toward the sky. He lowered it smoothly and slowly and when he sighted the largest smooth rock, he fired.

"Pffft" the arrow whispered and then, "plunk" against the stone. Perfect. Kevin retrieved his arrow and aimed again. On five out of seven tries, he made a bull's eye.

He was aiming for the eighth shot when a large bumble bee came out of nowhere, diving for his face. Kevin shooed away the insect and took aim again. Just as he was about to let go of the shot, the bee reappeared and dived at his face again. Just in time to throw off his aim!

"Pffft" went the arrow, but there was no "plunk." The arrow went sailing through the tiny window, right into the fortress, and out of sight.

"Oh, well," thought Kevin. "I've got all the time in the world. I'll just climb in and get it, and I can explore the building while I'm in there."

He hung his bow on a low tree limb and went climbing over the pile of stones and rubble. The rocks rolled under his feet, forcing him to crawl on all fours. What a pile!

And there was his arrow. Right in the center of the big room. He'd get it and lay it in the little window before looking around, so he wouldn't accidentally step on it.

He bent over to pick up the arrow and there, on either side of the arrow, were feet. The feet were wearing soft moccasins. As he stood up slowly, he saw the rough fabric of pants, a printed pattern of a shirt and then a face. The face was level with his, and it had a wide grin among its freckles.

"I'm Winston," the owner of the face told him.

"I, uh, I didn't see you come up," stuttered Kevin. "My name's Kevin. How did you get in here so quick and so quiet?"

"I didn't," Winston grinned.

"You what?"

"I said I didn't get in here quick and quiet. I was always here."

"But I looked through the window there," Kevin argued, "and I didn't see you."

"I know," Winston agreed.

"Were you hiding?"

"No."

"Then how come I didn't see you?"

"You hadn't shot your arrow through the window, yet."

"That window? What's that got to do with anything? I just missed my target."

Winston shook his head. "I made you miss."

Kevin grinned at the joke. "Not unless you turned yourself into a bee. That thing dived at me just as I let go. That's what made me miss."

The other boy smiled and nodded. "And I was chasing the bee toward you."

"But I didn't see you. Where were you?"

"I was there, but you had to come in here before you could see me."

Kevin looked carefully at Winston. He hated to ask, but he just had to know.

"Hey, are you magic? Like, are you not really here? Do I just think I see you?"

Winston grinned. "Of course I'm here and you see me. Any boy shootin' an arrow through the portal over there, and then comin' in, can see me."

Kevin nodded with satisfaction. Winston was a jokester. This was going to be fun. "Which camp are you staying at? I'm over at Number Twelve Beaver Road."

"I ain't over at no camp. I live here. I always lived here. Me and my folks and my baby sister. It'd be her that was the reason for us a'stayin'."

"Your baby sister? How come?"

"Yup. She couldn't help it, though, not bein' born yet."

Kevin narrowed his eyes and looked carefully at Winston. He was either for real, or he was going to a lot of effort for a joke.

"How long have you been living here?" Kevin asked him.

Winston looked up, thoughtfully. "Over a hunnerd summers that I kept track of."

"Hundred years?"

"Likely more'n that. I let some slip past me. There were times it didn't seem real important to mark down the time."

*Hmmmm,* thought Kevin. *Bet my dad would like to hear Winston's story.* He was always on the lookout for new and different ideas. Might even want to make a book out of it. Maybe he'd tell him later.

Kevin looked around him at the big room. It was different now. The broken wall was built back, solid and strong. There was no door to come in or to leave. A ladder made of poles was leaning against the wall and Kevin could see the end of another ladder on the other side.

There was a roof made of poles over one end of the room and a thick covering made of tree limbs and grass shaded the area below. Kevin felt fright bumps rise up on his arms and neck. Really weird! He looked back at Winston.

"You got no cause to be scared," Winston reassured him. "That's my house and my ma and little sister. You want to see my little sister?"

Kevin didn't know if he did or not, but he couldn't seem to talk so he followed after Winston.

The woman, Winston's mom, was humming softly as she gently rocked the hollow log of the cradle. She looked up at Kevin and smiled and Kevin smiled back. He looked in the cradle and saw the pink face of a baby snuggled into a ragged blanket. What should he say? All babies looked alike to him. He couldn't tell if this one was pretty or not. Winston came to his rescue.

"She's a good baby, don't you think?"

Kevin nodded. She wasn't crying and any baby that wasn't crying must be a good baby. He nodded again. "She sure is a good baby."

The boys walked away.

"Hey, Winston?"

"What?"

"You've got to tell me the truth, how come you're here. No making up anything, either."

Winston grinned. "I wouldn't be lyin' to you. We was a'goin' to the ocean to find gold. There was a place we called Calif... I forget the name of it."

"California?"

"Yep, that was it. We come all the way from Kansas City, takin' longer than we was thinkin' we would. Then cold weather came and one of the oxen broke a leg. We might'a figured a way to go on, Pa and me, but Ma knew it was gettin' time for the birthin' of my little sister and we decided to find us a place to winter over. Then we was goin' on to find the gold that was layin' on the ground. That's what folks said."

"Yeah? You lived in Kansas City, for real? I want you to tell me everything that happened, because that's where I live. What did it look like then? You, for real, lived in 1849?" Kevin was more than ready to go along with the joke.

Winston nodded.

"Tell me about it and don't leave out anything!" Kevin begged.

Winston's eyes shone with pleasure as he told his story.

"Kansas City was a big town. Must'a had a hunnerd houses. It had eight churches and four stores to buy stuff to wear and stick candy to eat. There was blacksmith shops and a lot of other shops.

"There was a newspaper office and my pa bought a paper every day for my ma to teach me to read out of."

"No school, huh?"

Winston shook his head. "I was a big boy, over ten years old. There weren't no need to be puttin' in school time, me havin' a ma to teach me words and numbers. My ma is smart. She can read anything that was ever wrote down. She read books thicker than a goat's hind foot. She was gonna teach me everything."

"Why didn't she?" Kevin asked.

"Well, it was mostly Pa. He got what they call Gold Fever."

"Got sick?"

"Nope, it wasn't sick in the body. It was more like sick in the head. He couldn't think of nothin' but that gold he kept hearin' about.

"Ma said to him we had everything a family could think of wantin'. We had us a two-roomed house and a wagon and a team of mules. We had us a little farm and I plowed the crops while my pa worked to build houses for folks with money. Ma said we did good, but Pa couldn't get that gold out of his mind. Ma said it was Gold Fever."

The boys had climbed the ladder up and over the thick stonewall.

Kevin saw a large, solid wooden wagon tied to a tree. A cow with wide horns chewed noisily on the nearby grass. He walked to the wagon. It was standing on the exact spot where he had stood when he shot the arrow. He reached out to touch the splintery wood of the wagon. It was real. A sharp splinter stuck his finger and brought out a drop of blood.

"It's a good old wagon," Winston commented. "Lot of them fall apart, comin' across the mountains, but that one didn't. Pa was gonna rub oil on it so it wouldn't rot. Don't know it he ever done that or not."

"You don't know?"

"Nope. He went on."

"He left you?"

Winston nodded. "He wasn't wantin' to and he shed tears but he had to go on without me."

Winston gazed dreamily into the distance, then turned back to Kevin. "I was tellin' about Kansas City. One day Pa brought home two oxen. It was Blackie, over there, and the other one was Daisy. Daisy busted her leg, but not till we got here. Pa sold our mules in Kansas City and then he sold our buggy and plow and a lot of other things so he could buy this wagon. We put everything we had inside and put the canvas top on it and Daisy and Blackie pulled us out of the town."

Winston paused and Kevin whispered to himself, "A covered wagon, can you believe it? He came here in a covered wagon!"

Winston grinned with pleasure. "Sure, a covered wagon! It was good to have a wagon and not be walkin' like a lot of folks did."

"Walking? Really, were there some folks walking to California?"

"If they had themselves no wagon, that was the only way they could go. So you can see, we was lucky to have us a wagon."

Kevin thought a minute. "You mean you had to sit there on that wagon seat, bumping along, all the way out here from Kansas City?"

"Sittin' there? Nope, not me. I was always seein' something like a rock or a flower or an animal I wanted to see up close so I'd jump down and go look. The wagon was slow and I could catch up to it, easy.

"I had me a dog named Curly and she'd run along under the wagon in the shade. There'd be times when Curly and me, we'd go chase down a rabbit for supper. Ma'd cook it on the campfire and we'd eat. Curly ate up the bones."

"Hmmm. What else did you do?"

"Ma, she would sing songs she knew from back in Kansas City, and she brought along a newspaper. I read every word in that old paper, probably a hunnerd times. I was learnin' to read in the Bible, too, but it had a lot of hard words."

Kevin sniffed a delicious smell. He realized he was getting hungry again. From somewhere inside the wall came the rich aroma of meat, simmered with vegetables.

"Say, that sure does smell good." He sniffed, appreciatively.

"You hungry? You can eat with us. We got plenty. This here's a good camp for huntin' something to cook."

"What about the bag limit?"

"The what?"

"The law that tells you how many animals you can kill."

Winston chuckled. "You're tellin' me a joke and I like to have believed you! With animals 'hind every stump and no lawman closer than a hunnerd miles, who'd there be to care what we kill to eat? Ain't nobody ever cared yet," he assured Kevin, "and we got plenty. Let's go eat."

The boys climbed back up the wall and then down again. The stew smelled even better up close.

Kevin's mom smiled and handed him a bowl made from a wooden gourd. With another gourd, one that had a handle, she ladled the stew into his bowl. Thick chunks of meat and colorful vegetables floated in the savory stew. It tasted even better than it looked.

"What else happened on the way here?" Kevin asked.

"Oh, lots of things. We came across the flat lands of Kansas in the heat of summer. There ain't nothin' hotter than the Kansas sun overhead in the summer.

"Then we came into the hills and it wasn't as fast goin' as Pa thought it was gonna be. Them hills got steep. There was times when it looked like the oxen couldn't make it. We put Ma's furniture out along the road to make the load lighter and went off and left it. Ma tried not to cry but her eyes was shiny and she didn't talk and she didn't sing like she used to do.

"Pa didn't talk much, neither. He just walked alongside the wagon lookin' at the wheels and listenin' to the noise they made. There was times at night he'd pour water over the wheels if we had enough to spare." Winston paused.

"Why would he pour water on the wheels?"

"To get 'em wet."

"Yeah, but why did he want them wet?"

- END OF EXCERPT -

# ADDITIONAL BOOK SERIES BY JOANN KLUSMEYER

**The Great I Am Bible Story Series for Kids**
*6 books*

**The Young Pioneers Adventure Series for Kids**
*5 books*

**The Wentworth Triplets Mystery Series for Young Teens**
*3 books*

**Footsteps in the Canyon Adventure Series for Young Teens**
*4 books*

**Burnt Tree Junction Historical Fiction Series for Adults**
*6 books*

**Ozark Mountains Historical Fiction Series for Adults**
*7 books*

**Taming the Wilderness Historical Fiction Series for Adults**
*4 books*

**The Sheltering Stones Historical Fiction Series for Adults**
*5 books*

**The Trilogy of Wishbone Hollow Historicial Fiction Series for Adults**
*3 books*

com/pod-product-compliance

'00

613147337 *